Red is the Colour

Mark L. Fowler

Print ISBN 978-1-912175-42-0

For Joe and Fiona, with love

CHAPTER ONE

Nobody had noticed the bone sticking out of the ground. The yellow diggers remained silent and the workers had left the site for the weekend, absolved of all guilt for what they had done; exposing a thirty-year-old evil to the fading summer light.

Josh Smith was walking his black retriever, Stan, along the canal towpath on a warm Sunday evening in June. With an air of resignation, the boy snapped the clip of the lead onto the dog's collar, and headed through the gate from the towpath down towards the subway entrance. The weekend was all but over. It was time to go home and get that homework done.

The two friends scurried through the empty subway that ran like a labyrinth beneath the giant roundabout. They emerged at the Wall of Death, the notorious accident black-spot, a monolithic curving structure segregating the main traffic artery from the adjacent foot path. From there they began the short climb up towards the ancient village where they lived.

At the top of the first climb was a plateau, a no-man's land that the villagers refused to lay claim to; a place of shadow that to outsiders marked the outer limits of the village itself. On the site where the old factory had stood, the process of demolition was almost complete. In a few months' time a *splendid new visitors' centre would herald another exciting chapter in the regeneration of the city.*

That's what the local politicians were promising, according to Josh Smith's dad. But for now, the place was one more graveyard housing the spirits of a great industrial past.

The usual shortcut, the un-named track leading from the plateau towards a rough and weary tarmac path known locally as

The Stumps, had been temporarily fenced off. Undeterred, Josh and Stan slipped beneath the barricade.

Moving carefully between the giant mounds of freshly dug earth, the two adventurers made good progress, crossing the forbidden site towards The Stumps, where the second barricade had been erected. As they edged around the base of the larger mound, Stan yanked fiercely on the lead, the sudden movement taking Josh by surprise and tearing the lead out of his hand.

The dog was sniffing around the base of the mound, and as Josh got closer he could see that his friend was licking at an object poking out of the excavated earth.

Nothing more than a rotten old stick, thought the boy. But the retriever was pulling on the 'stick', tugging at it for all he was worth and issuing a low growl as he did so. Didn't he realise there was maths and history to be done and parents already checking watches?

Stan seemed determined to have the treat and he was growling now with uncharacteristic menace as he wrestled with the dark thing that the ground refused to yield up.

Josh felt the first sickly tug of panic. They should not be in this place, stranded between the barriers festooned with warning signs proclaiming unspecified *danger.*

Darkness was closing in around them.

Josh picked up the lead and snatched hard enough to feel the leather cut into his hands. In an urgent, shouted whisper, he urged Stan to, '*Come on!*'

Still the retriever's fangs clenched tenaciously around the new find, while his master stopped to ease the pressure on his burning fingers.

The earth started moving.

The mysterious object was still clinging to some hidden thing inside the mound, something as yet invisible to the eye. Stan was swinging his head from side to side, determined to prise the find loose. His growl becoming savage.

Josh could see that the thing in the ground was not a stick, rather a bone, blackened no doubt by age and burial. More of the earth was sliding. Josh wanted to cry. At any moment, the hill might collapse and bury the pair of them forever.

Renewing his efforts, he hauled on the lead, his hands ready to burst into flames. But Stan was still not giving up the struggle. More of the bone was emerging, bringing with it whatever was holding it back and keeping it partially submerged beneath the dirt and rubble of a bygone age.

Josh let go of the lead and placed his hands under his armpits, squeezing away at the pain. '*Stan*, damn you,' he shouted, his eyes stinging with tears.

As more of the bone began to come loose, the boy could see that it was connected to something larger, something hideous. He wanted to look away, but found himself unable to do so. Instead, he stood transfixed, awaiting the extent of the revelation.

The scream was forming in the pit of his stomach. He could feel it rising into his throat with the realisation that Stan was holding triumphantly between his teeth the blackened skeleton of a human arm.

The dog was momentarily frozen by his master's guttural scream, though he still wouldn't let go of the arm.

In the awful silence that followed, as the scream died in echoes across the darkening city, Josh Smith watched the lower part of the mound collapse, allowing enough of the skull to break free of the earth to leave him in no doubt that the world was full of dark intentions and evil deeds.

All time went to the moon until sirens and flashing lights filled the summer night, the cavalry arriving on the scene thirty years late.

In fact, as Detective Sergeant Danny Mills was to observe, almost thirty years to the day too late.

CHAPTER TWO

DCI Jim Tyler picked up the phone.

'Jim,' said the voice on the other end of the line, 'I'm ringing to tell you that your fate has been decided.'

Tyler didn't respond. He listened and waited.

'Now, don't shoot the messenger. We've decided to let things simmer down for a while. You put that application in, good man. Staffordshire can use a guy like you, and they're a decent bunch.'

'I've arranged my own exile, if that's what you mean.'

'I wouldn't quite put it like that. You've made contingency plans, and very good ones. They've got Alton Towers. Your life could be complete.'

'Are you trying to be funny?'

'I'm telling you the way it is. The chief superintendent there is basically a good man. Graham's still crawling his way up the ladder but not forgetting where he came from. I did some training up that way in my previous life. I taught him practically everything he knows.'

'Graham Berkins knows the circumstances?'

'He's knows as much as he needs to. He knows exactly what he's getting and he's more than happy. Personally, I'm gutted to see you go, but sometimes politics prevail. You know the score. Stay off the sauce, Jim, control that temper of yours and that love – or should that be loathing – of authority—'

'And I just might fit in?'

'You might at that. Stranger things happen. Graham's having a tough time of it, what with staffing issues and regeneration blues. Detectives like you, Jim, with your experience and integrity are like gold dust. The city fathers in Stoke are getting precious – city on the cusp of change, millions pouring in, you know the story – imagining the rest of the world could care less what happens up there.'

'You sound well informed.'

'I'm fond of the place and fond of Graham. We go back a long way.'

'You should apply to move there yourself.'

'I'm too busy sorting out the mess down here. Move on, Jim, while you still can. If you can get past the moustache, you'll do alright with Berkins. He's awaiting your call.'

'Got a case to discuss already, has he?'

'You'll hit the ground running, there's no question of that. Too much time on your hands doesn't suit you, it never has. Keep busy and out of mischief.'

'Yes, Miss.'

Male laughter issued down the phone.

'I'm not expecting you to play by the rules, Jim. That's not the way you were made.'

CHAPTER THREE

D S Mills was still mourning the end of the football season. That and the fact that his wife's dream of country living had taken him out of the city, and miles from any decent boozers. If he was to kill the pain of the new mortgage, a good local was going to be – ah, what was the point?

He'd been putting in the hours when the call came. Not many murders on the patch and no reason to expect one now. Still, whatever it amounted to, this case had time-and-a-half written all over it. It might take his mind off the countryside, and make a start on that mound of debt that he could see stretching all the way to old age.

It didn't take Mills long to establish that the only wrong-doing for which Josh Smith and his dog could reasonably be held accountable was ignoring the warning signs at the barricades. 'A simple act of trespass punishable by nightmares of the recurring kind,' he told the constable guarding the newly erected cordon.

He looked at the boy with pity born of memory. *Shivering on a warm night, huddled in a regulation blanket, back turned against the grisly discovery already screened off from the prying eyes of the curious public.* Mills remembered that scene only too well.

Not many miles from there, in his own adolescence, he had once encountered a gruesome sight of his own. Mates playing on waste ground in the dying light, kicking a ball around until it flew into the adjacent bushes. The young Danny Mills, still holding on to a fading dream of playing for Stoke City, searching for the ball; his mates shouting after him, wanting to know what the hell he was playing at.

And then he had seen it. On the other side of a clump of stinging nettles; a dark shape lying next to the football.

Taking a stick to bash away the worst of the triffids, he had found himself suddenly staring into the unblinking eyes of a dead man.

A tramp, it turned out; a down-and-out, frozen to death. The police, that long-ago evening, had come charging across the waste ground with flashing lights, but also compassion. A blanket and a warm drink back at the police station, and a future career forming out of the haunting memory: that those uniformed heroes alone knew how to deal with terror and mortality.

Mills hadn't screamed that day, and at last his mates had come over to see what was so interesting. Josh Smith, on the other hand, had screamed loud enough to wake the dead, as well as the living; stopping Stan in his tracks, and giving the animal even now an attitude of nervousness not entirely explained by the plethora of flashing lights.

Mr and Mrs Smith had listened with alternating pride and embarrassment as DS Mills gently coerced their son to recount his grisly adventures. And when the story had been told to his satisfaction, Mills, momentarily feeling better about life, wrapped things up with what he thought to be a simple act of kindness.

'You shouldn't have crossed that barricade, you know that, don't you, son?'

'Yes, sir.'

'And you're not going to do anything like that again, are you?'

Josh Smith swore that he wouldn't, and then swore on behalf of Stan, too.

'You must be a Stoke City fan, calling him Stan,' said Mills.

The boy's face brightened. 'We both are. Hey – did you ever see Stanley Matthews play?'

Mills grimaced, and it wasn't entirely a stage-grimace either. 'How old do you think I am, son? On second thoughts, don't answer that. And anyway, show some respect: it's *Sir* Stanley Matthews. And now I'm going to let you into a little secret.'

He watched three heads crane forward, and even Stan appeared to cock an ear while keeping a nose and eye trained in the direction of the screened-off mound of dirt containing those interesting bones. 'Sometimes,' said Mills, 'a person does the wrong thing and, just the once, it turns out to be the right thing.' He took a moment to savour three baffled expressions. 'You see, something very similar happened to me, a long time ago. And do you know what?'

Three pairs of ears twitched expectantly, though Stan was at the same time giving his attention to the figures dressed in white, coming and going in the general vicinity of the bones. The dog let out a long growl, causing DS Mills to grin. 'He probably thinks it's finders-keepers.'

Nobody even smiled.

'Where was I?' said Mills.

They didn't have a clue, any of them.

'Yes, as I was saying, I learned my lesson, same as you. And, remarkable as it might seem, something good came out of it.'

Josh Smith's eyes widened. 'Do you mean I'm going to get a reward?'

'Don't push it, son.'

The moment was gone, and Mills quietly sighed, packing the recruitment talk away for another day before authorising a car to take the Smith family on the short ride home.

***

The constable manning the cordon was pleased to see Mills approaching, glad of the company and the chance to share some of his homespun wisdom about what a bad business this looked like.

Then he got on to the staffing crisis. 'I mean, with Dodds off long-term, and Jackson gone and what's-her-name – DC Clarke – still not sure if she's a flag or a balloon – we're in a right pickle.'

'That's not even the half of it,' said Mills.

'So, what are they going to do?'

'They're busing them in from all over the place.'

'What about the DCI post?'

'Filled. He's on his way.'

'Anyone we know?'

Mills told him.

'Jim Tyler? Not heard of him. From the capital, you say?'

'We're so bloody short up here,' said Mills.

'What a state we're in.'

'But the show must go on, regardless.'

'Trouble with the big city types, if you don't mind me saying so, is …'

The constable let his thoughts splutter out, scratching his neck as he did so.

'The thing is,' said Mills, 'we get what we are given.'

'Well, I suppose so. But we both know that you have to live here to understand this place. There's nowhere like it, or the people, for that matter. It takes a lifetime and it's never going to come out of books, no matter how many of 'em you get through.'

'That's a fine speech. Been working on it long?'

'Thank you. Actually—'

'I was being sarcastic, you dick.'

For a moment the officer appeared hurt, but he quickly recovered. 'I suppose he's highly qualified, this Tyler. Wonder why he wants to leave London to come here? Still, the question I always ask is – is he any bloody good?'

DS Mills looked at the constable and for a few moments saw himself reflected. The urge to denounce the outsider, the stranger; the redneck impulse that ran deep through the city. In that instant of dull recognition, he recognised the facts of the matter: Tyler had the gig, and none of them had any choice but to make the best of it. In subordination was of no use to a man with a family and a mortgage, not in the city and not in the country either.

Mills' tone hardened. 'Ours is not to question why, isn't that right?'

'Sounds about right.'

'Let's give the man a chance, for God's sake.'

From a higher place, a statement had already been issued to the fast-descending media. The statement was aimed at keeping the hounds at bay while prodding the memory of someone who, for whatever reason, had failed to realise that a loved one hadn't returned home sometime in the last three decades.

But the media had its own agenda. Statement or no statement, the city and the nation would wake up to a new horror story to enjoy over breakfast.

CHAPTER FOUR

When the call ended DCI Jim Tyler stood up and walked over to the small kitchenette. There was still beer in the fridge, kept back for emergencies.

So: they were letting him go and wasn't that just fine and dandy. He'd used his fists instead of his brain and let Greenslade get to him. But the truth was … *the truth was that not a single man or woman on the job didn't secretly envy his bottle, giving that bullying piece of shit the kicking he deserved.* He knew the deal: Greenslade had dropped the charges on condition. He had been persuaded to play ball to reap the rewards.

Tyler took out a beer and looked at the possibilities. He could end it now, get loaded and tell them where to stick it. There was satisfaction there, and plenty of it.

In the short term.

The trouble with that picture: he could see Greenslade's cretinous face, laughing the way bullies do, knowing that he had won.

Well – fuck that for a game of soldiers.

Gripping the bottle tightly he saw Green *twat's* rat-features forming like a demon on the far wall, and with a rebel yell launched the weapon, watching it smash in slow-motion, carpeting the floor with froth and broken glass.

***

Quickly Tyler got changed, and in five minutes he was running through the narrow streets circling the cemetery. Breathing hard and sweating heavily inside the hooded light grey top, he could have been mistaken for a local middleweight, taking in a good dose of petrol fumes to get him whizzed up for the showdown.

He didn't feel like a middleweight, though; more like Jodie Foster at the beginning of *Silence of the Lambs*.

For a second or two he let his imagination loose on the fantasy: setting out on the trail of some demonic serial killer and not fancying the odds.

It was better, or at least more heroic, than the reality of being a forty-something detective who had taken up running as part of the fight to give up drinking and losing his rag. A forty-five-year-old officer of the law who had worked his way up through the ranks, only to throw it all away because he hadn't been able to control his taste for the bottle or his anger at seeing injustice served at the highest level.

He was approaching a group of youths assembled on the pavement outside Wilson's Off-Licence. He saw them looking, and wondered which one would be the original smart-mouth.

As each in turn caught his eye and none looked away, Tyler felt the pressure building in his chest; the fight-or-flight dilemma turning every encounter into a matter of life and death.

The trouble with traumatic pasts, he thought. *They never let you go.*

He took the direct route, straight through the circle of scumbags, his heart pounding harder than the run demanded of a twenty-to-thirty-miles-a-week man on the right side of fifty.

With the anonymity of the hood and the uniform of the street he ought to be feeling a million miles from the sitting target status that had once been his lot as a uniformed beat-copper on the streets of East London. Now he had traded in those rags to play detective in the south and in the north of the big, big city.

Yet nobody knew anybody here, not really. Maybe he did need a change, even if that change came as a northbound exile to Stoke.

Tyler left the half-cut, spliff-dazed mob behind, already hearing their laughter at his heels; breathing hard against the brutal sound of it, and its connotations. Maybe it had nothing to do with him. Maybe the ghosts of the past really were dead and buried; and maybe one day he would actually believe that.

They weren't the kind he hated, not really. They couldn't hold a candle to the suits and ties in the top-floor offices of flawed mankind.

A few minutes and he was panting back into the flat that he had tried hard to call home, taking a shower and changing once again; leaving the beer and the shards of glass behind him and preparing to move on to find new adventure.

CHAPTER FIVE

After a short meeting with the chief superintendent, in one of the more reasonably furnished rooms at Hanley Police Station in the centre of Stoke-on-Trent, DCI Tyler met with the central team, shook a few hands and had his first encounter with DS Mills.

For those present that day in the CID office, witnessing the first meeting of Tyler and Mills, there seemed little to observe. Jim Tyler, at six-feet tall, lean and toned with neatly clipped raven hair, had extended a hand towards Danny Mills and smiled. Then Tyler had issued a simple, warm greeting, his softly spoken tone belying a quiet strength that more than a few had underestimated, often to their cost.

Beneath the apparent calm, a hidden storm raged almost constantly inside the DCI, discernible from something fierce that was occasionally glimpsed in the depths of his dark green eyes. A few among the assembled might have detected a certain edge to DCI Jim Tyler, cloaked by the effect of compassionate wisdom that he exuded. But most would have missed it.

His educated voice betrayed no accent, modern newsreader, rather than old-time BBC. He had been born and raised on a Leicestershire estate, moving to London to pursue a career as a police officer. Unprovoked, the edge resident in Jim Tyler was a subtle beast.

There was nothing pompous about the man, though many over the years had misunderstood him, taking a certain shyness that he had never been entirely able to shake off, as a sign of aloofness, even arrogance. A tinge of world-weary cynicism had crept in over recent times, often expressed in dark, dry humour. It had rubbed many up the wrong way.

The contrast with Danny Mills would not have been lost on the observers to that first, brief introduction. Mills was the shorter man, with a brutal crew-cut and a strong regional accent. He had lived his entire life in the Potteries, at least until his recent and somewhat troubled move into the surrounding countryside, courtesy of the demands of his family.

There were signs of a creeping middle-aged spread that Danny Mills remained in denial of, and it was born out of a passion for food of almost any description and a taste for beer that circumstances of late had caused him to neglect. For a man who loved his football, it had been noted by more than one colleague that the DS looked better suited to the game of rugby. But he had long given up playing sports of any kind.

There were rumours circulating in whispers that Tyler had arrived under a cloud. Mills was staying out of it. Gossip was toxic, and over the years he had seen it cause empires to fall and many heads to roll.

Following the short meeting with the new DCI, Mills had finished organising the team before taking the opportunity to drive home for a couple of hours, cursing every mile that the office was no longer a stone's throw away.

That auspicious day was promising to be a long one, and doubtless the first of many.

***

When Mills returned to Hanley Police Station, the dirty grey block that blighted Cedar Lane, Tyler announced that they would visit the site where the bones had been discovered, before making the drive out to the moorland town of Leek.

In Leek, ten miles to the north east of Hanley, there lived a forty-six-year-old woman who once had a brother. If that brother had still been alive he would have been forty-five years old. But thirty years ago, almost to the day, that brother failed to return home from school.

The boy, his sister and their parents had lived less than a mile from where the bones had been discovered. It was the first credible lead out of a sack full of hoax calls and sad, twisted flights of fancy. It still might go nowhere.

Another statement would have to follow soon and the pressure at the top was building nicely. Forensics weren't coming up with anything contradicting the mathematics suggested by the woman in Leek, though the pathologist needed to have his say and that announcement looked to be imminent. But so far, thirty years was shaping up to be a good estimation.

Which made the boy fifteen the day he failed to return home; and again, science had no problem with the figures, Pathology willing.

If the woman from Leek wasn't crazy, or otherwise mistaken, her brother had been pulled from a mound of earth by a black retriever named after one of the city's greatest heroes.

And if everything went on adding up, the dead boy was soon to be known to a news-hungry city as Alan Dale.

CHAPTER SIX

'I believe that the village was actually named in the Domesday Book,' said Tyler, watching his new partner observing the scene of crime officers still busying around the site where the body had been discovered.

'True,' said Mills. 'Except that this isn't the village.'

Tyler looked up towards the higher barricade, with the trees of the park billowing in early summer splendour. He admired the stunning explosion of colour before turning to look down beyond the lower barricade, to a strip of grim factory buildings crumbling alongside the busy city artery. *A city of contrasts,* he thought.

'The newspapers and the news stations seem to *think* this is the village.'

'Perhaps they should have asked the locals,' said Mills. He followed Tyler's gaze. 'That lot will be next, no doubt.'

'What's that— oh, I see. For the bulldozers, you mean. You don't approve?'

'Maybe they'll find a corpse or two there. That would really put us on the map.'

'Any reason they should *find a corpse or two?*'

Mills, visibly bristling, shrugged.

'Something the matter with your shoulders?'

'The village begins at the park gates, sir. The corpse was found in—'

'Stoke, I believe.'

'That's right.'

'Once the capital town of this *extraordinary collection, this quite remarkable city.*'

He watched Mills' eyes scanning his own for traces of irony and failing to find any.

'Sounds like you called in at tourist information, sir.'

'Does it? Maybe an outsider can see this place as it is now, and not as it once was.'

'What's that supposed to mean?'

In the heat of DCI Tyler's returning glare, DS Mills lowered his own.

'Finished, Sergeant? Good. I'm here to do a job, same as you. Come on. I need you to navigate the maze and get us over to Leek. Miss Dale is expecting us. She's been waiting thirty years, so the least we can do is arrive on time today.'

The two officers got into the car beyond the lower barricade now festooned with police warnings, and Mills pulled out into the stagnating line of traffic.

This part of the world was certainly full of surprises. Tyler had expected the ugliness, the testament to fading industrial splendour, but not the greenness, the rolling hills visible from practically every vantage point. Perhaps the entire city was filled with people who knew how to keep a secret; how to keep the rest of the world at bay.

If that's the case, he thought, *it doesn't bode well for the coming days.*

***

Mills drove back towards Hanley, taking advantage of the recent bypass to avoid the worst of the traffic. The narrow arteries of the city struggled to deal effectively with the weight of twenty-first century traffic, and the new flyover was generally regarded as a necessary deal-with-the-devil if the city was not to grind to a complete halt.

Skirting Hanley, it seemed an enigma to Tyler that within a few minutes they had navigated the bypass entirely and were already free of the congestion and out into open countryside. This was like no other city that he had laid eyes on. 'This truly is a miraculous place,' he said.

Mills didn't respond immediately. He eyed Tyler sideways and then asked, 'What do you mean by that?'

'I mean to say, one minute we're in the thick of it, the next minute, literally, the city has all but vanished. And it seems to perform this trick no matter which direction you take. How can this be so?'

'Look, sir—'

'No, you look,' snapped Tyler. 'I want your mind on the job, and I mean one hundred percent. I can hear your thoughts, man. The silence is full of them. When we're interviewing, I want you analysing the words, the pauses, and the look in the eye. I don't expect to find that you've missed it all because you're busy fretting over whether I'm trying to make some backhand jibe about your *heritage.*'

'The miracle is in the shape of it,' said Mills, not dropping a beat.

'What's that?'

'Stoke was never designed to any particular scheme. Six towns built themselves up in a ramshackle way, competing, expanding and finally converging. You couldn't sort the mess out if you wanted to. It happened to go long and narrow, hugging the water, serving industry and it never quite extinguished the countryside. I hope that answers your question.'

'Admirably,' said Tyler, impressed. 'Thank you for the orientation.'

'You are more than welcome.'

A journey of less than a dozen miles out of the city, most of it on the road northeast as it cut ruthlessly through the North Staffordshire countryside, brought the two officers into the town of Leek.

'The gateway to the moorlands,' said Tyler, as they arrived. 'And this time I do confess to stealing from a guidebook.'

Mills said nothing, but there was still an edge to the way that he didn't say it.

***

Sheila Dale sat in the front room of her small terraced house on the far side of Leek town, peering constantly through her net curtains in anticipation of the arrival of the promised unmarked police car.

When the car came into view the woman didn't hesitate. She was out on the street before the detectives had chance even to weigh up the neighbourhood. Net curtains were fidgeting at front windows on both sides of the street as Miss Dale shepherded her visitors through the front door and into her lonely world.

Sitting in the spartan elegance of the front room, Tyler thought the woman looked a good ten years older than she was admitting. He knew how the world could do that.

'Nice town, Leek,' he said. 'It's my first time. How long have you lived here?'

Dale looked nervous, her eyes moving between the officers, as though overwhelmed by the volume of company. Tyler wondered how long it had been since another human being had set foot through that front door.

'I moved out of the city after Mum died,' she said.

Tyler gestured to Mills, and the DS started to make notes while the senior detective conducted the interview.

Alan had failed to come home after school one afternoon in early summer. 'Just a few weeks before the main school holidays, it was. Mum and Dad never got over it. You never get over something like that.'

'I can imagine,' said Tyler.

The woman looked doubtful. 'For a time, Mum seemed to hold out, running on hope. She kept that up for a long time. It was her way of being loyal to her lost son. I think Dad was closer to Alan, though. I think Dad had more of an idea of what really happened.'

She asked if the two detectives would like a cup of tea, but Tyler answered for both of them, licking at dry lips but saying that they were okay for the moment.

'You say that your dad had more of an idea *of what really happened*. What do you mean by that, exactly, Miss Dale?'

'I think he feared the worst. That Alan wouldn't be coming back.'

She glanced at Mills, as though to tacitly enquire whether his colleague was in the habit of asking stupid questions. But Mills merely bit his lip and tried to smile politely.

'Dad basically pined to death. They called it a viral infection – I suppose they had to call it something. Maybe it was, and he was too weak to fight it. But I know that it was all down to what happened to Alan.'

Tears were threatening, her voice wobbling. 'He was dead within the year. I mean, within the year of Alan …'

The tears came down like a flood, and it was Mills' turn to ask if anybody would like a cup of tea yet. But Sheila Dale was rallying. 'Mum kept saying he would come back one day. She had all these fantasies about him going to London, America, even. Coming back rich. 'You'll see,' she used to say. 'You'll see I'm right. One day he'll be outside in his Rolls Royce.'

'But he didn't come back. I knew from the start he would never come back, not from where he'd gone. No coming back from there. And then Mum became ill about five years later.'

Tyler frowned. 'What do you mean?' he asked. 'About your brother *not coming back from where he'd gone?*'

'Well, isn't it obvious?'

She looked again at Mills for some assistance.

'We're a bit slow,' said Mills, trying to strike a genial note. 'We need things spelling out, I'm afraid.'

'Slow?' said Dale. DS Mills had already realised his mistake. 'I wouldn't say the police were so much slow as couldn't care less. Why should they, what's a poor working-class boy like Alan to the authorities?'

She took a few seconds to compose herself, blinking away the tears in the process. 'I'm sorry,' she said. 'I just don't think that much of an effort was made when my brother went missing. I think they missed their chance.'

She looked at the two officers, one to the other, and her expression softened. 'But I can't hold you pair personally responsible for thirty years ago, can I? That wouldn't be fair.'

Tyler allowed a short pause before asking again what she had meant by Alan not coming back from where he'd gone.

'He had nowhere else to go. He loved home, and he was happy there. Alan wouldn't have let his family suffer like that. He would have made contact.'

'You thought he was dead?'

'Do I have to spell it out?'

'Yes, Miss Dale. I'm afraid that you do,' said Tyler.

'Not exactly Holmes and Watson, are you?'

'We do our best. And I believe that DS Mills makes a lovely cup of tea. Perhaps it is time to test that belief.'

Mills made the tea while Dale told of how she had been working as a librarian when her mother became sick. Tyler thought how she looked like a librarian: the glasses, the thin, humourless face; almost a caricature of a librarian, in fact.

'I went part-time to look after her. She died less than two years later. Seven years after Alan went, it was. She was saying he'd come home one day, saying it right up until the day she died. But I think she'd given up believing it and I sometimes wonder if she ever really believed it.'

There was a faraway look in her eye, and Tyler wondered what exactly she was seeing. Mills, returning from his duties in the kitchen, took the opportunity of serving up the cups of tea. But all the time Sheila Dale's focus didn't shift. 'I moved up to Leek,' she said, still gazing into a past visible only to herself. 'I wanted to be away from it, but not so far away that I couldn't visit their resting places.'

A long pause followed, growing steadily into an awkward silence.

'Mum's grave. Dad's grave. I got a job in the library here, when my nerves allowed me to work at all. Four lives were ruined that day, not just one.'

'That day?' said Mills.

'June 16. It was a Friday, one week before the start of Potters.'

'Potters?' asked Tyler.

'An old tradition unique to the city of Stoke,' said Mills. 'Potters Holidays: Last week of June, first week of July.'

'I see,' said Tyler, slightly stunned by his sergeant's show of pride in explaining the concept.

'Rained every year at Potters,' added Mills. 'You could count on it.'

As though on cue, Dale was crying again. And even with DS Mills back in charge of drinks, this time the crying didn't stop.

The officers sat with their drinks until Tyler, recognising no sign of a break in the deluge, offered to come back another time. 'Is that okay? Miss Dale, is that okay?'

When Sheila Dale realised she was being asked a question, she nodded weakly, and put down the second untouched drink. 'I'm sorry,' she said.

'No reason to apologise,' said Mills. 'Not everybody likes my tea. It's an acquired taste.'

They were preparing to leave the woman to her freshly re-opened grief, when she gestured to them to wait a moment. Walking over to the walnut cabinet standing in the corner of the living room, she took out a sealed envelope and handed it to Tyler.

'You might find this helpful,' she said.

CHAPTER SEVEN

The officers stood at the top of The Stumps looking out over the city.

'This village,' said Tyler, 'would make an excellent base for a runner. There's always a hill to climb to get anywhere.'

Mills eyed him. 'Are you a keen runner?'

'I'm trying to be. There are worse ways of dealing with this job.'

Mills could think of better ways. A decent pint in a decent boozer being top of the list, and a season ticket at Stoke City wouldn't go amiss either.

'So, the million-dollar question: what do you think the chances are of Alan Dale turning up on his sister's doorstep with the Roller parked outside?'

Mills considered the question. 'About the same as Stoke winning the Champions League,' he said.

'I take it that's not a hopeful forecast.'

'I take it you're not a football fan.'

Tyler smiled. 'You follow the local team?'

'I try to. You get a choice of two teams, living here.'

'You must tell me more.'

And out of spite he did.

'Port Vale and Stoke City. Vale play in the north of the city. City used to play in Stoke, at the old Victoria Ground, the second oldest club in the country after Notts County. Nicknamed *The Potters*.'

'Fascinating,' said Tyler.

'City have a new ground now,' said Mills, carrying on regardless. He pointed to an impressive stadium, visible in the distance. 'They don't play in Stoke anymore.'

'They are the bigger club?'

'And the more expensive to watch. Hardly the sport for working folk these days, I'm afraid.'

'Perhaps you should change your allegiance?'

'You must be joking. The red and white stripes of Stoke City run through me like a stick of rock,' he said, and somewhat defiantly, thought Tyler. 'That's what my wife says, anyway. Vale aren't in the same league but the rivalry's still bitter.'

Not the only thing that's bitter around here, thought Tyler. 'I take it that you don't favour the under-dog.'

Mills cast a sharp look at Tyler. 'Don't get much time for football these days.'

'Overtime and country living?'

Mills' eyes narrowed. 'Anything interesting in the envelope?' he said.

Tyler ignored the question. 'And now the added inconvenience of thirty-year-old corpses turning up on the patch.'

He suggested they walk down The Stumps towards the higher barricade. A uniformed officer was still keeping guard and Tyler flashed his ID. 'Not many tourists around today?'

'School and work, I suppose, sir.'

'No doubt the coaches will be arriving later.'

'Wouldn't surprise me.'

The human remains had been removed and dispatched to the lab, but the SOCOs were still picking around in the dirt and the rubble of no-man's land between the barricades. The officers looked on, but there was little to see. The area where the body had been found was canvassed off, and watching the mysterious figures dressed in white observing their daily rituals wasn't much of a spectator sport, in Tyler's opinion.

The officers moved back up to the bottom park gate, just below the concrete posts. Tyler gazed up the path, through the two posts, trying to picture something. When he spoke, he did so without once taking his eyes off the path.

'So, what do we know?' he said. 'According to Pathology, a backward fall likely shattered the spine and fractured the skull.

But did he die immediately? Was he alone and was he conscious? The cheek bone was broken by means other than the fall. He may well be thirty-years dead and he may have died aged fifteen. According to Sheila Dale, his name is Alan. Thirty years ago, this place was a building site, the same as it is now.

'But was it murder?'

Tyler turned around, though not to look at his sergeant for answers to the questions fizzing through his head. He looked down beyond the patrolled barricade, then back up, through the posts. 'Come on,' he said. 'Just one lap today, I think.'

With Mills a yard or so behind him, Tyler made a single circuit of the small park, entering at the bottom gate, all the time looking back to gain a fresh perspective on the site where the body had been discovered.

Walking at a snail's pace, and constantly stopping to look back over the ground covered, he appeared lost in thought, confiding nothing, while Mills took the beating of the afternoon sun, which was doing nothing for his humour.

They emerged from the top gate, back onto The Stumps a few feet below the two concrete posts that, along with those at the bottom, had given the path its unofficial name.

'They were put there to stop cars trying to use the path as a short cut into the village,' Mills said, in answer to the question.

'Ingenious.'

'We know a thing or two,' said Mills. 'Contrary to popular belief.'

'Tell me, do you remember this place thirty years ago?'

'Not really,' said Mills. 'I lived in Longton. That's east of here.'

'Far?'

'Three miles or so.'

'Ah, Longton.'

'Something funny, sir?'

'I heard a story, a local legend, you might say. That there are Longton people who have never visited Tunstall, which, I believe, lies in the north of the city. You ever visited Tunstall?'

Mills didn't appear amused by the question.

'I mean to say, can such parochialism truly exist in this day and age? And here, in the very centre – the very *heart* – of the country?'

'It's as true as people from Tunstall never visiting Longton, I imagine.'

'I see. And never the twain … perhaps this really is a city like no other. What do you think? Maybe that explains the intense rivalry between the warring football clubs. Tribalism, I find that scary, I always have done. Would you say this was a city at war with itself?'

Mills took a deep breath that didn't quite suck all of the sour air out of the atmosphere. 'Thirty years ago, the site looked pretty much as it does today.'

'Coming back to you, is it?'

'Research, sir. I thought that it might be relevant to the present enquiry.'

'Good work,' said Tyler, still not acknowledging the acid tone. 'They knocked down a factory and built a pottery warehouse and outlet store. And now that's gone and next up is a visitors' centre, I believe.'

'That's progress, sir. I understand it was either that or more housing.'

'Not so good for attracting the tourists. Pottery on view in the Potteries – how could such a concept fail? But my guess is that now the place has blood in its soil, it will attract a good deal more, and not merely lovers of ceramics. What do you reckon?'

'I don't know about that, sir. All I know is they went bust. Not many new businesses have survived around Stoke in recent years. Everybody goes up to Hanley these days. This place has become derelict; a haven for druggies. With all the regeneration that's going on, or that's supposed to be going on, some chancer decided it would make a good location for building new houses. There's the park behind – I've seen worse locations.'

'And someone else decided a visitors' centre was the better bet.'

'Personally, I'd go with the houses.'

'Perhaps we should have another look inside that envelope, what do you think?'

'Can't see the harm in it.'

Back in the car, Tyler took out a pile of crisp A4 sheets. A careful hand had filled them up with black ink. He handed them to Mills and watched as the DS cast an eye over them.

But Mills was giving nothing away, and Tyler was soon gazing out towards the site below them, a place that Sheila Dale knew well. A place that had no doubt haunted her dreams these past years, one way or another.

'So, any thoughts?' asked Tyler at last.

Mills seemed to be mulling something over.

'Let's drive and think,' said Tyler.

With the pages tucked carefully back into the envelope, they headed back towards Hanley.

Winding their way through the heavy traffic, Tyler said, 'Perhaps we should have brought her in. Get the rest of the story and be done with it.'

Mills took his eyes off the road ahead and glanced at the passenger. 'You're saying Dale knows what happened? She knows who—?'

'She knows a hell of a lot.'

Something in Tyler's tone rang a strange note, and Mills couldn't help but be unnerved. 'What are you reading between the lines, sir?'

'What is there to read? Tell me, what is there, what's she telling us?'

'That's not a confession she's given us?'

Tyler looked at Mills. 'That's a remarkably astute remark.'

Mills let the compliment whistle past into the congested air outside. Then he said, 'It is a confession or else it isn't. And you've read it.'

'And so have you.'

The vibrations from the conversation were still resonating as Mills pulled into Hanley.

In sight of the police station, Tyler spoke again, but in a tone mindful of the echoes. 'Yes, I have read it,' he said. 'But not in that light. Come on, let's get a drink and take another look.'

CHAPTER EIGHT

The central police station looked every bit the ugly relation, standing across from the new court buildings, adjacent to the library and museum. Tyler had heard that the museum held the finest collection of pottery in the world; it was just that he didn't give a damn about pottery, fine or otherwise.

And neither, he suspected, did Danny Mills. The court buildings, splendid as they undoubtedly were, would no doubt play host to the same old dramas that the old buildings had; heroes and villains letting it all come down to which brief had the bigger brain, and was paid for from the deeper wallet.

Coffees in hand, the two detectives sat in the third-floor office, away from the hullabaloo, and went over the pages that Sheila Dale had prepared for them. They had an hour before CS Berkins arrived, a man renowned not only for a prize-winning moustache, but also a self-proclaimed ability to see the 'bigger picture'.

And he was going to have to make some decisions about what exactly the press and the media needed to tell the city and the nation about the late Alan Dale.

Alan was a few days off fifteen and one day he didn't come home from school. He attended River Trent High School and had done for almost four years. He lived all of his short life in the village of Penkhull at the geographical centre of the city of Stoke-on-Trent, and the oldest settlement in the city. Alan lived with his parents and sister, Sheila.

Alan was a quiet boy, bright but a little immature. He was what people might describe as naïve. He was too trusting. He was scared a lot of the time, too, because people like to pick on easy targets.

Alan wore glasses and his arms were almost as thin as the skin on them. He had skin that could barely conceal his frightened little heart beating in terror every time he took a kick or a punch or an unkind word.

He was good at making friends, but little by little I saw him losing the will to even try. People let him down every day of his short life but he still always did his best to smile and do the right thing like the lovely, shy boy that he always was.

The teachers at his school kept saying that he would do better if he concentrated. But how could a young boy like Alan concentrate when he was living in fear all the time? How could he?

His form teacher the year before he died was named:

MAGGIE CALLEER

Alan thought that she was kind. I went to the same school, though I was in the higher year, my last year. What I saw of Miss Calleer, I would say that she probably was kind. But she didn't do nearly enough, nobody did. Who was it who said, someone famous I think, that all it takes for evil to prevail is for good people to do nothing? Someone very clever indeed.

I believe that when Miss Calleer retired, she moved out of the city, but I don't think she strayed too far. There was only so much she could have done, but at least with her, Alan had a fighting chance.

Then Alan moved into the lion's den.

HOWARD WOOD

And Howard Wood was, believe me when I say this, an uncaring bully with a drink problem. Actually, I didn't know that he had a big drink problem back then, I only heard the rumours. But he was certainly an uncaring bully. He was Alan's so-called 'form teacher' for the last year of my little brother's life. He was also the worst thing that could have happened to Alan at that time. Or any time.

The Headmaster at the school was named:

FREDRICK WISE

Wise by name, foolish by nature. He couldn't see what was going on underneath his own stupid nose. Good at one thing he was, and that was defending his position. When my parents went up to the school and tried to complain about what was happening to Alan, Wise just made sure that nothing could ever reflect badly on his precious *school and, therefore, himself. He was a glory-hunter, a scoundrel who is now enjoying a fat retirement on the shores of Rudyard Lake. (I sometimes think that he lives too close to me for comfort and I haven't got it in me to wish him a long and prosperous old age.)*

Alan had a friend:

ANTHONY TURNOCK

Alan always called him Tony. Tony was what you would call 'the fat kid of the class'. Because of this he knew what Alan was going through, as he got some of it too. But Alan would never give them what they wanted, and so they never stopped.

They never stopped.

Tyler looked at Mills. 'What do you suppose she means by that?' he asked. 'What didn't Alan Dale give them that *they* wanted?'

Mills shrugged. 'I think she's trying to tell us that her brother was killed by these people, whoever they were – are. There's no confession in it that I can see.'

'Confession was your word, not mine.'

Mills didn't respond to that and Tyler turned the page.

Sheila Dale had documented the death of her father, her mother's illness, her time spent working as a librarian. 'She has a curious style. A curious lady altogether,' said Tyler. 'But look at this. This interests me.'

I went over to look at the place where they found Alan. Around the time that he went missing it was a building site, too. But they didn't close it off like they have done now. They left the path open so that people could take the short cut from the village down into Stoke and back, cutting between the allotments and the park.

One of my favourite memories is of me and Alan cutting along that path, down into Stoke on Saturday mornings to get the shopping from Stoke Market. In the village, in those days, there were lots of corner shops that served us during the week. But on weekends it was always the market in Stoke, because it was cheaper and the food was fresher, or at least that was the idea. On hot days we used to sweat bucketfuls carrying the shopping back up the steep path by the park, all the way to the top of The Stumps and all the way home.

The other day, when I went back there, I took the long way around and went back into the village. I went up to Alan's old school, my old school. Looking at that building I realised that I have no happy memories of that place, because of what it did to my brother.

It placed an angel amongst devils.

I hate it and I hate them. I hate all of them.

Alan did not walk home alone that day. He would have walked straight home, as he always did. He would have had no business around a building site where adolescent devils went to try and kill the pain of their own lives by inflicting evil on the innocent. They took him there and they killed him. One way or another they killed him.

You'll find all the answers to what happened to Alan by going back to that place, and to the legion that passed through it.

The final page was signed, *Sheila Dale.*

Tyler stood up, walked over to the window and looked out. It wasn't the best view he'd seen since arriving in the city. The bulldozers had certainly been busy, he thought, giving the impression that a bombing raid had recently taken place. Blink and you could be looking out on a scene from World War Two. Vast areas of debris dotted the landscape, providing intermittent impressions of desolation and abandonment.

'So, what do you reckon, then?'

'Sounds clear enough to me, sir. But what do I know?'

'I don't know, so enlighten me, please: what *do* you know?'

'She thinks that her brother was killed alright and probably by kids from his school, possibly from his class. This Howard Wood's class. But I get the impression there's something she's not telling us.'

Tyler didn't say anything, kept looking out the window. It was a good minute later when he said, 'Well, here comes the cavalry.'

***

Chief Superintendent Graham Berkins listened carefully to what Tyler had to say, and

even put off twiddling at the ends of his moustache until the DCI had finished. Then Berkins, fingers now firmly at the handlebars, was offered the opportunity to view Sheila Dale's written work, which he declined, bluntly.

A busy man, he was in the habit of making important decisions with speed and authority. The media had the scent and everything must be done, and done fast, to clear up the 'unfortunate mystery.' After all, Stoke-on-Trent was a place that was moving into the future, and dirty secrets from the past were the bread and butter of the media moguls, and a 'potential banana skin' to all that regeneration might promise. There was a lot at stake.

The ends of the moustache were rolling up beautifully as the senior man asked DS Mills to leave the room and get on with the business at hand, before concluding his address.

'You're a good officer, Jim, and we're happy, more than happy – I'd have to say delighted – to have you aboard. I personally believe that what happened in London highlights issues for which you simply cannot be held solely responsible. Off the record, I think you punched the wrong man, but I don't suppose that you would be even out on the streets if you had punched the right one.'

'That's kind of you to say.'

'It has nothing whatsoever to do with kindness.'

'It's still appreciated.'

'That's as maybe. In a nutshell: I admire your integrity, and their loss might turn out to be our gain. I'm aware that you have a number of … *personal issues.*'

'I'm addressing them.'

'Highly commendable. If you need any support, you only have to ask.'

'Thank you again. I'm certainly doing all I can.'

'Good man. You are about to show the world that Staffordshire will employ only the finest when it comes to bringing to justice those who transgress on these shores.'

Tyler hadn't remembered the county being coastal, and the thought distracted him to the point of almost missing the one about 'no span of time or distance hiding from justice those who attempt to defile the soil of our proud city.'

Tyler, wondering whether he was expected to dab an eye or jump to his feet and salute – perhaps both – listened in disbelief as Berkins promised that any resource required need only be asked for in the name of truth and justice.

Then a firm handshake, a brief but nonetheless serious eyeballing and a forthright nod, and it was all over.

God, the man is stressed, thought Tyler. *Close to the edge.*

***

He gave Mills the highlights and was surprised that his colleague seemed almost impressed. 'Oh, come on, man. He was trying out the speech before delivering it down there. And they won't believe a word of it any more than I did. The man's at breaking point.'

Mills joined Tyler at the window. A throng of people with cameras and microphones had gathered outside. Berkins was angling his neck to provide the right profile, one which did justice to the cultivated masterpiece between nose and top lip.

'Better get yourself a bath and hair wash this evening,' said Tyler.

'Sir?'

'It's back to school in the morning.'

CHAPTER NINE

They drove up through Stoke town centre, taking the wide sweeping arc past the still-secured scene, complete with media hopefuls diligently manning the lower barricade. 'Are you in the mood to be interviewed?' asked Tyler. 'Me neither. Drive on.'

Climbing Hartshill Bank, they turned into Wedgwood Road, and Tyler made the observation that there was not a single sign indicating that they were actually in Penkhull.

'More a state of mind is it, this mythical village?' he said.

'Sore point with the residents,' said Mills. 'The fight goes on.'

'The fight for recognition always does.'

At the end of Wedgwood Road they came to a T-junction. Mills pointed left. 'Heart of the village is up there; the school,' he said, pointing right, 'is down that way.'

It was just short of nine o'clock and the roads were still in the thick of the school run. As the car hesitated at the junction, a small queue had formed behind as Mills awaited a decision from the senior detective.

'Left, I think,' Tyler said at last. 'A little context might be useful.'

Mills pulled left into Trent Lane and up the short climb to the centre of the village. Turning right into the square, he pulled the car to a halt as instructed.

In the middle of the square was a small church, flanked on one side by a village store, antique shop, off-licence, chip-shop, hairdressers and launderette, and on the other by a row of incongruous houses that appeared to have been temporarily placed there.

'Many changes in thirty years?' asked Tyler, trying to get the measure of the odd mixture of times and places that surrounded him.

'Like I said before, sir. I wasn't around these parts back then.'

'No, of course. A Longton man. But all the same …'

'All the same, I believe that the church was still here.'

Tyler eyed him, and Mills caught a glint of steel.

'Alan Dale lived close to here?'

'About two hundred yards off the square.' Mills pointed back. 'Around that bend, half a mile on and you're down to the park and allotments.'

'So, the walk home from school, what, ten minutes?'

'Walking briskly, possibly. The lane up from the school is deceptive. I'd say fifteen minutes, unless you were striding out.'

'And as far again to where the body was found?'

'A bit less as it's downhill, once you get around that bend. A slow decline into Stoke.'

'In more ways than one?'

Mills didn't answer, and Tyler switched on the radio and tuned into the local station. The air waves were full of news and speculation following the statement from Berkins. 'Seems like there may have been a murder in these parts after all, by the sound of things,' said Tyler. 'Come on. Let's go and meet the headteacher.'

***

The ride down Trent Lane from the village square brought them to the school, the name of which had been left out of the press release. Tyler was glad of that. Fighting through a mob of cameras and microphones was far more fun on television than in the flesh. It would be a diplomatic triumph for the Head to get the information first-hand and in person. Grease the wheels a little, it all helped.

In the reception office, a secretary informed the officers that the headteacher, Miss Hayburn, was preparing to go into assembly and could not possibly be disturbed. Tyler sighed and flashed his card under the secretary's long and thoroughly powdered nose, and suggested that perhaps it wouldn't hurt for once if a deputy were to handle the formalities, and could somebody organise a pot of tea and perhaps a plate of biscuits for the nice policemen.

Mills thought for a moment and then went for it. 'You seem tense, sir,' he said, as the two of them were led towards the Head's office. 'I mean, if you don't mind me saying so.'

'I do mind you saying it, as a matter of fact. But anyway, these places make me nervous and I suspect that they always will.'

'Rough time at school, was it?'

'A concentration camp. But I survived. There, I've said it. In fact, on reflection, I've said too much and so now you must swear an oath of secrecy.'

***

Tyler and Mills were making a start on the hospitality when the door opened and a woman in her forties entered without knocking.

Busy, forthright, professional, thought Tyler. Miss Hayburn, headteacher at River Trent High, was making a favourable first impression.

Tyler liked her, and was even willing to admit, at least in his private thoughts, that some things had changed for the better. Here was a woman who you might just be able to bring your problems to. But then again, that might depend on what those problems were.

Miss Hayburn had heard on the news about the local discovery, and that 'foul play' was not being ruled out, far from it. But she had no idea that the dead boy was an ex-pupil of the school.

She appeared deeply shocked by the information and Tyler attempted to reassure her. 'Of course, you have nothing to worry about. After all, it didn't happen on your watch.'

He saw her shock mutate into an expression of firm resolve, and instantly recognised that it would be a mistake to ever get on the wrong side of this woman.

'Let me assure you,' she said, 'that you will have our full co-operation here at River Trent High. Anything that we can do to assist with your enquiries, you only have to ask.'

Tyler didn't need a second invitation, immediately requesting lists of ex-pupils and staff, along with full contact information where available. And Miss Hayburn was as good as her word, leaving the detectives to the refreshments, while she went to set in motion the process of information gathering.

Tyler, nibbling carefully on a single ginger biscuit, watched Mills demolish the remainder of the generous platter. The sergeant was a big man, he thought, and with his crew cut and sideburns would have looked the part of a formidable old-time copper in a uniform. But he had to watch his figure or else in a couple of years he'd be liable to start making noises getting out of a chair.

Mills, realising that he was being observed, stopped, mid-munch, the remains of a chocolate bourbon clutched guiltily in his fist.

'Very helpful,' said Tyler.

DS Mills discreetly swallowed the biscuit already in his mouth, while the remainder waved uncertainly until he lowered it to his lap. 'Sir?'

'Miss Hayburn. Very helpful.'

Tyler smiled, and Mills, taking this as an all-clear, demolished the last of the bourbon without further concern for the ethics of the situation.

'Did you enjoy your time at school, Sergeant?'

'It was okay. Not great. But not terrible either.'

'Were you ever bullied?'

'I can't say that I was, not really. I could look after myself pretty well. I was lucky, I suppose.'

'Indeed you were.'

'Why do you ask?'

'I'm curious, that's all. It's a common problem, I understand.'

'You mean bullying in schools?'

'I mean bullying in life. Is there any more tea left in that pot?'

***

The detectives were furnished with lists of personnel coinciding with the attendance of Alan Dale, and with particular reference to 1972. Mills, perusing the information while Tyler entertained Miss Hayburn with a diatribe on the 'current sad state of education in the country', interrupted. 'Howard Wood,' he said, and suddenly two pairs of eyes were scrutinising him.

Howard Wood, Alan Dale's last form teacher. Howard Wood, condemned by Sheila Dale in her notes. Still there, teaching at River Trent High.

'Would you like to speak to Mr Wood?' asked Miss Hayburn.

'Oh, yes,' said Tyler. 'Most certainly. But first you might like to paint us a portrait of the man.'

'Might I? To what purpose?'

Tyler thought for a moment, before returning to his diatribe on the nation's educational well-being, while Mills went through the remainder of the lists of old pupils and teachers, checking against the details given by Sheila Dale. At last Tyler came in again on the subject of Howard Wood, but still the headteacher was adhering to a strict code of confidentiality, protecting her staff with a subtle professionalism that the DCI couldn't help but admire.

'Did you ever meet Mr Wise, the headmaster here during Alan Dale's time?' Tyler asked her.

She hadn't. And neither did she wish to speculate on the grounds of gossip and reputation.

'Well, I have to say,' said Tyler, after the headteacher had again popped out of the office to burden administration with further requests for information, 'Miss Hayburn plays it with a straight bat. I can hardly blame her for that, though. Putting myself in her

39

situation, I would likely do the same, at least until I knew exactly what I was dealing with. Uncovered anything else interesting from your studies, apart from Howard Wood?'

'Not really,' said Mills. 'I wonder if Miss Dale knew the names – remembers any of the names – of the kids in her brother's class, apart from his friend Anthony Turnock.'

'I would imagine that she would have added them, if she'd thought they were significant.'

'So would I.'

'What are you saying?'

'Could be that she doesn't remember. Maybe we should ask her.'

'I'm sure we will.'

'We could do with an address for Mr Wise, too.'

'Yes, I was thinking of paying a visit. Any questions you would particularly like to ask him?'

'Be interesting to see if he remembers Alan Dale's parents visiting the school. And his thoughts on Mr Wood might be pertinent.'

'Lives on the shores of Rudyard Lake, then, our retired headmaster?'

'So I believe.'

'Close to Leek?'

'Too close for Sheila Dale, apparently. It's a nice drive.'

'Does the area have any connection to Rudyard Kipling? I'm fond of a bit of Kipling.'

'Did him at school,' said Mills, explaining how the writer was named after the area by parents who had fallen in love with the lake and its environs.

'This is a visit that I'm very much looking forward to. Thank you.'

'Don't mention it.'

They stood up as Miss Hayburn returned. 'At ease, Sergeant,' said Tyler, winking at the headteacher. 'He thinks he's here for detention.'

CHAPTER TEN

Penkhull, it seemed to Tyler, as they drove away from the school, was an island stranded up above the city. To get to it you either came by helicopter or else had to drive through pockets of traffic-congested ugliness, dead industry and urban squalor.

Many, according to Mills, really did make the journey by helicopter: the village bordered on one of the country's finest trauma units. Few days passed without some poor soul being airlifted into the domain of its expertise.

Mills had made the point that the trauma unit, complete with helipad, had come along too late to help the likes of Alan Dale, and Tyler had countered, suggesting that perhaps it would be a few years still before the unit would be capable of raising the dead.

At the top of Trent Lane, with the church and village square to the right, Mills turned left, as instructed, along the curving road to where Alan Dale had lived with his family. A row of terraces quickly came into sight, on the right-hand side. Mills pulled up at the side of the road.

Some other family is living there now, thought Tyler, looking out on the property. He pictured the comings and goings of ordinary people doing ordinary things in the magical ordinariness of real life. Love, laughter, excitement, disappointment, sadness and sorrow had existed here, as in all places and times, he reflected. But then something else had come along; something that wasn't in the natural order of things.

At last he gave the signal to move on, to the crest of the hill, Honeydew Bank, before beginning the descent towards Stoke town. Before reaching the town, close to the bottom of the hill, Mills turned along the street that led to the top of The Stumps.

Getting out of the car Tyler was again struck by the view over the city: its skyline of ancient churches, pot-banks, oases of green in the shape of parks and nature trails, and the quilt of patchwork emerald stretching beyond, towards the surrounding hills and the open country. He turned to Mills, who was standing at his side.

'On Friday 16 June, 1972, Alan Dale attended River Trent High School and, as far as we know, left for the last time after the bell rang at four in the afternoon. He may have returned home or he may have headed directly to this place, possibly taking the same route that we have just taken – on foot, of course, alone or accompanied. From his injuries, the ones to his face, at least, it's likely an altercation took place, close to the time of death. But Alan Dale's death, which almost certainly resulted from a backward fall, might still have been an accident.'

Tyler shook his head. 'Why don't I think it was an accident?'

Mills didn't answer, staring out on the view, wondering why he had never seen this side of the city before. When Tyler next spoke, it startled Mills out of a deep, nostalgic reverie.

'So, this city, scarred as it is by the *fallen remnants of a once-great industrial past,* failed to make an impression on the village in which we stand?'

'I don't think there were many pot-banks in Penkhull, if that's what you mean,' said Mills. 'I believe that the village was once mostly forest, but we are talking a while ago.'

'So I believe. Then a few thousand years later, some bright spark thinks the river would make a great place on which to build the world's greatest pottery town, and Stoke was born.'

'Sounds like you've been doing your homework, sir.'

'Do you think Miss Hayburn would be impressed with me?'

'You'd have to ask her that yourself.'

'I doubt things were quite that straightforward – historically, I'm talking about.'

'I'm sure they never are,' said Mills. 'But I do know that once the great industrialists got going, eventually the hill formed a natural barrier between the rich and the poor, workers down in the town, or on the village slopes, the pottery owners up on the hill.'

'You should write guidebooks in your spare time; do you know that. You have a natural gift.'

'If you say so, sir.'

'The Dales lived on the hill. Are you saying that we have a motive here? That all the other children, along with the teachers, had to make their way up the hill every day, and that they made life a misery for the little rich boy at the top?'

Mills couldn't help but smile. 'These days you don't have to be rich to live on the hill, and not even thirty years ago. Probably even less so then. I don't think the Dale family were rich. You don't have to put up with that kind of thing when you're rich, and neither do your kids.'

'Point taken,' said Tyler. 'And I'm inclined to agree. Let's take a look at Kipling country, shall we? *Jungle Book* was my favourite read as a child. How about you?'

'More the *Shoot* football annual. That and old Stoke City programmes.'

'You're not kidding?'

'I wouldn't joke about a thing like that, sir.'

***

Back on the road out towards Leek, Mills took a narrow turning a few miles short of the moorland town, Tyler waxing lyrical about the stunning countryside, and not letting up until they arrived at Rudyard Lake.

The lakeside had been one of the Sunday picnic spots that Mills fondly recalled from childhood, eating ice-creams on boat trips across the water and the tricks of memory placing an imprint of blue skies and sunshine into every one of those long-gone days.

They found the home of Fredrick Wise, retired headmaster, nestling up in the woods above the lake. An impressive wrought iron gate complete with intercom security system suggested to Mills an occupant of wealth and self-importance.

'Looks to me as though running those gulags was profitable even back then,' said Tyler.

'So you won't be sending your kids to River Trent High, then?'

'Other people have *kids*.'

'People like me, you mean?'

'I believe you have children.'

'Jessica and Harry.'

'High school?'

'Juniors. Ten and eight.'

'Doing well?'

'Jessica's a bright girl.'

'Set to follow in your footsteps, you reckon?'

'I reckon she would make a good teacher. Bossy little madam.'

'Harry?'

'Harry wants to play for Stoke.'

'Is that a possibility?'

'No, frankly. Doesn't like getting his kit dirty. A bit delicate is Harry.'

'Isn't he rather young to be written off?'

'You have to really want it.'

'As long as he enjoys playing, that's the main thing, surely?'

'I suppose it is at that.'

'But you would be proud to see him wearing the colours?'

'What parent wouldn't? But playing at that level – I don't think so. It hasn't dawned on him yet.'

'We can all dream.'

'Harry needs to get his finger out, one way or another. I was the same.'

'And look at you now.'

Mills was trying to weigh up the remark when Tyler asked him, 'What do you think of Alan Dale's old school, then?'

Mention of the dead boy so soon after discussing his own children, brought a chill to the bright summer air that Mills could have done without. Tyler let the question ride, walking to the gate and pressing the bell on the intercom. 'The sleek Bentley in that long driveway says daddy's home.'

The intercom crackled and Tyler announced himself. A few moments later the gate swung open and the two detectives walked towards the small mansion house.

Before they arrived at the door, Mills said, 'River Trent High has greatly improved, according to reports. I heard it had a poor reputation back in the day, though.'

'How poor?'

'I've heard people say that they wouldn't send their dogs there.'

The front door opened, and a stout, well-dressed man with receding, yet still tenacious, salt and pepper hair, appeared on the step.

***

Fredrick Wise had only the vaguest memory of Alan Dale, though an unrequited fondness for the high school that had formed the pinnacle of his formidable career. He had been in post as headmaster at the school from the autumn term of 1969, three years before the boy went missing.

'You remember the original enquiry?' asked Tyler, sipping at the tea provided by the diminutive Mrs Wise.

'Of course I remember. In those days, it was unusual to have the police visiting one's school. These days I believe it can be a daily occurrence.'

His wife shook her head in good old state-of-the-nation style. Wise went on. 'But a missing child was something out of the ordinary, and naturally we were concerned.'

'For how long?'

Wise looked bemused, and his wife reflected his bemusement like a mirror fashioned from the master's hand. 'I beg your pardon?' said Wise.

'How long were you concerned?' repeated Tyler.

Wise continued to appear baffled by the question, and Mrs Wise tried to help out. 'I think that the disappearance of a child is something that one never quite gets over,' she said.

'Do you have any children, Mrs Wise?' asked Tyler.

'I hardly see the relevance.'

Tyler pressed the point anyway. 'You see,' he said, 'I haven't any children either. And I wonder if, with the best will in the world, our powers of empathy can stretch to understanding the nightmare that families like the Dales must have gone through, in the circumstances.'

Mills, wondering quite what the DCI was playing at, was nevertheless intrigued by the awkwardness that he had so deftly created in that lavish sitting room. Mrs Wise was colouring up a treat, clearing her throat like there was a family of frogs living inside, and flapping her arms around, all but spilling her tea. But for the noble intervention of her husband, there might have been damage done to the impressively sumptuous carpet on which everybody present rested their feet with the utmost respect.

'Look, Inspector, I don't mind you coming here to gain some background on this whole business,' said Wise. 'But I don't see what the Dickens our personal lives have to do with anything.'

Tyler took a calm sip of tea. 'My curiosity gets the better of me sometimes.'

'What exactly is it that you want?' asked Wise.

Tyler finished off his drink, complimented Mrs Wise on the quality of it, before carefully resting his cup and saucer on the coaster that had been placed strategically on the adjacent mahogany coffee table.

'What do I want?' asked Tyler. 'I want to know what happened to a boy who failed to return home from school one day in June, 1972. I want to know if he was happy at school, and if not, then why not, and because of who. I want to know what kind of child he was, this Alan Dale, and about his final days. And most of all, I want to know about the last hours and minutes of his short life.'

The speech resonated around the room. Then Wise said, 'We have no children. We wanted them and my wife was once pregnant. She lost the baby and I nearly lost her. Now, does that answer that particular question, Inspector?'

Mills couldn't help himself. He was thinking of Jessica and Harry. He looked at Mrs Wise and thought: *What has she got, really? Living with this pompous, inflated oaf?*

With a nod from Tyler he explained that the purpose of their visit was not to upset anybody; that they were trying to build a picture of relevant events and people. As the boy had been last seen on his way home from school, anybody and any event connected with the school was potentially relevant to the enquiry.

'Thank you,' said Tyler, when Mills had finished. 'I couldn't have put it better myself.'

Mrs Wise smiled awkwardly and offered to make more tea, while Mr Wise took the opportunity of expounding on testaments to the successes of his headmastership.

'… I called it a day in, oh let's see, 1992. Twenty-three years.'

The second-round of refreshments was arriving. 'About five years overdue, I would say.'

'Dear!'

'Well, what kind of a job is it now? They're nothing but bureaucrats. No teeth in their heads. They need the army calling in these days.'

'Yes, dear. Quite.'

'Discipline's quite a challenge these days,' said Mills.

Tyler took a sip of fresh tea and looked ready to put the gloves back on. 'Was Alan Dale much of a discipline problem?'

Mrs Wise seemed to wince at the unpleasant reminder of why these two men were there.

'I had no direct contact with the boy, as I recall, which suggests that he was not *much of a problem*,' said Wise.

'Only the baddies tend to get noticed,' said Tyler, and he could see that Wise hesitated, unsure whether he should agree or not.

Tyler squeezed a little harder. 'Were there many *problems* at your school, Mr Wise?'

'I'm not sure what point you're trying to—'

'Bullying,' said Tyler. 'As old as civilisation itself, we're told. A problem in any institution, I would imagine. Anywhere that has so many people under one roof, whatever the ages – you read about it now, it was certainly going strong when I was at school. And I'm the same age as Alan Dale. So why should River Trent High have been any different? What was so special about your school, *Mr Wise*?'

'I'm not saying there was anything special! But I would never have tolerated bullying. I would have dealt with it, and dealt with it severely.'

'Are you talking about pupils, or teachers?'

The old headmaster was on his feet, his fierce expression suggestive of the iron with which he had commanded his charges all those years ago. 'Just what are you trying to imply?'

Tyler sipped at his tea, and waited for Wise to sit down. As he did so, Mrs Wise moved closer to her husband, and rested a hand on his arm. Then she gave Tyler a scolding stare.

As the frosty silence settled over the room, Tyler finished his drink before once again placing the cup and saucer of finest bone china back on to the highly polished coffee table.

'Do you recall Alan Dale's parents visiting the school, Mr Wise?' he asked.

'Visiting? How do you mean, parent–teachers evenings?'

'I mean visiting to speak to you. Expressing their concerns about the bullying that their son was suffering.'

'It was a long time ago.'

'You don't recall the visit?'

'We're talking thirty years.'

'And you are saying that you don't remember Mr and Mrs Dale coming to see you about their son?'

The eyes answered.

'I see,' said Tyler.

'See what exactly?'

Wise exploded, his wife grabbing at his arm and pleading for calm. She looked to be on the verge of tears. But the old headmaster was back on his feet, and the purpling rage must have been a formidable sight, thought Tyler, if you happened to be fifteen years old or thereabouts and found yourself the object of it.

Wise stood trembling with indignant anger, demanding an explanation. His wife joined him. Together they waited for the officer, this intruder into their home, to explain himself. But Tyler looked instead at Mills, and then nodded towards his wrist to indicate the time.

The two detectives stood up like choreographed dancers.

'Thanks for your time,' said Tyler. 'The tea was lovely. The china – local, I take it?'

He held out a hand, and the pressure of politeness forced the couple to take it in turn. Then Tyler made a remark about the uncertainty of the British summer, and turned toward the door, Mills following.

On the doorstep, Tyler said, 'I believe that Howard Wood was Alan Dale's form teacher.'

Wise appeared to flinch at the name.

'He still teaches at the school, apparently. I wonder if Mr Wood has any particular recollection of bullies in his class.'

'Why don't you ask Mr Wood?' barked Wise.

'We will certainly do that. But nobody springs to mind?'

'With regard to what?'

Tyler frowned. 'With regard to the death of a frightened little boy, what else?'

Mrs Wise was standing behind her husband, muttering something about a solicitor.

'Save your money,' said Tyler. 'Only the kind with things to hide need bother those busy people.'

To the retired headmaster he handed a card. 'Should you happen to recall Mr and Mrs Dale's visit, Mr Wise. Shortly before Alan Dale's death.'

CHAPTER ELEVEN

At River Trent High the bell was summoning pupils back for the afternoon session when Tyler and Mills arrived on the car park. In the unmarked vehicle, they waited for the surge of movement to ease before stepping out.

'Make you nervous?' asked Mills.

'What, kids? Don't they make everybody? I mean to say, with this weight of numbers, something tribal's bound to take over.'

'Are you winding me up, sir?'

'Why would I want to do that?'

'I'm sure that I don't know.'

'Your two – enjoy school, do they?'

'Mostly, yes, I think. I hope so,' said Mills, looking far from convinced.

'Parents look at the world differently, wouldn't you agree?'

'How could you know that, not being a parent yourself?'

'Isn't it possible that looking in from the outside fosters objectivity? Perhaps keeping my eyes and ears open teaches me all that I need to know about the world, and about life. But then I may well be talking bullshit. I concede the point: it is still not the same. On the other hand, I still have an ace card.'

'How do you mean?' asked Mills.

'Well, I was a child once, myself, wasn't I?'

'I suppose you must have been.'

Tyler glanced at the younger man. 'And I once had to spend time in such a place.'

'Didn't we all?'

'I had a headmaster not unlike our Mr Wise. We didn't get on.'

'I see.'

'What do you see?'

'Reckon he'll call you?'

'*What do you see?*' Tyler asked again.

'You obviously don't have much time for Mr Wise, sir.'

'Are you questioning my work?'

Mills looked uncertain.

'Well, Sergeant?'

'Are you saying that Wise had anything to do with what happened to Alan Dale?'

'I think that he played his part, yes. And no, I don't expect a call back.'

Tyler looked out of the car window, watching a boy tearing a sports bag out of another pupil's hands, before kicking it up the path as the other boy yelled after him.

'So, it's like this: a boy walks home from school, except he never arrives home. Or, to be precise, we don't think that he arrived home. His parents both worked and his sister was also at school, the same school but in the year above her brother.

'It's possible that he called at the house and went out again, though unlikely, at least according to his sister. According to Miss Dale, Alan was a home bird. The two of them ran errands, but mainly on Saturday mornings. After school Alan would go home and stay there.'

Mills stated the obvious. 'So why didn't he go straight home and stay there on that Friday?'

'What are the options?'

Mills thought for a moment.

Tyler cut in. 'I'm reading your mind. We're all trained to think about sexual predators lurking behind every bush. The local paedophile – that sort of thing has never gone out of fashion and I doubt it ever will.'

Mills almost winced at the dark statement, uttered as unchallengeable fact.

'He could have struggled with his attacker, sir. He had a broken cheek bone unrelated to the fall that likely killed him.'

'I'm not so sure that Alan Dale was the struggling type. It's possible that he overshot home, went down to the building site, was playing, fell and hurt himself, and then toppled over into the pit and was killed in the fall. A tragic accident, case closed.'

Tyler shook his head, unconvinced by his own scenario.

'Maybe he was on his own, nobody else to blame, and no witnesses. It's possible, like a lot of things are possible. But is it likely? I listened to Sheila Dale, I read what she wrote, and I saw something I didn't like in the eyes of Mr Wise.'

'You don't actually think—'

'I don't think Wise *actually* killed him, of course I don't. I stopped reading books like those a long time ago.'

Mills watched the last of the children disappearing inside the vast concrete structure. 'Looks like the coast's clear, if you want to chance it,' he said. But the sarcasm didn't draw so much as a flicker, and Tyler calmly opened the car door and walked towards the main foyer. 'They make a good cup of tea in schools nowadays,' he said. 'I'll give them that much.'

***

Miss Hayburn seemed surprised to see the two police officers back so soon, and greeted them with some news.

The administrative staff had been working hard on the chronology of Alan Dale's teachers and classmates. And furthermore, Maggie Calleer, who had been Dale's teacher prior to Howard Wood, had plenty to say to the detectives any time they were ready.

Tyler recalled reference to Calleer in Dale's notes. 'Kind' was the word that sprang to mind.

Miss Hayburn told the officers that Miss Calleer had recently retired, and that she had been an extremely popular teacher at the school. She kept in touch, and even attended concerts occasionally, supporting the school at fund-raising events. Tyler had the feeling that the two women were good friends.

A wave of optimism overtook him as he briefly imagined Maggie Calleer with an axe to grind with a certain ex-headmaster.

'While we're here,' said Tyler, 'I thought that we might have a word with Mr Wood.'

'Now?' asked Miss Hayburn.

'Well, I realise that he may be teaching, or about to.'

'I'm afraid that Mr Wood went home sick.'

'Nothing serious, I hope.'

'Complaining of a migraine,' said the headteacher, clearly torn between the poles of confidentiality and assisting the police as far as she could.

'Is he prone to migraines, or is he under particular stress at the moment?' asked Tyler.

Mills wondered if the DCI was about to make the subtext of his question explicit. But Miss Hayburn was no fool. The unspoken suggestion that Mr Wood had become aware of the police visit and subsequently fled into hiding, was allowed to hang in the air until refreshments were tactfully suggested.

While Mills contacted Maggie Calleer and Howard Wood, Tyler shared a pot of tea with the headteacher.

The conversation quickly turned to the old regime, and the legacy left by Fredrick Wise. But whether or not Maggie Calleer might turn out to be a woman with an axe to grind, which anyway seemed doubtful and nothing more than a temporary outbreak of naive and wishful thinking, Miss Hayburn was far too diplomatic to polish the blade in the presence of an inquisitive police officer.

'They were different times,' she said. 'I think that headteachers were more remote then. You know, summoned to deal with major problems and otherwise leaving the teachers to sort out the day to day matters. But from my understanding, speaking to those who worked under Mr Wise's leadership, I believe that had a major bullying issue been brought to his attention, he would have dealt with it directly.'

Tyler allowed an inward smile to manifest as the ghost of an outward, mild and polite one. He could see how Miss Hayburn had made it to headteacher. There was a politician lurking in there, and possibly even an honest one at that.

But still he didn't feel inclined to let the point go so easily. 'This enquiry is at an early stage. The picture is far from clear. But, hypothetically, if a child died as a result, directly or indirectly, of the actions of others at the school, then surely it would reflect, would it not, rather negatively on the man at the top?'

'Hypothetically, yes, of course. Hypothetically, anything might happen as a result of something that might or might not have happened in the first place. Hypothetically, we might assume almost anything and then root around for facts to fit those hypothetical assumptions. Of course, I wouldn't really expect that to happen in the context of a modern-day police enquiry. How's your tea?'

'One more hypothesis,' said Tyler.

'Just one?'

'If a child went missing on your watch, how long would it take you to forget all about it?'

Miss Hayburn seemed about to say something when Mills appeared at the door. 'A word, sir?'

Tyler excused himself.

Outside in the corridor Mills reported that he had made contact with Howard Wood. 'Reckons he's too unwell to receive visitors at the moment, sir.'

'That bad, eh? What about Calleer?'

'Only too pleased to speak to us, and at our convenience.'

'She remembers Alan Dale, then?'

'Remembers him very well.'

'Local?'

'She lives a few miles out. I took the liberty of telling her that we're on our way.'

'They all seem to retire outside the city,' said Tyler. Mills didn't respond.

'I'll tell Miss Hayburn that we're leaving. See you in the car.'

Tyler went back to finish his tea, and to find out what wisdom Miss Hayburn had been about to impart on the subject of lost children.

'People deal with tragedy in different ways,' she told him. 'It's easy to condemn with hindsight, to make something out of nothing.'

He thanked her for her help.

As he strode out to the car he was cursing the timing of Mills' interruption.

You give a politician time to think and the truth goes to hell.

CHAPTER TWELVE

Heading east towards Longton, Mills had turned into a tour guide, pointing out his old school, even the street where he had spent most of his early childhood, before passing the small police station and reflecting on the many happy years he had spent there. When they passed the Gladstone Pottery Museum, he threatened to take Tyler along when they had a spare hour.

'You would make a local of me? Do you think I'm worthy?'

'Not for me to say, sir. But in your spare time I could at least make a tourist of you.'

'You're very proud of where you live, aren't you?'

'Is there any crime in that?'

'Maybe I'm envious.'

The city was receding already. Vistas of green were opening up all around as they passed through Weston Coyney and beyond, approaching Cellarhead crossroads.

'I live close to here,' said Mills.

'Not exactly a city boy, are we?'

Mills felt a strong urge to defend his move out of the city, but resisted, letting a grunt suffice by way of explanation. It wasn't exactly prudent, these days, to police the streets where you lived. To keep on doing the job you needed distance from it, a place to escape to, and even more so when you had a young family to think about.

His wife had told him that much and told it many times. It had been part of her argument for moving in the first place. He had to admit, there was some sense to it, though it still didn't help when it came to finding a decent local, or paying the bills. Or finding a decent school where your kids—

He glanced at Tyler but kept the thoughts to himself. It was either obvious enough or else impossible to explain. Perhaps it didn't really matter which.

A little short of Cheadle they took the turn-off and were soon approaching the village of Kingsley Holt. On the far side of the village, a tidy terraced cottage, neighbour-less on one side, opened its door as the unmarked car parked up outside the neat front garden.

'You found me,' sounded a cheerful voice as the detectives entered through the front gate. 'Maggie Calleer,' said the equally cheerful-looking woman, holding out a hand to the two officers in turn, before ushering them inside.

'Drinks?' she asked, before leaving them to make themselves comfortable in the small sitting room while she disappeared into the kitchen to boil the kettle.

Tyler cast an eye over his surroundings. 'I don't know about Kipling's parents,' he said, catching Mills' eye, 'but my guess is the great man himself would have preferred it.'

'What's that, sir – Kingsley over Rudyard?'

'Understatement over ostentation. I bet the tea will be better, too. China cups are for looking at, not drinking out of.'

'*Prefer beer mugs myself,*' *said* Mills, as Maggie Calleer brought the drinks through.

***

Miss Calleer had been retired two years, holding out to the tender age of sixty. She had entered the profession straight from college, serving for five years at her first school, the rest of her career spent at River Trent High. She had never married and had no children – and liked bangles and bracelets, by the look of it, thought Tyler. A charity-shop chic that didn't go at all badly with the carefree '60s elegance. More than anything, he noticed, was an abundant aura of *kindness.*

'So, how are you finding retirement?' asked Tyler.

'I recommend it,' she said. 'I loved my job, but I love my freedom too. I can spend all day reading, or walking, with no one to answer to other than my own conscience.'

'Which is always clear?' asked Tyler.

'I believe that you would like to ask me about Alan Dale.'

'You remember Alan, then?'

'I remember him,' she said. 'He was in my form the year before, well, you know.'

She described a shy, introverted boy with a 'lovely smile that could have charmed ducks off the water' but acknowledged that Alan probably wasn't the cleverest child in the year, certainly not in academic terms. She underlined that he had 'something about him, something marking him out. In his own way, he was a very bright spark. That was part of the problem.'

Tyler asked her to elaborate.

'What I mean is, unless you can handle yourself ... well, in my experience a child generally has an easier time of it if they blend in. Surviving school requires the average child to be something of a chameleon. Alan didn't blend in anywhere. He was different, and the difference was unmistakable. I don't think the poor lad could have done a thing about it.'

Tyler asked her to explain what exactly was different about Alan Dale, but the retired teacher was having difficulty nailing it.

Then her face lit up.

'Let me give you an example,' she said. 'I remember one day giving the class a poetry exercise. I asked them to write a poem about what they did at the weekend, or on holiday, something like that. Most would have written something silly, no doubt, because they felt awkward about doing the exercise at all. Others might have rehashed an idea that they'd heard in a song, or an advert. Something that would be instantly familiar.'

'What did Alan write?' asked Tyler. 'It's a tall order, I realise. Recalling what a pupil wrote thirty years ago.'

'Well, that's just the point,' she said. 'I *can* remember. I can remember like it was yesterday. Alan was simply never bland.

While he did his best to blend in, if something caught his imagination, he couldn't help but shine.

'He wrote a poem about a tree standing alone in a park. The tree had no friends until one summer all the birds came and built nests in the tree. It was a beautiful poem.'

'But not appreciated by everybody else in class?' said Mills. 'Who read the poems out?'

'I did. The class laughed along with the dafter stuff, and the derivative nonsense. I didn't identify the authors, but most of the class gave themselves away through sniggers or gestures, showing how proud they were, or ashamed. I read Alan's poem and, I tell you, I was almost in tears.

'When I'd finished reading it out, there was a kind of stunned silence. Most hadn't a clue what to make of it. I read it out a second time, and they probably still didn't get it, the majority of them.

'But they *were* getting who had written it. It wasn't the sort of thing that you would expect a – what was he then? – a fourteen-year-old boy to write.'

'You think,' said Tyler, 'that he would have suffered for that poem?'

'I'm sure of it. A girl might have got away with it. Things were very different back then.'

'They certainly were,' said Tyler, remembering only too well. 'Boys didn't do things like poetry, at least not without a direct order from above. Sorry, go on, Miss Calleer.'

'What you say is right. That macho thing – quite ridiculous, when you stop to think about it. And you see, a cleverer boy than Alan would have, how can I put it? He would have found the wavelength operating in that classroom. He would have joined in the spirit of things and written rubbish.

'But Alan was naïve; he had an idea and he ran with it. I don't think it would have occurred to him that it might have consequences.'

Tyler moved on to the subject of the old headmaster. He asked what Frederick Wise was like to work for.

'Old school,' she said. 'Very old school. You saw him in assembly and the kids saw him if they were in trouble. And usually that meant big trouble. Otherwise, ivory tower 'don't call me, I'll summon you', was his style.'

'Would he have taken bullying seriously?' asked Tyler.

She thought for a moment. 'That depends.'

'On what?'

'I think he had, like I say, an old-fashioned mind-set. An attitude that people ought to be able to stand up for themselves. Sort out their own problems.'

'Might he have turned a blind eye – if it wasn't causing an obvious disruption?'

Calleer looked uncomfortable with the question.

'And if it was?' asked Tyler.

'Then he would have shown them who was boss. Not exactly a pacifist, Mr Wise. He didn't take prisoners. The kids feared him, that was clear enough. If somebody threatens to beat the living daylights out of you, I think that you have a tendency to fear them. But that's not what I, personally, would call respect. More a matter of survival. That isn't how you sort out the bullies, not really.'

'Were there any bullies in your class?' asked Tyler.

'I think I know where this is heading.'

'Then perhaps you can tell me, because I haven't the faintest idea.'

'You think Alan Dale was the victim of bullying, and that one of his tormentors may have been responsible for his death.'

'And what do *you* think?'

Again, she looked uncomfortable, and the silence stretched out until Tyler at last intervened. 'I mean,' he said, 'it is, at least, an interesting hypothesis.'

'You mean that you haven't considered it yourself?' she asked.

'Well,' said Tyler, 'clearly you have.'

She thought for a few moments. 'Yes,' she said, 'I suppose I have. I've considered a lot of things. But I'm not sure about what I think happened.'

Tyler watched her carefully and then he said, 'At least you have given it some thought. I'm not sure that your old boss did.'

When she didn't respond, Tyler said, 'You didn't like him much, did you?'

'I didn't see a great deal of him, to be honest.' She hesitated again, and then seemed to come to a decision. 'I think that children deserve the very best. Children are vulnerable, all of them, no matter how tough they act.'

'Though some are more vulnerable than others?' said Tyler. 'Like Alan Dale?'

'Yes.'

'You think Wise let him down? You think that he let Alan Dale down?'

***

While Calleer made a second round of drinks, the two detectives sat ruminating over what the retired teacher had said, and what she hadn't said. When she returned Mills took the cue to freshen up the room with further talk of retirement and the consolations of the stunning countryside that surrounded them. In the course of the conversation he told her that he had two children of his own, both of school age, while Tyler remained outside the conversation, drinking a mug of tea and brooding silently.

At the same time he listened.

He listened intently as the conversation meandered around the education system, local school options, discipline in the classroom and in society generally. Topics debated by politicians and a multitude of experts on countless TV and radio shows, arguments going around in circles as people tried to solve conundrums and contradictions a sight older than most of them realised.

'Bullying,' said Calleer, 'is not something that happens only in the classroom, or in the playground. It is not confined to children.'

'I hope you're not referring to the police force,' said Tyler.

'It all comes down to power, in the end,' she said. 'One person exerting it over another. Forming a gang, or an organisation, to gain the whip hand.'

Tyler nodded.

'You know,' said the retired teacher, 'I sometimes think that the history of bullying is the history of human relations.'

'Bit strong, don't you think?' said Mills.

But Tyler didn't think so, not at all. He liked Maggie Calleer. She spoke a language that he understood. And he wanted to hear more of it, to gain the full extent of what her time with the likes of Frederick Wise had taught her.

'I think that bullying is endemic in society,' she went on, encouraged by the senior detective. 'A lot of it is probably unintended, to some extent, and the perpetrators would be absolutely horrified, in a lot of cases, to realise that they were in fact acting as bullies. But that doesn't stop it being harmful. On the other hand, you have the sadists. You have those who know absolutely what they are doing. And they're a different breed altogether.'

'And did you come across many of those during your time at River Trent High?'

She laughed. 'You don't miss an opportunity, do you?'

'I don't tend to,' said Tyler. 'And poor Sergeant Mills here will be taking his children out of school altogether by the time we've finished.'

The room fell silent.

And Tyler knew that the door had been loosened.

Calleer took off her glasses and massaged her eyes, as though to coax the faces from the darker recesses of memory. 'There were one or two, yes.'

'Can you remember their names?'

Her mind was evidently whirring, and not merely through the act of trying to remember.

At last Tyler said, 'The school have been putting together lists of personnel and pupils at the school during the early 1970s. If you can't remember the names off the top of your head, you may recognise some of them when you see the lists.' He paused for a moment. 'You have to understand that this is a very serious matter that we are investigating, Miss Calleer.'

'I don't need reminding of the seriousness. A dead fifteen-year-old boy – I don't need lists to remind me. I'm not senile quite yet, thank you all the same.'

'It was a long time ago,' said Mills, trying to defuse some of the tension in the room.

'Thank you,' she said. 'But when you teach a class for three terms, you tend to remember them. At least, human nature being what it is, you tend to remember certain ones. The difficult ones always prove to be the hardest to forget, for some reason.'

'And who were the difficult ones that year?' asked Tyler. 'Who stands out from the class of '72?'

It turned out that there were two persistent troublemakers, both of them in trouble regularly and for behaviour that included bullying. 'They thrived on trouble, those two. It went against the grain to send pupils to see Mr Wise, but I happily made exceptions where that pair were concerned. I don't know that it made the slightest bit of difference, mind you. You beat a savage dog and it doesn't stop the thing from biting people. If anything, perhaps it makes it worse. But it got them out of the classroom for a while, and some days it was a matter of survival.'

'Not just for the children, then?'

'I could hold my own. I was never a pushover.'

'I have no doubt,' said Tyler.

'These two – they picked on Alan Dale?' asked Mills.

'They picked on practically everybody.'

'I'm sorry,' said Tyler. 'I didn't quite catch their names.'

Calleer took a breath. 'Steven Jenkins and Douglas Marley,' she said. 'There, now you have it.'

She appeared to ease back in her chair, as though the worst was over.

'They didn't single out Alan Dale?' asked Tyler.

'They had the temperament of wasps: they'd sting whoever was closest to hand.'

'Were there any other trouble-makers in your class?' asked Mills.

'That pair were the most obvious. There was another lad, Phillip Swanson. But he was more of a crafty one. He was the type who would make bullets for the likes of Jenkins and Marley to fire.'

'Any others?' asked Mills, busily making notes.

'I'm scraping the barrel a bit now, but Martin Hillman was another in the Swanson mould. Harder to weigh up though. What you might call a dark horse. He didn't get into trouble; he was far too smart for that. But I saw the way kids like Swanson got others to do their dirty work, and I sometimes wondered about Hillman. I don't miss much, and I didn't back then.'

'Dirty work?' asked Tyler.

'I think that a lot of teachers, especially with large classes, don't always recognise what's going on. They see the Jenkins' and the Marley's of this world and that's it.'

It was time to start wrapping up the interview. But still Tyler had one more name to conjure with.

'You worked with Howard Wood, I believe.'

'He's still there.'

'What was he like to work with?'

'I didn't have a lot to do with him.'

'What do you remember about him?'

'He was a keen football supporter, I know that much.'

'Nothing more than that?' asked Tyler.

'Like what?'

'You tell me.'

'I didn't like him.'

'Was he a bully?'

'I don't know that he was. Some people, well, you just can't warm to.'

'Mr Wood taught Alan Dale the year after you, isn't that right?' said Mills.

'I believe so, yes.'

'Were the boys you mentioned all in Wood's class that year?' asked Tyler.

'Now you are pushing it. There weren't many changes made, generally speaking, so probably, yes. They had a streaming system. I taught a class in the middle stream. Theoretically, a child could move to a higher class should they perform well enough.'

'And move down if they underperformed,' said Mills, remembering the system only too well. 'Bit like football.'

'Like a lot of things,' said Calleer, ignoring the football analogy, 'it might have looked fine in principle. In practice, you start shifting children around on performance and you end up with an administrative nightmare. It could lead to other problems too.'

'And not very PC these days, moving anybody downwards,' said Tyler. 'Nobody fails anymore. It isn't allowed.'

Something occurred to Mills. 'Wasn't Alan Dale bright enough for the top class?'

'That's a very good question. Alan Dale was top class material, despite his quirkiness. Sharp, though not academic. In some respects, I think that he was quite brilliant. But you have to understand that most children, in a situation like that – I mean, where you can be 'promoted' – would be too fearful of reprisals. Like I said, it pays to blend in and not be seen as a trailblazer. He wasn't the only one.'

'What do you mean by that?' asked Tyler.

'The entire system was a nonsense really. I mean to say, I keep my ear to the ground and I know for a fact that Martin Hillman is a successful businessman these days, a councillor too, though not locally. And Phillip Swanson, he's a social worker, I'm told. Either their potential wasn't recognised or they chose to play a game.'

'A game?' said Tyler.

'Well, you know, keeping their heads down, under the radar. If you stay invisible you can get away with almost anything.'

'I see,' said Tyler.

'Actually, as I recall, both of those boys picked up in their final year, knuckling down. It sometimes goes like that, in my experience. When you see that the end is in sight you sprint for the line, so to speak.'

'How come you were aware of their 'knuckling down' when you were no longer their teacher?' asked Tyler.

'I was quite good friends with Jill – Jill Maynard. She taught those children in their final year. Sadly, Jill passed away a few years ago. She never got to her retirement, it was so sad.'

'A lesson there for us all,' said Tyler. 'I'm sorry to hear about your friend. Did she have much to say about Hillman and Swanson?'

'Nothing that I haven't already told you. I think, like me, she saw Swanson as being rather sly and Hillman as, well, difficult to get the measure of.'

'And do you think Alan Dale would have recognised the danger of 'promotion', as it were, above the need to get away from the … reprobates?' asked Tyler.

'I don't think I can even begin to answer that. There are what you call 'reprobates' everywhere, in every class, in every stream. I know that must sound terribly cynical, but there you are. When you have forty children in your class, you remember something about most of them, but you hardly have the time to *really* get inside the minds of any of them.'

'You say,' said Tyler, 'that there were – that there are – reprobates everywhere, in every class. I'm sure that you are right, but I want to be clear: are you suggesting that had Alan Dale moved school or class he might have survived?'

Calleer showed the palms of her hands. 'I don't know what happened. I don't know who was responsible.'

'I suppose,' said Tyler, 'that I am asking if you think that the danger came from any one specific place. Or person.'

'If I had my suspicions, I would tell you.'

Her face had clouded over and Mills wondered if she was about to cry. 'You know, it breaks my heart,' she said, 'to think of that boy doing his best and not having his talents recognised. And it's every bit as depressing imagining him underperforming so that nobody noticed him. God, the tragedy keeps getting deeper.'

'Would he have known that he was destined for Howard Wood's class?' asked Mills. 'I mean, if he remained in the middle stream?'

'There were two classes in that stream. So he would have realised that there was at least a fifty percent chance.'

'At least?' said Tyler.

'People always imagine that the odds are in favour of the worst-case scenario. Howard Wood was a bit of what you might call a man's man.'

'You think he was a bully himself?'

'You've asked me that already.'

'And now I'm giving you the opportunity to reconsider the question.'

'Howard Wood was Stoke City mad. If you were a football fan and showed a spark of meanness, you were probably okay with Howard Wood.'

'Would you say that putting Alan Dale in his class sealed his fate?'

'It's always easy to be wise after the event.'

'Is that a "yes"?'

She sighed, heavily. 'How can anybody know that for sure?' she said. 'I've often thought about little Alan, about what might have happened to him. I hoped that he somehow escaped. That he found a different, happier life somewhere else. But I didn't think the chances were high. I imagined that he probably took his own life, and if he did, then I think that there are a lot of us to share in the blame for that.'

Calleer's head appeared to hang in shame. Then she looked up at the two detectives. 'Do I think he was killed? One way or another, yes, I do. In my opinion, for what it's worth, a little boy was made so unhappy that his life had to end at fifteen years of age.

'I don't know whether somebody actually took his life, that's your job to find out. But even if they did, and you find them, I don't think it relinquishes *our* responsibility. We still let Alan Dale down, all of us, each and every one of us, and we have to live with that for what remains of our lives.'

For a few moments nobody moved or said anything.

Breaking the silence, Maggie Calleer asked if the officers had any more questions.

It was time to go.

CHAPTER THIRTEEN

On the drive back they passed close to where Danny Mills lived with his family, on the outskirts of Cheadle. As Tyler had expressed an interest Mills turned off the main road, entering a short lane before pulling up outside a small semi-detached house.

'That's home these days,' said Mills, with an expression and a tone that appeared ambiguous. Tyler was trying to weigh up the curious mix.

'Does it have a serviceable kettle?' he asked.

The house was empty, and when Tyler expressed surprise that the clan were not present to greet the weary policemen, Mills launched into an explanation of how his wife would still be on the school run.

Tyler observed that schools had clearly extended their hours over the years.

'She's likely taken them into town. I think they might have been promised a trip to the cinema, thinking about it. With me being on this investigation, it's a case of see you when I see you.'

Tyler held up a hand to assure Mills that he didn't have to explain his family arrangements. And anyway, all this talk was getting in the way of the sacred art of tea-making.

Mills suddenly brightened. 'We could go for a pint after we knock off.'

Tyler appeared to lick his lips for a moment, and at the same time his demeanour tightened. 'I'm not sure that's such a good idea,' he said.

'Another time, then,' said Mills. 'No worries. I'll make a brew.'

The senior detective looked around the lounge, at the abundant photographs of family featuring two apparently perfect children, while the sergeant went through to the kitchen. He faintly heard Mills tapping in numbers on a handset, followed by an audible impatience and the termination of the call.

He wondered whether his sergeant's wife – she looked quite beautiful on the photographs – might be in trouble later for not having her phone switched on, or for failing to hear it. In his experience, it was always the little things.

As he listened to Mills knocking around in the kitchen, putting together the drinks, he remembered the minefield of little things from a previous lifetime.

***

'How long do you think Berkins will give us?' asked Mills, handing Tyler his drink. 'We could end up interviewing half of Staffordshire and still not be sure that a crime was committed.'

'I'm fully expecting to,' said Tyler. 'If what Miss Calleer says is true, half of Staffordshire is in some way responsible.'

He took a sip, savoured it on his tongue, and nodded his approval. 'But you're quite right. Priorities move on, and quickly. A full-tilt summer crime wave and I can well imagine a misadventure outcome. There's nothing quite like fear to remind the public about priorities – not to mention the city fathers.'

'Sir?'

'Oh, come on now. The press have put an angle on this, and an emotive one at that. A city that cares enough about its citizens to turn over every last stone to find justice for a fifteen-year-old boy who didn't come home thirty years ago …'

'Do I need to go on?'

Maybe he did. Mills didn't look at all convinced.

'Okay, it's prime cut now, and so Berkins is giving us the time. The new visitors' centre may end up with a plaque dedicated to Alan Dale, and a good result would be a godsend to the department. But it's a fickle world. All that public emotion won't count for a thing if Jack the Ripper comes to town.'

'That's hardly likely.'

Tyler groaned, a little too heavily. 'What I mean is, thirty-year-old crimes don't have the public looking under their beds. That's all I'm saying. Anyway, I'll authorise some shift workers to track down those classmates. If we can get locations on the scallywags Calleer gave us, we'll visit those as soon as. Be interesting to see what they turned into.'

'And Howard Wood?'

'I want to see if he turns up at school next week. I have my doubts. But we'll visit either way. Look, we've got a busy weekend ahead of us, why don't you take the rest of today – I can find my way back to Hanley, just about.'

'Thanks,' said Mills, 'but my car's at the station and the buses out here – the drivers don't tend to make special arrangements for officers on serious enquiries.'

'You're not in danger of becoming a workaholic?'

'And not an alcoholic at this rate, either.'

'Indeed,' said Tyler, clearing his throat unnecessarily.

'Anyway, if the family have gone out …'

Tyler caught the sadness, or was it anger, and asked Mills if he wanted to talk about it.

The speech was already fully formed in the mind of Danny Mills. The one about leaving his roots behind, and despite his wife's argument about not living on your work patch, at the end of the day he was still in Staffordshire – only not the part of it that he loved.

And how was having less money going to make them feel happier and why couldn't people get on and enjoy what they had instead of feeling the pressure to try and become what they are not. Being away from friends, family, football, pubs where everybody knows your name, if not your rank. Having a son and a daughter bullied at school because daddy's a policeman, something that never happened in the city, not once.

Having a wife who he loved with every bone in his body, but who couldn't for the life of her see what the deal was about moving *just a few miles* – oh, he had the speech alright. The problem was, he was sick to death of hearing himself reciting it.

When Tyler asked again if there was anything that Mills wanted to talk about, Mills looked blank and replied, 'Not that I'm aware of, sir.'

They made the journey back to Hanley in silence, Tyler not even making his customary remarks about the abundant greenery of the city as it welcomed them back.

***

At the station, faxes awaited them from Miss Hayburn. Her administrative staff had worked overtime to furnish the investigating officers with a comprehensive list of all the children in Alan Dale's year, highlighting those who had been in Howard Wood's class. Looking through the list, Tyler put a mark next to the names of those singled out by Calleer. It would be down to his team to research the whereabouts of the grown-up children.

After organising the task and briefing the team on priorities from the list, he noticed Mills on the phone. And he quickly recognised the easy manner and the secret coded humour passing between two people still enough in love to care for such games. *Kissing and making up.* Tyler remembered those games, though they hadn't lasted anywhere near long enough.

He was remembering a lot of things, lately, and the memories were digging away again at that empty pit inside that he was longing to fill with the forbidden sauce.

Forbidden to him, at least. It was time to get back on track; useless memories could only take him back to a time from which he'd spent too long escaping, and too long yearning to return to. He needed to run some of it off.

Mills, sensing the presence of the senior officer, wound up the call with a staged formality that wouldn't, reflected Tyler, have fooled the cleaning lady. Matter of fact, there had been many a police station cleaning lady, in his experience, who could have given the average detective a good run for their money when it came to instinct and insight.

'So, was it the cinema?'

'Missed them by a few minutes, sir. They'd only popped into town.'

'Surprised we didn't pass them.'

'We did.'

Tyler felt the weight of those two words fall like a slap in the face. Why *should* Mills point out his family to the man sitting next to him in the car – the man who merely happened to be a senior colleague? Why should Mills share anything of his private life?

'Why don't you go home,' said Tyler, a sense of remorse overwhelming him. 'There's nothing more to be done here tonight.'

'I could pitch in on that list, sir.'

Tyler raised a smile, and flicked through his notebook to something that he had written down after visiting Calleer. 'It's too easy to have regrets,' he said.

'What's that, sir?'

'Something someone said. Listen to this: I know you've heard it once already.'

He read from his notebook:

'I tried too hard to give people the benefit of the doubt, I did then and I do now. What someone was thirty years ago – some change, grow out of it, or even into it. But some don't change at all. And who's to know? Easy to be wise afterwards, it always is and it always will be. Yes, I'm hard on myself sometimes when I look back – and why shouldn't I be? I hated injustice then and I hate it now, but the question always remains: did I do enough? Things don't get better or worse, the world just goes round in circles and nothing really changes at all.'

Tyler looked up. 'Quite a speech, wouldn't you say.'

'Miss Calleer.'

'And coming right before telling us that some things do change for the better. And citing the excellent job being done, as we speak, at River Trent High by the excellent Miss Hayburn.'

'I can still help out on that list.'

'I'm losing patience with you. Lists. Good God, man, you're a detective sergeant, and you have a family. Goodnight … Danny Mills.'

The sound of his name uttered by the DCI made him want to laugh. Instead of laughing, Mills did as he was told and went home.

***

Tyler's living accommodation lay on the outskirts of Hanley. It was hardly a palace, though he had slept on worse beds in his time. The flat was a runner's dream, though. Every time he entered it, he found himself donning his running gear and heading out again to pound the pavements until he no longer had the energy or the desire to find a pub or an off-licence or a face that he could sink a fist into.

With the late-evening's hard miles behind him, Tyler lay on the single mattress, alone in the darkness, trying to beat away the returning ghosts that seemed intent on reminding him of how different existence had once been.

When Kim had come into his life.

He had been a bobby on the beat with visions of grandeur. An early marriage to the job, though it wasn't long before he and Kim were living together. A three-way relationship, that's what she had once called it, and perhaps more than once. And then one day she came home with news indeed: she was pregnant. Except that the great Jim Tyler, preparing to take his exams, wasn't so sure how wonderful the news really was.

'It isn't a good time, that's all.'

'I thought you'd be happy, Jim. I thought it was what you wanted.'

'What *I* wanted?'

'We don't have to stay living here; we can get a decent mortgage between us. Find somewhere—'

'But not right now, that's all I'm saying. The timing couldn't be worse.'

'I'm sorry to have inconvenienced you.'

'We could have talked about it. We could have planned things properly.'

'But life isn't always like that, Jim. Sometimes life just *happens*.'

And on it went. How could she have done this? Everything had been going along fine, hadn't it? There was time for all the family stuff later on, when his career was established, when both their careers were established. What was the hurry?

'How could I do this? How could … *I … do this*? Can you hear yourself? There will never be the perfect time, Jim, don't you see that? Is that what you're waiting for? You wait forever for that and it doesn't come. I didn't plan this, but it still might be the best thing that's ever happened to us.'

Was his look so accusing? So transparent?

He apologised. Blamed it on the stress he was under at work, and the exams coming up. Of course she was right.

He said the words but did she believe them? Did he even believe them? He made up for it a dozen times over, and when he passed his exams with flying colours, he took her to Spain, their first trip abroad together and, as it turned out, their last.

Kim miscarried in Spain and the awfulness of that time broke completely what hadn't already been broken. She made a full recovery, physically, but whatever they still had together never made the journey home. With hindsight, he came to see that it had never made the journey out there in the first place.

They split up and didn't keep in touch. For a time, he wondered what had been so urgent about passing exams and gaining promotions, but the doubts didn't last. With Kim gone, his temporarily abandoned sense of ambition was refuelled and re-ignited, and he quickly developed the art of burying himself alive in work. And it was only on rare occasions that he wondered how far he would have to go to lose the feelings of inadequacy that seemed to wait for him in the quiet and in the dark.

He became relentless; obsessive. When he wasn't working himself to the bone, or studying, he was visiting the corporate gymnasium. He found a chest hiding under the skin and bones, and in no time other muscles were popping up to see what was going on.

Kim would hardly recognise him. It was that thought, more than any other, that could make him want to cry.

But as DCI Jim Tyler lay on his bed in the darkness, on the outskirts of Hanley, he could no more cry now than he could back then.

Shortly before the incident at work that pre-empted this current exile, he had bumped into Kim on the street. He hadn't seen her in years. And in all of those years he had never found another like her and he knew that he never would. In some dark chamber of the heart, all that time ago, he had arranged the ceremony and taken the oath, consigning himself to a single life.

And now the screw had been turned again. It had been his day off. He had turned a corner and suddenly she was there, in front of him. She was married and recently found herself to be pregnant again, her third child.

They were strangers now, on an old familiar street but living in different worlds; yet it seemed that she wanted to tell him her news, proclaiming it proudly. And tell him she did, adding that this time he might approve because she'd done things in the right order: marriage first, baby second, career a long way down the line. He had to respond with something. He said that yes, this time he did approve because this time it had nothing whatsoever to do with him.

And he had walked away with a momentary sense of victory; of restored pride.

And it lasted all of a minute.

That day he almost did cry.

Almost.

***

On the Sunday evening DCI Tyler went to bed late. It was a week since the discovery of the corpse of Alan Dale. He had been out pounding the streets again, running through the city, trying to gain some clarity on the case and at the same time trying to exhaust the demons inside him clamouring for retribution and the balm of alcohol. He had finally fallen asleep, exhausted, lying on top of the single bed with dark dreams for company.

The phone was ringing.

It was Chief Superintendent Berkins, no less. Suspected murder of a forty-five year-old male found dead in his flat.

The age registered in some remote region of Tyler's mind, though not in the conscious part.

Steven Jenkins, his body discovered in the flat in which he was apparently living, surrounded by enough illegal substances to start a small empire. A neighbour had called the police after hearing a disturbance; the woman had gone around to check that everything was okay after hearing a car screeching up the road, in the aftermath.

But everything had not been okay.

Steven Jenkins.

Now the registration was a conscious one. 'You may have to put the other case on a back-burner,' said Berkins.

'Actually, we might not have to,' said Tyler.

'What's that?'

'I'll get over there straight away.'

'That's what I thought you said.'

When the call ended Tyler rang Danny Mills.

CHAPTER FOURTEEN

The scene of flashing lights was a mile or so out of Hanley town centre. Steven Jenkins, it turned out, had been DCI Tyler's near neighbour.

According to the woman who had made the discovery, Jenkins had been a frequenter of the town centre most weekends. She seemed to know his routine remarkably well for somebody who 'only lives next door. Not close, nothing like that. 'It was even more remarkable considering Jenkins had only been living there for a few weeks.

The neighbour was telling Tyler that she had occupied the flat for more years than *he'd* seen, before embarking on a potted history of every tenant who had lived next door.

At the risk of appearing rude, Tyler tried to restore some focus to the woman's boundless erudition on the subject, and she responded with a promise to be as helpful as was humanly possible on this, clearly, the night of her life.

Steven Jenkins had been a presentable young man who favoured denim in the day as much as in the evening. Friday, Saturday, Sunday and Tuesday were his usual nights out, leaving the flat usually around eight and returning in the early hours, and usually alone.

Though preferring to keep herself to herself, the neighbour had spoken with Jenkins on a few occasions, and found him to be 'more sociable than the average man of his age. Having said that, I saw him only yesterday and it was like getting blood from a stone getting a simple "hello". Sharp, he was, too – when he did speak.'

'Sharp?'

'Like he had things on his mind. Big things, I would say. Nervous, he was. Living on his nerves and his cigarettes. I know what it's like.'

No, she wasn't sure what exactly Steven Jenkins did for a living, but he always went out early in the morning, same time every day, Monday to Friday, back late afternoon and casually dressed; jeans for all weathers. Didn't drive – didn't own a car, at any rate. Never noticed him using the bus stop down the road, and so as likely as not he worked locally, though she had never come across him in the town during the day.

Tyler gently nudged her observations on the life of the late Steven Jenkins back towards the previous evening, and she apologised for running off at the mouth. It was the shock and all that, she explained. 'He usually returned to his flat to have something to eat before going out for the evening. Except last night he didn't. It was very late when he did come back.'

'Did he return to his flat alone?'

'As far as I could tell – not that I go about minding other folks' business, you understand.'

'Of course not.'

'But I didn't hear voices. I'm a light sleeper. It doesn't take much to wake me. I suppose, living on my own like I do, and not having much company, I tend to listen out. Bit like having a son, you might say. In a way, I mean.'

She looked awkward, as though she had let out some treacherous secret, exposing the terrible truth about herself.

Tyler waved a hand, as though to dismiss the need for further explanation. It wasn't easy to admit to loneliness, he knew that. Not a socially acceptable condition. If this neighbour felt assured to hear the safe return of the man next door, treating him in her fantasy world as some quasi-adopted son, then where was the sin in that? The world was short of good neighbours, in every sense of the word.

'So, when Mr Jenkins did eventually return, as far as you know he was alone?'

'I would say so. But then I must have dozed off.'

Again, the woman appeared guilty, as though admitting that she had been negligent. As though her lack of vigilance had made her somehow responsible.

The next thing she heard, she told Tyler, was a 'commotion going on. I must have been in a deep sleep. It's these tablets the doctor's been giving me.' Again the caution, as though she was giving too much of herself away; the need in her to qualify insatiable. 'On prescription, naturally,' she said. 'I wouldn't take any of these things like they do today.'

'Naturally,' agreed Tyler.

'And neither did that young man.'

'What's that?'

'Take things like they do today. Mind you, you can't tell these days. Some of them look so respectable. It's drugs all the time, what you hear in the papers and see on the telly.'

As though a reality that the woman had been fighting against was finally seeping through, she said, 'Do you think this might have been about drugs? I hope not.'

Tyler looked into the woman's filling eyes. Steven Jenkins was dead; murdered in cold blood. What difference did it matter to his neighbour whether drugs formed part of the equation or not?

Was it fear of the unknown? Did people feel safer, believing that some kind of order remained active in the world, if murder could be explained in old fashioned terms, whatever they might be? That the man next door is killed for love, money, some pub argument about football, maybe, then the world can keep turning. But drugs … and the universe is set to explode.

'So, you awoke hearing sounds from next door?'

'Like I say, Inspector – you did say 'Inspector', didn't you? Like I say, those tablets—'

'You were telling me about what awoke you.'

'That's right, but I was in such a deep sleep that I couldn't get my bearings at first. I thought I'd left the telly switched on or something, but then I remembered that I hadn't been watching it that evening hardly at all. Thought it might have been Mr Jenkins – Steven – next door – his telly, I mean.'

'What exactly did you hear?'

'I'm sorry, but I don't really know. It was over before I was properly awake. Then I heard a car start up outside and I got out of my bed. The car made such a noise as you never heard in your life.'

'You saw the car?'

'Not really. It was up the road and gone and I'm not very good with cars, to tell you the truth.'

Tyler heard a cough behind him and he turned around to find Danny Mills.

***

Mills hadn't been asleep when Tyler rang. He'd been lying in bed, next to his wife, listening to the calm sounds of her breathing. Thinking about the case; his imagination bringing Alan Dale back to life; trying to see the boy and understand some of the torment that he might have been subjected to.

He'd thought of his own son, Harry, and his daughter, Jessica. About the bullying that he and his wife had found out about and tried to nip in the bud, talking to the headteacher and respective form teachers.

He knew from his own memories of school days, that it wasn't always evident what was going on in a child's mind. Neither he nor his wife had noticed any worrying signs for more than a week now, but might they be missing something? Were their children going through some dreadful daily ordeals that they were too frightened or ashamed to talk about?

Short of hiding in the playground bushes and bugging the classrooms, how was it possible to be sure? And was that kind of paranoiac feeling a normal part of being a parent, or a symptom of encroaching mental illness brought on by the stresses of work and life in general?

His mind had drifted back to Alan Dale. If the boy had died directly – or indirectly, for that matter – as a result of bullying, was he tragically unlucky or had his idiosyncratic nature marked him out?

Not fitting in had never been a recipe for an easy life. If you stood out from the crowd because you were fat, thin, tall, short, spotty, the wrong kind of clever or stupid: whatever the differences, it could be the call to arms for the bully, and a guarantee of years – a lifetime, even – of misery for the victim.

He could see the dead boy, but as a living, frightened soul begging for someone to save him, to intervene on his behalf.

When the call came, Danny Mills might as well have been asleep, so deeply was he involved in the nightmare, conjuring up the dead boy.

Mills was taken to one side and quickly briefed. Steven Jenkins had been found naked, clutching a large bag of cocaine, his throat cut so deeply it had almost taken his head off. There were other substances found in his flat.

'Any questions, Sergeant?'

'Dozens.'

'Any that can't wait half an hour?'

'Just the one.'

'Fire away.'

'Do you believe in coincidence?'

'About as much as you do.'

Tyler asked Mills to take over with the neighbour while he went to make calls. When he returned he saw Mills still engaged with the woman, her mouth firing on all cylinders. He set about relieving the ear-bent sergeant, calling for reinforcements in the form of an available constable.

They watched as the neighbour was assisted back to her flat. 'Let the SOCOs do their dealing and count your lucky stars. That kettle will be in for a hell of a night. So, what do you know?'

Mills repeated the neighbour's account, Tyler hearing nothing that he hadn't already.

'I think we can probably rule her out,' he said with a weary tone. 'Of course, you know what happens next. The press will have a field day juxtaposing the two events: the thirty-year-old mystery of a dead schoolboy and the brutal killing of his classmate. *Then and Now: A Bloody History of the City of Stoke-on-Trent.* The irony is that they won't see the possibility of a genuine connection. Not yet.

'When we resume the trail that leads from River Trent High, we must be cautious and discreet, and not a little open-minded.'

'I don't follow?'

'We must be wary of assuming that there *has* to be a connection. We might be seduced into missing something even more obvious.'

Mills frowned.

Tyler closed his eyes, and for a few moments seemed to become lost in whatever tangle was absorbing him. 'Guilt can do strange things to a person. The corpse of a missing schoolboy comes up out of the ground and with it likely a multitude of dirty secrets, of one kind or another.

'And so, when somebody is murdered, a short time after the discovery of the dead boy, or what's left of him, the curious mind starts to consider possibilities. When the police are digging around already, does someone have a vested interest in keeping somebody else quiet?'

Mills looked about to say something when Tyler cut in.

'We let scene of crime do their work with the late Steven Jenkins and we put out an appeal for witnesses who saw anyone coming to his flat or leaving in a hurry and we go door-to-door. And we pray that something comes in on the getaway car, if that's what it was. So, what's the order of the day? The teacher of the dead pupils, or the classmates? Or should I say *surviving* classmates?'

'I had Howard Wood down as next on the list, sir.'

'And I see no reason to change that. I'll visit Wood later while you follow up this end.'

Tyler was getting into his car when Mills said, 'Looks like Jack the Ripper turned up after all.'

CHAPTER FIFTEEN

oward Wood was still off sick and not feeling receptive to visitors when Tyler rang him to make arrangements.

Wood maintained that as he was off work, any visit would have to wait. Tyler made it clear that while he had no wish to compound the effects of the migraine, or to become infected with the alleged stomach virus now afflicting the teacher, he was prepared to risk it. The visit could *not* wait.

Tyler had little trouble finding Wood's flat. He was becoming familiar with parts of the city, even if the ramshackle lack of design was still baffling. *Oh well,* he thought, *with any luck, I won't be around long enough to grasp it.*

***

Wood's home was in Hartshill, bordering the west side of Penkhull village. Following the main road that curved up out of Stoke, passing the site where Alan Dale had been found thirty years too late, the turn off was on the right, just beyond the Jolly Potters public house.

Howard Wood answered the door in pyjamas and dressing gown, and with a pained expression that suggested the glare of the sun was something his eyes had been unused to for a long time.

The teacher was sipping at a beaker of water as he ushered the detective through to the curtained lounge. He asked if Tyler would like a drink. He declined.

The lounge was a gloomy affair and smelt of stale tobacco tinged with something distinctly sour. Tyler suspected that the sour odour was old alcohol dying on the sick teacher's breath, and wondered if this was the man's idea of a cure.

'I take it that you are aware, Mr Wood, that the body of a schoolboy was recently discovered in this area.'

Wood spoke gingerly, as if the effort came at a high price. 'I'm aware.'

Tyler asked Wood if he knew that the boy was Alan Dale, an ex-pupil at River Trent High, and taught by Wood himself in the final year of the boy's life.

'Yes,' said Howard Wood. 'I vaguely recall him.'

But the memories seemed vague indeed, and the teacher remembered almost nothing about the boy, save for the fact that he once existed and had made up the numbers in his class for a while.

Tyler raised the subject of bullying and asked Wood if he had found it much of an issue at the school. Wood said that he hadn't encountered much of that sort of thing.

'Are you saying, Mr Wood, that *that sort of thing* was not an issue back in 1972 – or now?'

'Well, both. Why do you ask?'

'You don't recall *any* incidents?'

'Working with children, you learn to expect problems. That goes without saying. Most problems sort themselves out. You know kids – friends one day, enemies the next. I find a laissez-faire approach works best on the whole.'

Wood seemed to be forgetting his discomforts, his tone starting to reflect exasperation at the detective's questions. Tyler had the feeling that the teacher's sense of security was growing. No doubt he believed, as so many had, over the years, and often to their eventual cost, that had the police come armed with an ace card of some kind, it would have been played at the start of the interview.

Content to let Wood lower his defences further, Tyler maintained his slow probing in the least officious manner that he could muster.

'Would you say that the school has changed a lot over the years, Mr Wood?'

'Everything changes.'

'For better or worse?'

'Some better, some worse.' Wood grinned. He thought he was in the presence of an idiot, and an air of superiority was oozing out. *Perfect*, thought Tyler. But the DCI wanted to see a little more before he was ready to pull the rug out.

'Mr Wise,' said Tyler. 'You remember him?'

'Of course,' said Wood, almost incredulously. 'My memory isn't quite that bad yet.'

'I'm pleased to hear that. Mr Wise seems to be a very different character from the incumbent headteacher.'

'You've met him, then?'

Tyler registered the flicker of interest. 'More of a disciplinarian, I would imagine.'

'Fred Wise, you mean? It was different then. You had something to threaten them with.'

'And did you ever have to threaten any of them, Mr Wood?'

'What are you getting at? Are you talking about this Alan Dale? Like I say, he was one of many. I don't recall him being a problem.'

'Were any of your class, that year, *a problem*?'

'Kids know who they can play up, and who to behave for. You have to let them know which side of the fence you're on. Having said that, I was never big on the discipline thing. Kids respect a person if they think that person understands them; you don't have to make them afraid of you. Like I say, I didn't have any problems because the kids basically liked me.'

'And you don't recall anyone giving Alan Dale a particularly hard time?'

'No, I don't.'

'What about Steven Jenkins?'

Tyler, peering through the gloom, watched the self-satisfied grin disappear in a frenzy of blinking. Wood picked up his tumbler of water, taking a few sips and appearing to experience a relapse, falling again into the jaws of whatever condition was afflicting him.

'You remember Steven Jenkins?'

Howard Wood took on more water, his fingers trembling as he drained the beaker dry. 'Was he in my class?'

'You don't recall?'

Wood recited the name out loud a number of times, as though trying desperately to bring the person to mind.

'Let me see if I can help,' said Tyler. 'Steven Jenkins was known to be a trouble-maker. A bully, according to some.'

'Maybe this Steven Jenkins grew out of it by the time he came into my class.'

'His reputation would have gone before him, making you at least aware of him, I would imagine.'

A light seemed to come on inside the stricken teacher, illuminating the room. To Tyler it seemed that Wood was either playing a clever game, or else had in that moment solved a tricky dilemma.

'Actually, now I think about it I do recall Jenkins. And he could be a handful, you're right. It's becoming clearer now.'

'Good.'

'Steven Jenkins did have some issues with Alan Dale.'

'You're recollecting Alan Dale more clearly now, too?'

Wood was on a roll. 'I had to punish Jenkins on, I think, at least a couple of occasions for incidents concerning other pupils in the class.'

'Alan Dale?'

'Yes, I think it was. In fact, I'm almost sure of it.'

'I see,' said Tyler, trying to keep the scepticism out of his voice. 'But at the time, when Alan Dale went missing, you didn't dwell on the fact that Jenkins may have been causing problems for the missing boy?'

Wood didn't say anything to that.

There is something too convenient here, thought Tyler. Jenkins dead and suddenly the teacher remembers punishing him for bullying Dale. Not *big on the discipline thing*, but putting in a shift where it counted. Howard Wood, practically the hero of the hour, in fact. Yet there's no-one around to challenge the hero's testimony.

'Mr Wood?' prompted Tyler.

'I really don't remember what I thought,' he said. 'It was a long time ago. I don't feel well.'

Tyler watched the performance, complete with pained expression, a hand nursing the stomach region, then the need to lie down in the dark a while – alone, of course. On a stage, it would have gained respectable reviews, though hardly any statuettes.

'Just one more question, Mr Wood. Then I will leave you in peace, at least for now. Are you aware that Steven Jenkins was killed during the early hours of this morning?'

Again, Tyler observed the reactions of Wood closely, and saw all he needed to see.

Howard Wood wasn't aware; Tyler would have put his pension on it. The man was slippery. He might have had a more fulfilling career on a stage than in the classroom, if indeed the two careers were entirely exclusive. But he didn't know, ninety-nine against one, he didn't know that Steven Jenkins was dead.

And yet, at the same time, he didn't seem altogether surprised.

***

It felt good to be out on the street. The thought of having to share a classroom with a man like Howard Wood was an odious one. Strange, though, that Miss Hayburn would keep such a thing as Wood on her staff. Could it be the man had hidden qualities? Perhaps it was as difficult to get rid of teachers now as it was then.

He wondered how Danny Mills was getting on.

CHAPTER SIXTEEN

Mills had made good progress tracking down the class of 1972. It helped having someone like DC Brown around. Brown could switch on a computer and organise a database in minutes flat. *He's wasted on the force,* thought Mills. *The likes of Eric Brown could be earning a mint at Microsoft and without the stress.*

Steven Jenkins, it seemed, had not been the first to follow Alan Dale to an early death. In the intervening years, no less than four from the class of '72 had succumbed.

Not that there was any suggestion of foul play in the other cases. Cancer, heart disease, a traffic accident and a freak wave on the Greek mainland had done the business.

Brown reckoned there ought to be a survival prize. 'I could set up a programme, if you like,' he told Mills. 'You outlive the rest of your classmates and you're called back to your old school. Then you go up in assembly and collect your certificate: The Longevity Award.'

'Nice idea,' said Mills. 'Why don't you get on to it?'

'But what if your old school no longer exists?' asked the young DC, teasingly.

'Don't be pedantic.'

'No, sir, right, sir.'

'Sarky bastard!'

Many of the survivors were still in the area, and Brown thought that worthy of the observation: 'You can try leaving Stoke, but it gets you in the end.'

'Thank you,' said Mills. 'That's very astute and helpful.'

'We do our best, sir.'

'That's your last warning.'

Maggie Calleer had already given the names of the 'troublesome ones', as she recalled them, most notably Douglas Marley and the now late Steven Jenkins.

'Looks like leopards really can't change their spots,' said Brown.

'That's hardly fair,' said Mills.

'Isn't it?' said Brown. 'It is in my experience.'

'Well, that's as maybe. Looks like Mr Marley has psychological problems, though hardly a textbook monster. I mean to say: two hospital admissions for overdosing and a history of self-harming. Where's your compassion?'

'And one occasion of domestic violence – that we know of. His partner, or whatever you want to call her, had significant facial bruising and two broken fingers.'

'He maintained that she attacked him. That he was defending himself.'

Brown gave Mills a look. 'That's certainly what he *maintained*.'

'It happens.'

'I'm sure it does.'

Douglas Marley was living in a hostel in Stoke, not a hundred yards from where the body of Alan Dale was discovered. 'Significant?' asked Brown. But Mills was learning the art of not jumping to conclusions, using the recently acquired Tyler method, and said nothing.

Then there was Phillip Swanson. The sly one, according to Calleer. A social worker based in Newcastle-under-Lyme, and living out beyond the town in the village of Audley. 'Looks like he's a reformed character,' said Brown.

'In what sense? In a lot of people's books, being a social worker's a step down the ladder from convicted terrorist.'

Brown smiled. 'But then we're more enlightened than some, aren't we, *sir*?'

'Anyone in mind?'

'The place is full of rednecks – take your pick.'

'Are you referring to the city, or this police station?'

Brown laughed. 'I couldn't possibly answer that.'

Martin Hillman was living in Derbyshire and running in the forthcoming local elections there. Maggie Calleer's *dark horse*. 'According to his old form teacher, Hillman was a sneaky one, same as Swanson if a tad harder to nail down.'

'Well, maybe that's how she's funding her retirement.'

'How do you mean?'

'Successful politician with skeletons in the cupboard. Hillman might be paying her off to keep her mouth shut. Big house she's living in, is it?'

'One problem with your theory: what part of keeping her mouth shut involves giving us his name?'

'Perhaps she wants out. Has she asked about protection yet?'

'Brown.'

'Sarge?'

'Shut up!'

The silence lasted for as long as it took Mills to visit the gents.

'Here's one Calleer missed,' said Brown when the DS returned to his desk. 'Robert Wild. Currently on probation for theft and minor assault, and undergoing his third period of rehabilitation for drug and alcohol problems. Living in the north of the city. Tunstall. A small army of estranged children scattered far and wide across the landscape.'

'The future is assured,' said Mills, grimly.

The remaining boys from the class were living in the city, doing various jobs and with various sized families to support. The girls appeared to have scattered further afield, two having emigrated, one running a hotel business in Cornwall, a couple living in Scotland and as many in the capital. There were two teachers among them, and a fair few working in the NHS. A small number had clung to the remains of the local pottery industry, and there was even a police officer, who appeared to be having herself a decent career in Northumberland.

One person was still unaccounted for, however. Someone Sheila Dale had mentioned in her notes. Alan Dale's one friend at school: Anthony Turnock. *The fat boy.*

***

Tyler walked in and asked if anybody was thinking of making a brew. Brown obliged while Tyler asked Mills for an update.

As the tea arrived, Tyler announced that there would be a briefing later and asked that the word did the necessary rounds. Perusing the information assembled by his colleagues, he seemed about to impart wisdom.

'So, what do you think?' said Mills.

'Not a bad cup of tea, I have to confess – but then I *was* spitting feathers.'

'Howard Wood not forthcoming with the refreshments?' asked Mills.

'I wasn't desperate enough. I tell you, I don't like that man, not one bit. Not that we leap to conclusions, you understand.'

'I understand,' said Mills. 'I did the two-day course on it. And now I'm learning from the master.'

Tyler gave him a look.

Brown came over. 'Found him,' he said. 'You can run but you can't hide. I give you … the fat boy.'

'Congratulations,' said Tyler. 'Local?'

'Fenton,' said Brown. 'That's—'

'Allow me,' said Tyler. 'Fenton lies between Stoke and Longton.'

'Speaking like a native already,' said Brown.

'Does he work, this Turnock?' asked Mills.

'Small pot-bank coming into Longton,' said Brown.

'Try and speak to him today, before the briefing,' said Tyler. 'Thank God for fat boys.'

'Sir?'

'He might be the most reliable resource we have. We'll carve up the rest of the visits later. But make Turnock a priority.'

CHAPTER SEVENTEEN

Sheila Dale picked up so quickly that Tyler wondered if she hadn't been sitting waiting for his call. He asked how she was bearing up.

Her brother had been dead three decades, and, it seemed to DCI Tyler, the woman had long given up hope of any news but the worst kind. Still, the actual discovery of Alan's body was bound to bring to the psychic foreground all the raw and complex feelings accompanying any traumatic loss. It didn't take a trained psychiatrist to see that and Dale didn't need it spelling out.

Even when there's no glimmer of hope, the mind plays tricks. And without the evidence of an actual body, in dreams and in waking fantasies, a cruel and irrational hope can persist. He knew it, chapter and verse.

Dale wanted to know how the investigation was going, and he told her more or less the truth: that they were making slow progress and looking for as much information as they could get their hands on. When she said that she would do anything she could to help with the investigation, he wondered if she wasn't intimating that she had more to tell him. He sensed that something had changed. She sounded stronger, he thought.

He asked if he might visit her again, later that day, and she agreed.

Tyler put down the phone and pondered.

***

Anthony Turnock was at work but agreed to meet Danny Mills. He asked if they could meet at his home in Fenton during his lunch break. It seemed a reasonable enough request. In the interim, Mills set about scaling the foothills of the paperwork mountain.

***

Dale opened the front door as Tyler approached. Before he'd taken a seat, she offered him a drink, which he accepted gratefully.

Sitting across from her, back in that spartan front room, it seemed to him that little progress had been made since his last visit. And yet a picture was building all the same.

In answer to her question he told her that he had been to see two of Alan's teachers and his old headmaster, Mr Wise. That there were others that he still needed to speak to.

'Apart from Anthony Turnock, do you recall the names of any of the children at the school – in Alan's class? Was there anyone that your brother might have mentioned?'

She took a drink, a polite sip, as though she were the guest in the room. 'Alan was a shy boy, a very private boy. He never wanted to cause a fuss. He preferred to suffer in silence.'

The pain in that last sentence was grotesque, thought Tyler.

'Your parents went up to the school to see Fredrick Wise. Do you know if your parents had any names, boys, or girls, for that matter, who were giving Alan a hard time?'

'My parents knew Alan was being bullied because of the cuts and bruises.'

'Did your brother sustain a lot of cuts and bruises, Miss Dale?'

'He always seemed to be coming home with something. And it was becoming more frequent towards … the end.'

'Any serious injuries?'

She appeared to hesitate. 'Not particularly serious, like I said – mainly cuts and bruises, you know the sort of thing. But there were a lot of them, and almost every day.'

'And how did your brother account for his injuries?'

'That's the thing. He would always say that he had fallen over in the playground, or that he had injured himself playing football, or something like that. But Alan didn't like playing sports, unless they made him, of course. But there was no way he was getting all of those injuries by accident.'

'And did your parents believe what Alan told them?'

'I think they did, at least to begin with. They probably thought they had the most accident-prone child in the world.'

'So, what changed? Did Alan say something to your parents?'

The sadness in her eyes was almost too much to look on. 'Alan never said anything. But I knew that something was wrong and I told them.'

'What did you tell them?' asked Tyler.

'I said that Alan was having a hard time at school. They'd noticed that he was more quiet than usual, and had been for a few days. When they asked him what the matter was he said that it was nothing. So eventually I couldn't stand it and I said that Alan was getting picked on.'

'Did you witness Alan being picked on, directly?'

'I never saw anyone actually hitting him, or anything like that. They were craftier than that. They weren't quite stupid enough to do anything when anyone might be watching. They knew that they might get into trouble, I suppose. So, they were always sneaky about it.'

'And you're certain that Alan never mentioned any names?'

Again, she seemed to hesitate. 'Never,' she said. 'Apart from his friend, Anthony.'

'When your parents visited the school, do you know what followed from that? Was any action taken?'

'I shouldn't have thought so. At least, not at first. Wise didn't want anything damaging the good name of the school and his own reputation. Because we didn't have any names or any proof of anything, he assured my parents that he would be speaking to Alan's form teacher. And that if anything surfaced then the guilty party would be punished. That's what he said, apparently.'

'And was this assurance enough for your parents?'

'They were very old fashioned. They would have seen an authority figure like Wise as being a man of his word. A man of integrity. That's a laugh.

'I think they would have expected that justice would be done, if the culprits could be identified. But the trouble was that Alan wouldn't come forward with anything and Wise said that without that his hands were tied.'

'Do you know if justice was done?'

'My parents kept asking Alan, and I did, too. It was like getting blood out of a stone most of the time with my brother. He was scared, though. I think he was afraid that if he gave them any names, if he told them about what was going on at that place, that it would have made things a lot worse for him.'

'It must have been very difficult for you, knowing that Alan was being bullied but nobody doing anything about it.'

'It was horrible. I felt so helpless. I asked them – my parents, I mean – about going back up to the school because things were getting worse. And that's when Alan said that two boys in his class had been summoned to Mr Wise's office and had come back looking very sorry for themselves.'

'When was this, Miss Dale?'

'It was close to when my brother went missing.'

'He didn't give the names of the two boys?'

'Like I said, he never mentioned anybody except his friend, Anthony.'

'Do you think Alan was telling the truth? Might he have been saying what your parents wanted to hear?'

Dale smiled. 'You are a very perceptive man. I don't know, not for sure. But I was there when those conversations were taking place, and at the time I believed Alan.'

'You believed him?'

'I did, yes.'

'How could you be certain, Miss Dale?'

'I couldn't, of course. But I believed him because of the way he said it. And I remember thinking that there might be reprisals.'

'Reprisals from the two boys?'

'Wise had quite a reputation, and the boys genuinely feared him. I think he would have dealt severely with somebody, anybody, if he believed that his position was being compromised. Just so that justice could be seen to be done. He wouldn't want anything coming back on him or his precious school. I'm sure it would have been properly documented in case our parents or anybody else had taken the matter further. That's what I imagine, anyway, for what it's worth.'

'Thank you,' said Tyler. 'That's interesting.'

Tyler thought over what Dale had said, pausing to finish his drink and to frame the question: 'Does the name Steven Jenkins mean anything to you?'

***

Mills arrived a few minutes early, and sat outside the terraced property. Fenton was something of an enigma, he had often thought. Regarded as one of the towns making up the city, yet it seemed curiously devoid of any tangible centre. He thought of the area around the magistrate's court as the heart of the town, but wondered if that wasn't down to the job he was doing.

He recognised the figure walking briskly along the road towards him, even though he had never seen Turnock before. The grown-up version of the boy who had once been Alan Dale's best, and possibly only, friend might not be exactly a contender for the fattest man in Britain, but the bouncy gait and jowly features betrayed a man with no history of being thin. He looked nervous and was keen to disappear inside the property with his visitor, and Mills obliged.

The inside of the property suggested a confirmed and lifelong bachelor. It didn't look as though the man had accumulated much in his life, and for a moment Mills felt an empathetic sadness, and a sense of being blessed in this life after all.

'I've got about forty minutes,' said Turnock, breathlessly. 'Is that enough?'

Mills nodded. 'If we get straight to business.'

Mills let the man begin with his own memories of Alan Dale, painting a familiar picture of a classmate subjected to the worst horrors of the so-called education system back in the day. It seemed to Mills that the grown up 'fat boy' might be describing scenes from a war story, in which fear and danger marked out every day. A game of survival, relentless and without mercy. Yet in their clandestine friendship, some secret respite had been born in the knowledge that at least they were not suffering entirely alone.

The man had a kindly, affable face, with a smile that seemed warm and genuine. But the way it remained glued to his face, regardless of the context, regardless of the twists and turns in the conversation, quickly became unnerving. It suggested an almost-pathological eagerness to please, and a desperate need for urgent approval.

So far there had been no mention of any names, and already Turnock was starting to glance at his watch. It was time to end the preliminary sketching and come up with a few faces.

'Do you remember the name of your class teacher, Mr Turnock?'

'Which one?' he answered, and rather lamely, thought Mills.

'The year that Alan went missing. 1972. Your penultimate – your next to last – year.'

'I know what penultimate means, sir.'

Mills blanched at the mild rebuke, and at the use of the word 'sir'. Turnock looked about to apologise.

'You don't have to call me "sir", by the way. Actually, that's what I'm supposed to call you.'

'Mr Turnock's fine. Tony, if you prefer. I really don't mind.'

It wasn't quite the discussion of names that Mills had been hoping for, and again the man was eyeing his watch.

'So, do you recall your class teacher that year, Mr Turnock?'

The name came out like a reluctant blasphemy. 'Mr Wood, you mean?'

Mr Wood, it seemed, had given Alan Dale a hard time indeed. Given both of them a hard time. Mills was intrigued to hear why that might be.

'He said that he didn't like boys who wouldn't stand up for themselves. I once told him that some of the others were picking on Alan, and he gave me a right good hiding in front of the class. Said he didn't like tell-tales, either. I didn't tell him again.'

'Can you remember the names of any of the others in your class?'

'I can remember all of them.'

It didn't surprise Mills to hear that. The man had an anorak quality about him, a trainspotter's eye for every kind of detail that the average person easily missed or else discarded. Fear and humiliation, too, tended to leave their marks in the memory, making names from a difficult time impossible to forget.

Turnock was looking at his watch again, and Mills assured him that they had another ten minutes and that he was quite prepared to give Anthony a lift back to work and be discreet on all counts.

Mills could almost feel the tremors emanating from inside the grown-up fat boy, the dark fear hidden behind the thin mask of that perma-smile. Thirty years on, a grown man, and still afraid of being found out telling tales. It took all the remaining time to extricate the names, one by one, beginning with Steven Jenkins.

***

Sheila Dale thought that she remembered the name but couldn't be certain. 'I think so,' she said. 'It does ring a bell. Alan never mentioned any of them by name, like I said.'

'But, Miss Dale..?'

'One day after school I waited around near to the school gates. Out of sight, you understand. I had a bad feeling that something was going to happen. There were two boys who always seemed to be picking on somebody or other when they came out of school, and I wondered if they were the two that had been in trouble with Wise.

'I saw those two get Alan's friend, Anthony, down on the ground and start hitting him and taunting him. I asked another kid who those boys were, but the child was too frightened to say anything. But I heard the name Jenkins, I'm sure that was the name, and I even went into the school to report what I had seen.

'I saw Mr Wise himself. He didn't recognise me.'

It was a big school, thought Tyler. He wondered whether Miss Hayburn could remember the names and the faces of all the kids under her command. Maybe she could at that.

Dale stopped talking, carefully placing her teacup and saucer on the little stand next to the chair. Tearfully she said, 'I let them down that day, Alan and Anthony.'

'In what way did you do that?' asked Tyler.

'Wise could be very intimidating. The girls rarely had anything to do with him, directly, but he had a manner about him. I remembered him from assembly, and I lost my bottle that day. He asked me if I made a habit of policing his school at home time, and he made me feel stupid and I didn't pursue it.'

'Do you think it would have made any difference if you had?'

'Who knows? But I should have tried to do more.'

'Miss Dale, are you aware of what happened to Steven Jenkins?'

'Happened? What do you mean?'

If she knows, then her acting is right up there, thought Tyler. And anyway, the idea of this quiet-spoken spinster cutting the throat of a naked man clutching a bag of cocaine, and zooming away at high speed, was too ludicrous for words.

***

Anthony Turnock said that he mentioned Steven Jenkins first because he was always the one who seemed to do most of the hitting. He wasn't the biggest or the brightest, but he was always trying to make a name for himself.

'A big Stoke City fan, he was. He asked us one day who we supported. I could tell he was spoiling for trouble, so I said that I supported Stoke even though I couldn't care less about football. He punched me in the stomach and told me I was just being a creep. Alan didn't say anything and so Jenkins kept on saying that he had to name a team or else he would get a right good kicking.'

Turnock paused. 'I don't know why he didn't just say Stoke, and be done with it. But that was Alan. He could never make life easy for himself. So, he said Chelsea.'

'Chelsea?' said Mills. 'Why them?'

'I asked him that myself, later, and he said he'd heard of them and that he liked the colour.'

'He knew that they played in blue?'

'It was because of that song the fans sing. *Blue is the Colour*. They'd played Stoke in a cup final a few weeks earlier and everyone had been on about it. It was a massive thing, all over the school and the city too. You couldn't get away from it. That's the only reason Alan knew anything about them, I imagine.'

'So, when Alan said *Chelsea..?*'

'Jenkins eyeballed him and told him that in this city, if you didn't support Stoke, then you didn't deserve to live. That people who support other teams are traitors and should all be tortured and killed and their corpses dumped in the sea.'

'And what happened?'

'I remember Jenkins saying: *'Red is the colour, you better remember that.'* Then he called over one of the others. We were in the playground. I think it was Douglas Marley. He was another big Stoke City fan. Him and Jenkins made Alan repeat what he had said: *Red is the colour.* And then they started kicking Alan until the whistle blew, and I think a couple of them got sent to the headmaster.'

Turnock hesitated. 'No, I don't think it was Douglas Marley.' He thought for a minute. 'It could have been Robert Wild or Phillip Swanson, they were both Stoke fans too.' But Turnock didn't seem convinced. 'It's bugging me now,' he said. 'I think I'm getting things mixed up.'

'Don't worry about it,' said Mills. 'If it comes back to you, get in touch.'

'I think that was one of the reasons that Mr Wood had it in for us.'

'What's that?'

'Because we weren't interested in football.'

'Mr Wood was a football fan?'

'Never missed a match. He was always going on about Stoke City. When they beat Chelsea in that cup final he brought a programme in to school and passed it around the class. That's likely how Alan knew Chelsea played in blue, that and the song.'

'And Alan liked the colour and he told them he supported Chelsea,' said Mills, almost to himself.

'They never stopped after that.'

As good as his word, Mills drove Alan Dale's old friend up the road, dropping him off discreetly around the corner from the small pot-bank where he had worked since leaving school.

***

Sheila Dale, hearing the news about Steven Jenkins, didn't respond at first. Then the words tumbled out, gathering momentum. 'The good Christian thing to do, I believe, is to forgive and forget. But how can you? How can anybody witness what happened to a timid, harmless, inoffensive little boy like Alan and not feel a sense of *justice*?

'I'm sorry, I shouldn't talk like that. I can't help it.'

Tyler asked if she would like another drink. She declined, and he licked at his own dry lips.

'If there's anything else I can tell you …'

Tyler said that they would perhaps be best leaving it there for now, but that he might need to come and see her again.

'Do you think you will find them?' she asked.

'Find who, Miss Dale?'

'Whoever did that to Alan? Whoever took him down The Stumps and did that to him. Not every fifteen-year-old boy has to be a hooligan to get through the day.'

She looked close to breaking down. 'Do you think that Steven Jenkins was involved? Do you think that he killed Alan?'

'What do you think, Miss Dale?'

'It's the wrong kind of solution,' she said. 'It answers one question and asks a much bigger one.'

'I don't follow.'

'If this Jenkins killed my brother, then, yes, it is so tempting to imagine that justice has been done. But the truth is, you see, I don't think that there's a single person in this world who would have cared enough to have done that for Alan.'

Tyler wanted to say, *Not even you, Miss Dale?* In the end he held onto the thought, draped as it was in conflicting connotations of love and vengeance.

***

From his car Tyler rang Mills, and listened intently to the sergeant's report of his interview with Turnock.

'So, you don't put him down as the noble destroyer avenging his friend?'

'I think it's highly unlikely,' said Mills. 'But it's a funny old world.'

'It's certainly that,' said Tyler. 'I once read a story about someone turning up half a lifetime later and murdering an old enemy who lived hundreds of miles away. No apparent motive, the perfect crime – at least in the pages of fiction. And between you and me, I once thought long and hard about putting that principle into practice myself.'

'I take it that you put the idea on a back burner, sir?'

'A back burner, yes.'

The silence down the line became loud and ominous, and Mills broke it. 'Turnock said something very interesting about our old friend Howard Wood, though.'

'Did he?' said Tyler, his mind still running an ancient spool from the archives of his own past. 'Then you'd better tell me about it.'

Mills related the anecdote about football allegiance, and how this had intensified the problems Alan Dale was having at school.

Tyler stopped him. He recalled the conversation a few minutes earlier. Something Dale had been saying – a reference to football? *Hooligans.* He hadn't attached any significance; thought it merely an expression, a reference to the thuggery that existed everywhere in the world, throughout history.

Tyler ended the call quickly. He got out of the car and knocked lightly on Sheila Dale's front door.

CHAPTER EIGHTEEN

At the briefing Tyler gave what some regarded as a master class in the 'stating of the bleeding obvious'.

He wanted the interviewing officers doing the rounds of the class of '72 … 'to raise the name Howard Wood, along with pupils on Maggie Calleer's list, and to note *all* observations made by the interviewed persons. Naturally, all officers will focus on anything pertaining to Alan Dale on the day, or the preceding days, of his disappearance.'

He wanted an open style of interviewing, to allow possibilities to emerge, though using prompts where necessary regarding highlighted individuals.

'With regard to Steven Jenkins, again let them do their own remembering first. Let's see what comes out, what conclusions are leapt to, if any. I do not want any leading towards an investment in scenarios that happen to be resident in *your* heads. *Open minds*, okay? That's the key thing. Then by all means resort to direct questioning.'

Somebody asked about media coverage.

'Jenkins' name is out there now. Most people will, I imagine, be putting two and two together when they hear the background on the Alan Dale case. The media haven't made the connection explicit, but they will and soon. It will be interesting to see what two and two equals in the minds of the class of '72.'

An old Ford Fiesta had been found abandoned less than two miles from Jenkins' flat. Fibres inside the flat matched those found in the abandoned vehicle. Tyler acknowledged the possibility of a professional job, a contract killing, perhaps; again he expressed caution in leaping to conclusions: it was also possible that somebody was choosing to give that impression.

Contrary to the belief that was fast developing at the station, Tyler hated stating the obvious. But this wasn't television, and the road he travelled doing this job was paved with years of stating it. Let them talk; it came with the territory.

Mills was given the trip to Derby. 'I think the ex-patriot has to be yours,' said Tyler. 'You can ask if he still finds the time to visit *the Beloved City.*'

***

When the briefing was over Tyler told Mills about the curious conversation with Dale after he'd returned to her house.

She had, naturally enough, appeared surprised to see him again only minutes after he had made his exit, but welcomed him back in nonetheless. He'd been thinking about the reference she had made to hooligans, and it had set something itching at the back of his mind.

Mindful of his sergeant's remarks over the phone, about what Anthony Turnock had said regarding football allegiance intensifying Alan Dale's problems, he had raised the subject of Alan's final days again and watched Miss Dale's reaction carefully. She'd hesitated, not for the first time, either, he'd noted. It seemed to him that she was trying to decide on the next course of action.

Then she had started crying. A deluge, like before. Tyler sat it out; waited for her to regain some composure. Without warning, she launched into her tale.

Close to the time that Alan went missing, two days before, in fact, Alan had returned home from school complaining of not feeling well. He was late returning home, and she remembered that vividly. 'Alan always came home promptly. I was the same, though we never walked home together.'

Tyler asked why that was, and Dale explained that Alan had been picked on in the early days for walking home from school with his sister.

'I had started my homework but I was aware that he was late. I was starting to get worried, and then he suddenly turned up. I remember feeling very relieved, like I'd sensed something was wrong but had been trying to keep my panic under control, and now I could let go.

'But when he came in the house I could tell that something really *was* wrong. I asked if he was alright and he said that he wasn't feeling very well and wanted to lie down. He went straight up to his room and I followed him upstairs. I was concerned about him.

'When I got upstairs I could hear him sobbing. I stood outside his room. He was breaking his little heart, he was. I called his name, but either he didn't hear me or else he was ignoring me.'

Dale had broken off from her tale, struggling to keep herself together.

'I opened his bedroom door – to see if he was okay.'

'*And I saw him.*'

'Take your time,' said Tyler.

'It was horrible,' she said, her eyes screwed tightly shut, reliving the scene. 'He was getting undressed to get into bed. From his back down to his knees he was a mass of red marks– I've never seen anything like it. I must have gasped, because he turned around. I said, 'What have they done to you?'

'He was angry at me, going into his room like that, and he was shouting at me, telling me to get out, but then he stopped and he ran to me and he held on and I didn't think he was ever going to stop crying. When he finally stopped, it all came pouring out of him.'

She paused again, opening her eyes and looking straight at Tyler.

'The day before, they had been taunting him about being a traitor to his city for not supporting his local football team. And on the way from one classroom to the next they started calling him names, filth like you never heard in your life. They were doing that when they turned the corner and bumped right into

Mr Wise. Two of them, the main culprits, were singled out. Wise ordered them both to his office.'

'Was Steven Jenkins one of them?' asked Tyler.

Dale nodded, blotting her eyes with a tissue.

Tyler ran through the other names. She thought it could be Hillman, the other boy, but couldn't be certain.

'Part way through the next class – Howard Wood's class – the two boys returned, extremely subdued, explaining to Wood where they had been and why. Wood had, according to Alan, glared at him – glared at Alan, but nothing more was said. The boys gingerly returned to their desks and it was apparent to all that Wise had made a job of dealing with them. Some of the girls were giggling and making gestures about their ordeal.

'The following morning, Wood was talking to the class about some match he had been to, and about the importance of having pride in your heritage. That the red and white stripes of Stoke City were something to carry with your head held high.

'After school they rounded on Alan and said that it was time he was initiated into the colours of his *real* team. They wouldn't let him go home. They walked him past his house and down the hill to The Stumps.

'There were a few people playing in the park and one or two working in the allotments, but those animals who took him down The Stumps told Alan that if he shouted for help it would be the worse for him.

'There was demolition work going on. They were knocking down one eyesore in preparation for another.'

The great symbol of the rebirth of the city was how Sheila Dale had put it, with a sneer as she said it, bitterness and anger bleeding out of her.

'And now they're doing it again. Nothing changes.'

'What happened next?' Tyler had asked her.

'They told him that they were going to make a Stoke City fan out of him if it killed him. They reminded him that Mr Wood had said that you had to wear the stripes of your city proudly.

Then one of the boys – one of them who Wise had punished – exposed himself, revealing the marks left by the headmaster. They said that it was *his* turn now.'

At that point Sheila Dale had dissolved again into tears, her body heaving in grief and disgust.

Tyler gave her time to regain her composure, and finally she told him that it was the only time Alan let any of it out, and that he begged her not to say anything to anybody.

"Please don't tell Mum and Dad,' that's what he said.'

'Why do you think he said that?'

'He was terrified. My brother was as traumatised as a soldier on a battlefield. Have you any *idea..?*'

Tyler looked at her, his own memories mixing with the obscenity that she had described, and then he lowered his head. 'No,' he said. 'I have no idea.'

'They beat him, those boys took it in turns to beat him. They acted like savages. There were five of them, and I don't know the names of any of them except for Steven Jenkins and maybe that other one that you suggested, but I don't know. Alan wouldn't tell me, but I knew the name Jenkins and later I heard that other one, I think.'

'Heard from whom, Miss Dale?'

'Oh, I don't know, I can't remember. But they were all to blame, every one of them.'

'Alan told you there were five of them?'

'And those who weren't hitting him, they watched and not one of them showed an ounce of pity. They chanted while they were doing it: 'What is the colour? *Red is the colour.*' Over and over, they did. And Alan held me that day in his bedroom as he sobbed his heart out. Can you imagine, for one moment, the hell that he must have been living through?'

Tyler had to look away from the fury and pain, impotently shaking his head, and lowering it again respectfully.

When she had stopped crying, in the quietness of the room, the stillness, Tyler looked up. Sheila Dale was looking at him, breathing deeply, as though gathering her forces a final time. Tyler had felt every muscle tense in preparation for what she was about to impart.

'And then my poor little brother said something that will haunt me to the end of my days.

'Alan said, 'Don't cry, it's over now. It's done with.''

***

Afterwards, Tyler had sat in his car and mulled it all over. He thought of the neighbourhood bullies and the string of sadists parading as teachers, who had tormented him for close on five years, a chunk of his childhood forever tainted and troubled and in so many ways unredeemable. How he had vowed to leave that estate forever, to climb out of it, and rise above it. In his final years at school he'd buckled down and at college he worked himself into university. And the zeal didn't wane; it was like an engine, over-revving for fear that it might stall, become immobilised; in fear that in failure he would be dragged back into the nightmare from which he had escaped.

And then he met Kim.

And his sin had been not to tell her of his ghosts and his nightmares.

His ambition had split them apart, because she never really understood where he had been coming from. If he had found the courage to tell her that; to let her know what was driving him, instead of hiding it away like a dirty secret and denying it even to himself …

Tyler had pushed the thought away, steering his mind back to the words of Sheila Dale. And as he sat in his unmarked car outside her house in that narrow street in Leek, he had dwelled on the greater sins that had been inflicted upon an innocent young boy, until he found himself crying for the first time in a long time.

When Tyler had finished telling Mills about his visit to Leek, minus the part about the tears, he said, 'So you see, half this city has blood on its hands. What they did, what they didn't do. Like any other city. The world we live in.'

'Do you think,' said Mills, 'that they took Alan Dale back to that place two days later to finish the job?'

'I think it's one of a number of possibilities. But I don't want to confront anybody with that scenario just yet. I'm interested to see what accounts of those evil days are given voluntarily.'

'She didn't recall any of the other names?'

'Hillman was a possibility.'

'Hillman? I doubt he'll admit to being there,' said Mills. 'Councillors, aspiring MPs don't generally own up to having skeletons in the closet.'

'I think you're probably right about that,' said Tyler. 'But it'll be interesting to see how high this man's defences are built. Could be that he drove the demons from his system that day, in the summer of '72. Turned his life around, saw the light, you know the story. Maybe others thought it would be fun to take their turns having sport with a terrified, traumatised boy. We might even find out.'

***

In the late afternoon sunshine, Mills headed east, passing the Britannia Stadium, home of Stoke City FC. He had a thought to fly in the face of his circumstances and buy himself a season ticket. Buy the whole family a ticket and be damned. So what if they didn't end up going half the time? What was money when you didn't have any? What was money against such a life-affirming act of defiance?

Tyler, meanwhile, drove west out of the city, bypassing the town of Newcastle, and on towards the village of Audley. He was due to interview a social worker, a protector of children who, thirty years earlier, had possibly witnessed the death of one.

CHAPTER NINETEEN

Mills found Councillor Martin Hillman every bit as keen to help in person as he had been on the phone.

Hillman had heard about the unearthing of his 'old classmate – the Dale boy' – and of the 'terrible tragedy of Steven Jenkins' who he seemed to recall as being 'a somewhat troubled young fellow.' These things came to try us, the politician and businessman told Mills. It could be a harsh world, but one did what one could, and tried not to dwell on such dark realities. 'You'd go mad if you dwelled on all the tragedy that surrounds us.'

'You wouldn't want to do that, sir,' Mills had advised, though secretly he doubted Hillman was the type to lose much sleep over the misfortune of others. He appeared every inch the regulation business type, and a politician of high ambition. But Mills resolved to keep his prejudices at bay, and to obey DCI Tyler's confusing maxim, his parting comment as the DS had left the station for Derby, about only *partially* judging a book by its cover.

The house was a small mansion by Mills' standards, and set in a beautifully landscaped garden. Martin Hillman had not married, though the gleaming Aston Martin out in the drive suggested, at least to Danny Mills, that female companionship might not be lacking should its owner feel so inclined.

Again, Mills tried not to allow his feelings to intrude on his professionalism, tough as that could be sometimes. It was an ongoing battle. The bitterness rose up from time to time, but at least these days he was beginning to recognise it for what it was. And a part of him that he was slowly growing accustomed to, was proud to be making progress.

Still, for the present enquiry, the subject was irrelevant, and Mills resolved to put it out of his mind. One final time for luck, he reminded himself about prejudices and the covers of books.

***

Hillman had done well in his end of school exams, and following a two-year A level stint at a local college, had been the first member of his old class to reach university. Three years at Nottingham doing business studies … 'and I never looked back. Not bad for the product of a single parent family, wouldn't you say?'

His father had disappeared into obscurity when Martin had been too young to remember him. His mother had always 'valued the merits of a solid education. She was a solicitor, so I suppose that was to be expected.'

'Where did you live?' asked Mills.

'Hartshill, actually. Nice little cul de sac near to where they built the trauma unit.'

'You still go back to visit your mother?'

'Sadly, she died. I was at university at the time. I don't have any relatives in the area, or anywhere else, for that matter. I have no ties. I'm what you might call a free agent,' he said, with a wide smile. 'I decided to make Nottingham my home, and more recently I moved across to Derbyshire. Business commitments and political ones too, these days. I love this area and, frankly, I have nothing to go back to Stoke for.'

'You don't keep in touch with friends?' asked Mills.

'I'm probably beginning to sound like a rather sad case,' said Hillman, 'but I didn't make any friends back in the Potteries, to be honest. My life is here, and I'm happy with that state of affairs.'

'So, you don't have any contact with your old classmates, then?'

'God, no!' said Hillman, looking somewhere between amused and appalled at the very idea.

'You didn't get on with your classmates, I take it?'

'They were alright, I suppose. But we were just kids. You don't choose the people that you share a class with. You're forced into a rather unnatural situation, in my opinion, and you simply try to make the best of it.'

'Not the happiest time of your life – school?'

'Like I say, it was a part of life that one has to cope with the best one can.'

'And you don't go back to watch Stoke City play?'

Hillman laughed, long and loud. 'You are kidding?'

Mills didn't say anything.

'You a City fan yourself?'

'I have my moments,' said Mills. 'I understood that, as a child at least, you were quite devoted.'

'Me? Are you kidding? One or two of them in my class were regulars because their parents were regulars, their fathers, at least. Steven Jenkins used to go with his old man, and he was always going on about Stoke City, as I recall. It was a long time ago.'

'So, you were never really a fan?'

Hillman frowned. 'Are you sure that you're talking to the right person? My mum hated football. She used to say that grown men with nothing better to do than kick a ball around ought to be drafted into the forces. And she thought that people who paid good money to go and watch were even more reprehensible. I happen to think that she was probably about right. Anyway, what are you, the football police?'

Hillman laughed again, and Mills let it go.

'When was the last time that you visited the city, sir?'

'Oh, you lose track.'

'But not recently?'

'You know, it's so long ago now that I would have to get an old diary out to check.'

'But you haven't been back to the city in the last few days?'

Intelligence shone out of those dark grey eyes, thought Mills, as he waited for Martin Hillman's response. And when it came, it surprised him. At least, one aspect of it did.

'Oh, I've been far too busy for nostalgia. Meetings like you would *not* believe. Business meetings, council meetings, none of them exactly five-minute affairs either. I had a right humdinger last night. I mean – Sunday evening! Is there no rest for the wicked?'

'I wouldn't know about that, sir.'

'Well, let me tell you – it went on until well past midnight.'

'Really,' said Mills, noting the remark, but unable in the heat of the moment to grasp why it rang such an odd note.

Mills asked for details of the meetings, names of others present, the usual. Hillman didn't bat an eye, assuring the officer that he would have all the information faxed over first thing in the morning.

Then Mills asked if Hillman had any memories of Alan Dale.

'Not really. I mean to say, it's tragic, obviously, whatever happened to the poor little sod, but–'

Hillman broke off. 'Do you really think that he was murdered?'

Mills didn't answer. Hillman was evidently the type used to running things. If you weren't careful, you ended up telling the Martin Hillmans of this world more than they told you. 'So, you have no particular memories relating to Alan Dale?'

Hillman appeared to make an effort of remembrance, but when he came back with nothing at all, Mills asked him if he remembered any bullying at the school?

'Well, of course I'd be lying if I said that there wasn't any. I can't imagine a school without bullies, to tell you the truth. It's the way things are, I'm afraid. It's the nature of things.'

'You do remember incidents of bullying, then, sir?'

'I hope that this doesn't come across as being rather snotty,' said Hillman, 'but I tried to rise above such things. There were a few rough types in the school, but if you kept your head down and got your work done … I never had any real problems that I recall. How about yourself? Which school did you go to?'

Mills resisted the diversion. 'Alan Dale – did he have any problems with any of the other children, that you can recall?'

'What kind of problems?'

Mills tried to conceal his growing impatience. 'Can you recall anybody giving Alan Dale a hard time?'

'Like I say, I tried to stay out of that type of thing.'

'Do you recall the headmaster of your school, Mr Hillman?'

Again, Hillman appeared to be searching back into the dense mists of time. 'Actually, I do,' he said. 'Can't bring his name to mind, though. It really was a long time ago. It's quite frightening when you stop to think—'

'Does the name *Wise* ring any bells?'

'That's the fellow! Not that I had a great deal to do with him.'

'Then you don't recall being sent to his office, along with Steven Jenkins, for picking on Alan Dale?'

Hillman looked shocked to the core. 'Me? Who told you that?'

'You were not punished by Mr Wise for—'

'I was not punished by Mr Wise for anything. I had nothing to do with him. He was there in assembly and other than that I never saw him. Like I say, I kept my head down and got my work done.'

'Were you friends with Steven Jenkins?'

'I think 'friends' would be pushing it. I kept myself to myself.'

'You never played football, or talked about football together?'

'I tried to avoid kicking footballs and talk of kicking footballs. Sometimes you had little choice, but I did my best to keep both activities down to the bare minimum. My mother, likewise not being a fan of the game, as I've already explained, or of any sports, for that matter, was rather adept at writing sick notes, bless her. She wanted, I think, to keep me out of the way of the barbarians.'

Mills didn't say anything, and a thick silence quickly descended.

Hillman erupted again into laughter, but to Mills it rang false and hollow.

'You must excuse my sense of humour, really you must,' said Hillman. 'I don't really think of all sports enthusiasts as that, of course I don't. I think my mother knew a lot about the dynamics of the playground, and she supported my individuality admirably, I would say. I told her that I had no time for football or for gruelling cross-country runs, and I imagine that she was nothing but proud of me. And so, rumours of an impending asthmatic condition flaring up and causing problems for the authorities – my mother was a fine solicitor, and she knew how to write a letter that would count. I rarely had to take part.'

'And you didn't show any interest in Stoke City Football Club?'

Hillman grinned. 'I have already established that I had no interest in football, but I wasn't a fool either. I knew how to play the game of … *blending in*. I could have named the team and I kept an eye on fixtures and results. It's what one does to keep ones head below the parapet, but nothing more.'

'You remember Stoke City winning the cup, sir?'

'1972,' said Hillman, not missing a beat, his intellect shining out of those dark eyes again in beams that were unsettling DS Mills. 'That *was* the year the boy went missing, wasn't it?'

'You've not forgotten, then?'

'The police were at the school, asking questions, naturally; and it was mentioned for weeks on end in assembly, right up to the holidays.'

'Potters,' said Mills.

Hillman laughed again. 'What a fine institution that was: *Potters' holidays.*'

'Alan Dale went missing very close to Potters.'

'What point are you making, Detective Sergeant?'

He wasn't. He was floundering, clutching at straws, wondering what it was about Hillman's earlier comment about late night meetings that jarred so.

Then seeing it: *the eureka moment.*

Sunday evening, late. When Steven Jenkins was getting his throat cut. A general question about visiting Stoke over the last few days followed immediately by the prompt delivery of an alibi for the night that Jenkins had been murdered.

'Detective Sergeant?'

Mills tried to remember what he'd been asking. Holidays, yes. 'The investigation would have started before the Potters break and continued during and after, all the way up to the big school holidays.'

Hillman looked puzzled. 'So, your point? It was a big thing; the police coming to school, a child missing – I would be hardly likely to forget something like that, now, would I?'

'But you don't recall anything about Alan Dale, or anybody giving him a hard time?'

Hillman was checking his watch. *A persuasive man,* thought Mills.

But Mills hadn't finished, and pressed on, asking about other members of the class; going through the list of names. Did Hillman remember any of them?

They rang faint bells, some of them, he said. But it was a long time ago.

'What about your form teacher that year?'

'Ah,' said Hillman. 'Now I do remember him. That would be Mr Wood.'

'What do you recall of Mr Wood?'

'The thing that I recall about Mr Wood, he was a little different to the rest of the teachers.'

'In what way different?'

'I think that he tried to treat us as adults. He was less formal, less rigid than most of the others. Some would like that, and some not, I suppose.'

'And you, sir? What did you make of him?'

'He was alright. I never had a problem with him.'

Mills again tried to hide his exasperation.

'Was Mr Wood a football fan – a Stoke City fan?'

Hillman seemed to hesitate. 'I don't really remember,' he said. 'He could've been. Is it important?'

It was Mills turn to hesitate. 'Probably not, sir.' Then, for some reason, the instinct to be mysterious stole over him. 'But you never know, sir,' he said. 'Not at this stage.'

He saw the question mark rising in Hillman's eye. Both men looked at the other, as though waiting for something to give way. Mills wondered if Hillman was going back over what had been said, trying to fathom if a cause for doubt had been raised. A mistake of some kind made, some giveaway.

Mills watched carefully, even as Hillman started up the small talk and the need to get on. He wouldn't have relished meeting a man like Martin Hillman across a poker table. Here was a player who gave away only what he wanted to give away.

And yet that hesitation about Howard Wood.

What could it mean? Or was he looking too hard? Wood was a teacher clearly remembered by many as being a football fanatic, and a keen Stoke City supporter. Had Hillman been caught on the hop? Could he genuinely not remember that aspect of Howard Wood, or had Hillman not thought through the ramifications of appearing to clearly remember what might have been a defining characteristic of the teacher?

The air, still stained with the enigmatic remark that Mills had made, crackled until finally Hillman held out a hand, and Mills thanked him for his time.

Councillor Hillman promised again to fax the information about meeting dates and times to the number on the card which the detective had given him, and then it was goodbye.

It was a good drive back and it was getting late. Already Mills was thinking that Douglas Marley would have to wait until morning.

***

While Mills had been over in Derby, Tyler had enjoyed a drive out to Audley to see Phillip Swanson. He had enjoyed the drive, anyway. North Staffordshire was proving to be something of a wonderland, and not the dump that at least three country-wide studies had concluded whilst trying, for some reason unknown, to establish where the real armpit of the nation lay.

The time spent with Swanson, however, had been less enjoyable.

Phillip Swanson had separated from his wife and three children, and the ex-Mrs Swanson had taken her clan back to her native Dublin. She had worked as a social worker, and met Swanson whilst cohabiting with another member of the profession. Living close to Swanson in the Stoke area, she had hopped literally from the bed of one social worker and into the other, and Tyler couldn't help but conclude that they could be an incestuous lot.

Swanson asked if he might smoke, and Tyler told him that he was at liberty to do as he pleased in his own house. The subtext of the remark, that he would much prefer it if Swanson didn't, appeared to go unobserved, and no amount of theatrical coughing by Tyler made the slightest difference.

The social worker nervously lit up a cigarette and inhaled deeply, apparently in an attempt to steady himself for the ordeal ahead. Tyler wondered if this was a normal day for Phillip Swanson, and if so, how he managed to get through the weeks and months. The man seemed surprisingly insensitive, thought Tyler, and insensitivity jarred somewhat with his expectations of someone in a so-called caring profession.

Still, he was prepared to give the man the benefit of the doubt. Perhaps Swanson was unduly nervous. Perhaps he had something on his mind, something to hide.

He kicked off with some preliminary remarks about the beauty of the area, but all he could seem to draw from Swanson was a look of deep suspicion. Experience suggested that this interview was either going to be hard work, or else an early jackpot was on the cards. He wasn't hopeful.

Tyler got down to business. 'You attended River Trent High School during the early 1970s, is that correct?'

The man nodded, puffing vigorously on his cigarette.

'Is that a yes, Mr Swanson?'

'Yes.'

What felt like half-a-dozen smokes later, it had been established that the man's memory of his school days was extraordinarily dim.

He did remember an Alan Dale, 'the boy who went missing, wasn't he?' but insisted that he had nothing whatsoever to do with him. He remembered the teacher Mr Wood, who was 'okay', and when prompted he recalled Martin Hillman who was bright and got on with his work. One or two others could be a laugh and there were one or two who gave everybody a hard time. In the latter category, he singled out Douglas Marley and Steven Jenkins.

On the subject of Steven Jenkins, the mists appeared to clear, and Swanson, now in a rhythm, was eager to heap the troubles of the world at the door of that particular ex-classmate.

'Do you recall Jenkins picking on Alan Dale?' asked Tyler.

'He picked on everyone,' said Swanson. 'He was always in trouble, usually for bullying, fighting, that sort of thing.'

'You don't recall him *targeting* Alan Dale?'

Swanson appeared to think deeply for a minute. 'Actually, now you mention it, yes, he did. And sometimes he would pick on him after school.'

'In what way did he pick on him?'

'Threatening him, hitting him. He used to go the same way home.'

Tyler watched Swanson light up another cigarette. 'And do you believe that Steven Jenkins might have been responsible for what happened to Alan Dale?'

'What did happen to Alan Dale?' asked Swanson.

'That's what we're trying to find out,' said Tyler.

It occurred to Tyler that Swanson wanted to ask something, but had thought better of it. At last he said, 'I didn't think about it at the time; but now that you mention it, I suppose it is possible, yes.'

Tyler leaned forward. 'Could you explain exactly what you mean by that?'

Swanson pulled heavily on his cigarette, his eyes darting nervously to and from the detective's solid gaze.

'I – if something happened to Alan Dale,' he said. 'If, I mean, someone did something to him … I think Jenkins was the sort.'

'Are you saying, Mr Swanson, that you believe that Steven Jenkins might have been responsible for the death of Alan Dale?'

Swanson lit another smoke off the dying embers of the last one.

'I don't know about that,' he said. 'I don't know what happened.'

'But you believe it might be a possibility that Steven Jenkins was, in some way, responsible for the boy's death?'

Swanson didn't answer.

'You said that Jenkins was 'the sort'.'

Swanson took in another huge lungful of smoke, and blurted it out. 'I don't know what happened and I didn't see anything and I didn't hear anything – but if anyone killed that kid, I think that someone like Steven Jenkins might have been responsible, yes.'

'Bit convenient, though, wouldn't you say?' said Tyler.

'I don't understand,' said Swanson. 'What is?'

'Why, the person responsible for the death of Alan Dale, getting killed himself so early in our investigation?'

Unease gathered like a storm. 'Convenient? I don't know what you mean.' The man looked like he needed to light another cigarette, the trouble being that he still had one going. Tyler kept the pressure on.

'I don't know,' said Swanson. 'I mean, Jenkins did pick on Alan Dale.'

'*And?*'

'Going home the same way …'

'You mean, down *The Stumps*?'

Swanson was nodding vigorously. 'Steven Jenkins lived down in Stoke.'

'And where did you live?'

'Penkhull.'

'Near to the park?'

Swanson nodded. 'Yes.'

'So, you would walk that way home too?'

'Not with him.'

'Who with, then?'

He had to say something, but the clouds appeared to be closing in around him, and not only the ones filled with nicotine. Whatever he said now he had to stick with and both of the men in the room knew it.

'Usually I would go the other way.'

'Other way?'

Close to where Alan Dale had lived, a fork in the road provided two options for those living in the park area of the village. The right fork sloped down Honeydew Bank into Stoke, with the option of cutting through the streets towards the park. The left fork swept over in the direction Hartshill, with a choice of zig-zagging down through the maze of streets, also to the park.

Steven Jenkins favoured the long slope down Honeydew Bank, continuing into Stoke, where he lived; unless a game of football had been arranged, in which case he would head over to the park. Swanson was admitting to sometimes going that way, yet at the same time detaching himself from that option.

Trying to keep his choices open, thought Tyler. He asked if Douglas Marley and Robert Wild sometimes went that way, and Swanson said that he thought they did. They lived in Stoke, he thought, and played football in the park.

'But you were not so keen on playing in the park after school?'

'Not really. Sometimes.'

'And so what was the other route – the one you say that you favoured?'

Swanson spelt it out. At the fork in the road beyond Dale's home, the alternative to the Honeydew Bank descent was to turn left by the infant school and walk towards the hospital complex. Then, a couple of hundred yards short of Hartshill, take another right and drop down through the streets, coming out by the park though not at the entrance adjacent to The Stumps.

'Did anybody else walk that way?' asked Tyler.

'A few.'

'Nobody in particular?'

'I don't know what you mean.'

Tyler remembered that Martin Hillman had lived in Hartshill. That route would certainly be the most direct for him. *Thinking like a native*, he thought. 'Did Hillman walk that way?' he asked Swanson.

'He might have done. I think he lived over that way.'

'He wouldn't have taken the other route?'

'I don't imagine so.'

'But you didn't tend to walk that way with him, even though he was a classmate?'

Swanson paused, as though deliberating on which path lay the lesser of two evils.

In the end, hedging his bets, he appeared to find resolution by taking the middle ground. 'I might have done a few times, but we weren't really big mates.'

What a surprise, thought Tyler.

'You didn't have any 'big mates' at school?'

'No.'

'You haven't kept in touch with anybody from your class?'

Swanson eyed the detective. 'No.'

'And you haven't recently come across anybody from your class?'

The question seemed to fall like a bombshell into the room, and Tyler half expected Swanson to run for the door. Instead, fumbling for another cigarette, he shook his head.

'Is that a 'no', Mr Swanson?'

'No, yes, I mean, yes, it's a 'no'.'

Tyler watched the man ignite another smoke.

'You have trouble with your nerves?'

'Yes, sometimes. I'm off work at the moment.'

'I'm sorry to hear that. How long have you been off?'

A few days, it turned out. And Tyler couldn't help thinking about Howard Wood's recent period of sick leave, and doubted the coincidence.

'Your old class teacher, Mr Wood, still teaches at the school.'

'Does he?' said Swanson, with as much disinterest as he could muster.

'You didn't know that?'

'Why should I? It was a long time ago.'

'Big Stoke City fan, apparently.'

'Who?'

'Your teacher. Mr Howard Wood.'

'Oh, right.'

'Not a fan yourself?'

'Of Wood or City?'

'Both.'

'Wood was alright, I suppose. I used to go to the match, but you move on, don't you? Find other things.'

'How old were you when you *moved on*?'

Swanson was puffing away furiously. 'I don't know. Is it relevant?'

'It could be.'

Swanson fell silent.

Tyler again edged forward in his seat. 'Do you think' he said, 'that supporting the wrong football team is a good enough reason for beating someone to death?'

Tyler wound up the session, but indicated that he might need to visit again. The news seemed to come as a nasty shock to Phillip Swanson, who, on extinguishing his cigarette, promptly fumbled for another.

As Tyler walked out to his car, in the cooling evening air, he felt the sense of relief that comes from leaving a place of intense suffering.

CHAPTER TWENTY

'Anything interesting to report?' Tyler asked Mills, ringing on his mobile.

Mills mentioned Hillman's pat presentation of what he was confident would turn out to be a rock-solid alibi.

'That's the trouble with detectives,' laughed Tyler. 'We have such suspicious minds.'

'How did you get on with Swanson?'

'Good question. If I'd told him we were investigating the murder of the man in the moon, I think he would have looked guilty. So many layers of it, it's hard to know if the man's a serial killer or in need of a change of profession. He also has a penchant for the convenient option. He fancies the late Steven Jenkins for the death of Alan Dale.'

'That would be convenient.'

'Swanson tried hard to distance himself from the rest of his class. Portrayed himself as having little to do with any of them, then and now.'

'Seems to be a common theme.'

'Hillman, too?'

'The loner who got on with his work. Eyes down all the way to the Houses of Parliament.'

'See no evil, eh? Sounds like a natural. Anyway, I'm outside the offices of Mr Robert Wild.'

'Offices?'

'Make that doss house. Do you know Tunstall at all?'

'Coming from Longton, how could I?'

'Sarcasm suits you – did anybody ever tell you that?'

'My wife might have mentioned it.'

'Right, it's getting late. I'll see Wild and call it a night.'

'I was down to see Douglas Marley. I called the hostel and Marley won't be going anywhere. Is tomorrow okay on that one?'

'Tomorrow's fine.'

'I'll write up a full report, but one other thing I should tell you. About the incident Sheila Dale mentioned – Jenkins and Hillman in trouble and getting a thrashing off Wise.'

'What about it?'

'Hillman has no recollection. He said he never got sent to Wise for anything, and of course he would never have picked on or bullied anyone.'

'What were you even thinking about suggesting such a thing?' said Tyler. 'I think I'll visit the school again in the morning. They might have records.'

'What kind of school did *you* go to, sir?'

'One that kept records.'

'Got your name in the book, did you?'

'That's classified, I'm afraid. Goodnight.'

***

Robert Wild appeared friendlier and more coherent than Tyler had imagined. The inside of the house was as inviting as the outside, but the company was an improvement on what he had left behind in Audley. There was roguishness to Robert Wild, but a sense of humour laced it.

Wild reckoned he'd had his share of life's problems, what with difficult women and people over the years plying him with just about every variety of drugs and drink that the world, or at least the city, had to offer. But he was turning his life around, he said, working for a local builder. 'Suits me, you see, working. I don't get into bother when I've got plenty on. And working with that slave driving bastard – sorry about that, officer.'

'Are you trying to give up cursing, too, in this new life of yours?'

Wild laughed, and it was toothy and infectious.

Tyler started the time travel, whisking the tanned imp back to River Trent High. A familiar pattern emerged straight away.

'Didn't have much to do with any of them, tell you the truth.'

A class full of loners, thought Tyler. *But was that a teacher's dream or nightmare?*

'Wood was a bit of a laugh, bit of a nutter. Always going on about Stoke City. I used to go to the match myself, same as the old man at home, but you get bored with it.'

'Bored watching football?'

'Well, no, I don't mean that so much. But when you're younger you get obsessed sometimes, some do, at any rate. Like, fanatical, you know. Take it a bit too serious. I mean, it's only a bloody game, when all's said and done. Anyway, I'm closer to the Vale now, living up this way.'

Tyler remembered what Mills had told him about the city's football rivalry.

'You mean Port Vale?'

Wild nodded. 'You not from round here?'

'I'm learning.'

'Try this for size: Chuck a bow aggen a woe, yed it, kick it an bost it.'

Tyler looked suitably baffled. 'Not Latin, is it?'

'Old pottery slang. It's about throwing a ball against a wall, heading the ball, kicking it and bursting it. Something like that.'

'I see. Like I say, I'm learning. It may take a little time, by the sound of it.'

'Well, good luck: it takes a fucking – sorry, it takes a lifetime.'

Hoarse laughter followed, and Tyler couldn't help but smile.

'I mean, all that aggro over football, makes no sense. Women – now there's a reason for a good punch-up.' More laughter and apologies followed, and DCI Tyler tried to steer a course back to the investigation.

'Don't remember Alan Dale at all,' said Wild. 'Long time ago.'

But despite the years, he seemed to remember Marley, Swanson, Hillman and Jenkins, in turn, despite having 'little to do with any of them'.

'Marley was a character all right. Thick as a brick, he was. You could lead him into anything. Always getting the stick off Wise, that one. Water off a duck's arse, though. Where there's no sense there's no feeling, isn't that what they say ..?'

'... Swanson was a bit daft too, come to think of it, but not as bad as Marley. I mean, Marley was just fucking crackers, whereas I think Swanson had a bit of an edge to him ...'

'... Martin Hillman was a strange one. Hard to suss him out, to be honest with you. Kept his head down, did that one. Bit different from the others. One of those where you could never be sure what was going on, what they might be thinking. But I heard he was doing alright. Can't think who told me. Good luck to him, I say ...'

'... Steve Jenkins, yes I remember Steve. He was a bit daft, too. Not Marley-daft, of course, nobody's that daft. But he was daft enough. I think he had a few trips to see Wisey, too, but then who didn't? I think we were all head cases in them days, the bloody lot of us. It was the seventies, crazy times.'

Wild grinned, remembering a past life.

'Maybe what's-his-name, the one who did well—'

'Martin Hillman, you mean?' said Tyler.

'Him, yes. Maybe he was the exception.'

'Was he ever in trouble with Mr Wise?'

'Who knows? It didn't take much, same as I said. But to be honest, I don't think he was the sort to get in bother.'

'Too much of an angel?'

Robert Wild laughed. 'I wouldn't say that about any of us. No, I don't mean that he was goody-goody, more that, oh, I don't know what I'm saying. Maybe he was just a bit too clever. The clever ones never get caught, do they?'

'That's an interesting thought,' said Tyler. 'Are you aware that Steven Jenkins was found murdered?'

'Bloody hell, yes, I am, as a matter of fact,' said Wild, a little taken aback by the abruptness of the question. 'On the news. I was thinking, I'm sure I knew someone once with that name. When I realised it was local, I thought: I bet it must be him. Well, bloody hellfire – if you'll pardon the French.'

It seemed a long shot that Robert Wild might recall the time of Alan Dale going missing, but then police work was often full of surprises. Tyler asked the question.

Becoming lost in thought, his eyes closed, and squeezing away at his temples for all he was worth, Wild said at last, 'Now you mention it, bloody hell, yes. That lad did go missing. Hey, they gave him a hard time, some of them. There was a fat kid in the class, too, can't think of his name.'

'Anthony Turnock?'

'Could be, I can't remember. But he certainly got some, I tell you – the fat ones always did. I remember – that's right – I remember them taking that other lad, what's-his-name?'

'Alan Dale.'

'Him, yes. They were taking him down to that park they sometimes played football in. I used to go that way home sometimes myself, living in Stoke, though most times I cut straight down the bank. You won't know where I mean, not being local, I suppose.'

'Was this close to the time Alan Dale went missing?'

'God, now you're asking. Now you *are* asking.'

Tyler leaned forward, blood buzzing, beating the deep reserves of tiredness and frustration back.

'You say that they were taking him down to the park, Mr Wild?'

'To tell you the truth, now I think about it, I was going that way a few times round about then.' He gave the detective a coy smile and looked about to wink at him for good measure. 'I was a bit keen on one of the girls who lived backing onto the park. It was worth the detour, know what I mean?'

Now he did wink, but seeing that Tyler was less than conspiratorial, he rubbed at his eye as though the wink had been the result of a foreign object that had mysteriously blown in.

'When you say, 'taking him down to the park', would you say that he was going willingly?'

'I don't get you.'

'What I mean is: was Alan Dale being taken against his will?'

Wild, still rubbing at his eye, looked uneasy. 'I was a bit distracted, you might say. Like I said, I had other things on my mind.'

'Of course, I understand,' said Tyler. 'I don't suppose you can remember who was *taking* Alan Dale to the park?'

Wild thought for a moment, his fingers back at his temples. 'Steve Jenkins was definitely one of them.' He nodded, confirming the point. 'Definitely Jenks. I think Marley and Swanson were there too.'

'Anybody else?'

'It was a long time ago, and, like I say, I wasn't exactly taking that much notice.'

'But you did notice,' said Tyler. 'Thirty years later, and you remember that at least three boys from your class were taking Alan Dale down by the park. I think that is a remarkable feat of memory.'

Wild grinned. 'Why, thank you – thank you very much, sir.'

'My pleasure,' said Tyler. But though Robert Wild seemed eager enough to please, despite trying a few more angles, a few more ways to dislodge the blocks that the years might have put in the way of the man's powers of recall, Tyler couldn't seem to get any further.

It was time to call it a night; get some rest and see how things were adding up come the fresh light of a new day. He made a final recap, but Wild still wasn't making any connection between the deaths of the two ex-classmates.

As the two men stood up, Wild seemed to freeze, his face exhibiting an expression of dumb amazement. 'Now I get it,' he said. 'You think that Steve killed that lad and now somebody's killed Steve for it?'

Tyler didn't comment. He watched something unfolding, forming on the man's sun-scorched face. 'Thinking about it, when they were taking that lad down by the park, it *was* close to the time it happened. I'm sure of it.'

'Close to the time what happened, Mr Wild?'

'I remember the headmaster in assembly, old Wisey, saying that the police wanted to speak to us – all the kids, I mean. They wanted to know who was doing what and where. I was worried about telling them what I was up to, I can tell you.'

He seemed about to try out another wink, but had a brief rub at his eye instead.

'But I tell you the God's honest truth: I never put the two things together before. I mean, him going missing and them taking him down that path. 'Cos they were up to something, you could tell. Suppose I should have done something about it, looking back and all that. But you know how it is.'

Tyler knew but remained silent on the matter. He watched what might have been fleeting regret register on Wild's life-kissed features. But quickly the emotion transfigured into another memory from that long ago, eventful day, and the beginnings of a smile shone through, quickly dampened when he caught the detective's eye.

'And you think somebody got Steve for killing him? Wow.'

Tyler gave it a final shot. 'Can you recall who else might have been walking down that path with Alan Dale? You've mentioned Steven Jenkins, Phillip Swanson and Douglas Marley.'

'Shit!'

'Excuse me?'

'Sorry about that. It's just …'

'Please go on, Mr Wild.'

'It's just that – you don't think Marley and Swanson had anything to do with Steve's death, do you?'

'What do you think, Mr Wild?'

'Oh, I don't know about anything like that. I haven't seen any of these people in ages, and it was all—'

'Yes,' said Tyler. 'It was a long time ago. What about Martin Hillman? Might he have been there?'

'I don't think he lived down that way.'

'But could he have been there that afternoon?'

'You never know. Quite a lot of kids went down to the park in the summer, but Hillman didn't usually get involved in stuff like that. Too bright, know what I mean. Not the sort who'd get his hands dirty. Be at home working on his career, I would have thought.'

Not the sort who'd get his hands dirty, thought Tyler. He wondered how much Wild remembered about that *dark horse.*

'How many were with Alan Dale that afternoon, Mr Wild?'

He was rubbing at his eye again. 'Like I say, I was a bit, you know …'

'Distracted, yes, I realise that. More than three, would you say?'

'I would think so.'

'As many as six?'

'Possibly. No more than that.'

Tyler asked for the name of the young lady who had been the cause of Wild's distraction on that long-ago summer afternoon.

Wild had the name clearly tattooed on his heart.

'Pam,' he said. 'Pamela Scott. Say, I'm not likely to get into any trouble on account of … any goings on?'

'I think a complaint would have been put in by now,' said Tyler. 'I wouldn't worry unduly on that score.'

'I wonder what Pam's doing these days.'

Tyler was wondering the same thing.

***

That night Tyler dreamed of the perfect murder.

He arose one sun-filled morning, bought a train ticket to a faraway city where a man lived alone in a house with a red door on a quiet street. He had done his research discreetly, and from a distance, so the man would have no idea that later that day he would have a visitor from the past.

A boy he had tormented; a boy who had survived the torment and grown to be a man.

Tyler rode the train that beautiful day, and he got off at the town where the man lived. He had thought about this day for so long, rehearsed the course of it so many times behind closed eyes, and everything went like clockwork.

Walking down the street where the man lived, the bright red door at the end came into sight, and the boy who had become a man found that his heart was racing. He knocked on the door and waited, the blood thumping so heavily in his chest that he thought the other man's neighbours must hear it.

At last the man came to the door.

The strong, animal looks had gone, replaced by a frailty so pathetic and unexpected it made Jim Tyler want to laugh.

Had the years alone done this? Or had imagination raised this creature so high, only for the cold splash of reality to bring him down from a stature he had never really claimed? Or was he, Jim, looking, in reality, at the same thing but through different eyes, no longer the helpless child?

The man didn't recognise him and, baffled, asked if he could help. Tyler asked if he might be allowed inside the property. The man questioned him and Tyler said that he had some important business to discuss. This thin man appeared so kindly that for a moment Tyler wondered if he had come to the right address.

He was invited inside.

The house, so neat and inviting from the outside, with its brightly painted red front door, was on the inside a grim prison from which, by the pallor of the man, there appeared little hope of escape.

Once inside, and with the front door, that deceiving bright red front door, firmly closed against the outside world, Tyler said that he had known the man many years ago, as a boy.

It took a few moments, but at last the recognition broke through. Yes, the man remembered him.

But something wasn't right.

The man ought to be full of foreboding, realising at last what he had done and the price to be paid for it.

Yet none of this was happening.

The man offered refreshments, as though it was a thing of wonder that an old friend from the past should go to such trouble to look him up and visit.

Tyler's plan began to unravel. A lifetime's hate had brought him here. It was a perfect plan and a simple one. But as he stood there, it was all changing.

Jim Tyler was facing the most difficult decision of his life.

While the man went into what perhaps had once passed for a kitchen, to make the drinks, Tyler tried to make up his mind. Could he go through with it? Should he turn around now and leave, the mystery remaining behind him forever?

He asked himself the question: *Had things really been so bad?*

Had he exaggerated his past – was he insane, a psychopathic killer working out some deranged fantasy?

What if he sat down with the man, confronted him about the past, and see what happened next?

The man was coming back.

Decision time, Jim.

Something had changed in the man.

Maybe, remembering, he had seen what fool stood in his house, and filling up a mug with poison he was going to end what he had started a lifetime ago. Or maybe he had remembered all along, waiting for this moment all of these years, a destiny about to be fulfilled; the boot now on the other foot.

Or the same foot?

Jim Tyler was confused.

He felt the fear grow. He had been lured here, so far from home. Lured to this fairy-tale landscape, entering the nightmare …

The eye of the storm …

He felt his hand slip into the pocket of his coat, and tighten around the shaft of metal within …

***

Tyler woke up, the scream fully-formed in his throat, waiting to come out. Bathed in sweat, he looked at the clock. It felt like he had barely fallen asleep, and yet already half of the night had been eaten away.

He was thirsting for a drink, the urge to go out and find it overwhelming. He quickly dressed in his running clothes and ran out, through the streets, trying to exhaust the cravings.

On returning he stood under the shower, his breath returning, the calmness coming in dribs and drabs. DCI Jim Tyler, twenty years a police officer, held the past in check, the thirst for poison, retribution, and tried to focus on the present investigation.

As tiredness finally overwhelmed him, he lay down on the bed and accepted that he would have to close his eyes and be transported again to the faraway city and the red door and the ghosts of a dark, unshakable past.

But none of this happened. On waking to the alarm Tyler had the feeling that he had been making love to Kim again in his dreams.

CHAPTER TWENTY-ONE

The hostel was quiet when Mills arrived that morning. The senior officer on duty was expecting the DS, and Marley's notes were ready to hand. Mills glanced over them and said, 'So where's the man?'

'He's out the back, having a smoke.' The officer filled in some of the gaps and Mills jotted down a few notes of his own.

Douglas Marley had been at the hostel for a few weeks as part of a rehabilitation scheme to get him back to independent living. He had a long history of mental health problems, culminating in two hospital admissions following overdoses of prescription drugs. Prior to the admissions, the police had been called to the flat Marley had been sharing with a woman who had recently been imprisoned for drug trafficking.

Mills recalled from records at the station that when the police were called out to the flat, the woman was found to have facial bruising and two broken fingers. Yet Marley maintained that he was in fact defending himself. That she attacked him.

'He still does maintain that version of events,' the officer told Mills after the DS had raised the subject. 'It's one of his favourite stories. He tells it at least once a week and he occasionally gets requests for it. Nobody believes him, of course.'

'Do you believe him?'

'Who knows,' shrugged the officer. 'I've heard stranger things. The way he tells it, she made a bit of a mess of him. Bruises to his neck and face suggestive of being repeatedly struck with a heavy object. Apparently, she kept a baseball bat in case of intruders. Could have been a marriage made in heaven,' said the officer. 'Or somewhere else. I'm not aware of any other violent episodes. More of a self-harmer, at least these days, as far as we know.'

Mills asked if there had been any incidents of any kind whilst Marley had been at the hostel.

'Actually, apart from something curious a few nights ago, Doug has been an absolute delight. I would say that we have seen some real progress and he's due for review fairly soon. Who knows, but there could be hope for our Mr Marley.'

'What happened a few nights ago?' asked Mills.

Marley, it seemed, had wandered down to the town centre, as he did most evenings, to sit on one of the benches near to St Luke's church. 'Sometimes he might scrounge some money to buy cider, other times he'd sit and smoke and just have the crack with the 'other dossers', as Doug himself tends to put it. And by 'crack', I mean a laugh and a joke, nothing heavier than that, at least not these days.'

'Progress,' said Mills.

'But on Saturday Doug comes back early and he looks shaken up. I mean, something had really frightened him. The officer on duty that night wrote in the report book – hang on, let me find the part …'

Mills waited while the officer took forever to find what he was looking for.

'Ah, here we are. *Smell of alcohol yet no clear sign of inebriation. Slight tremble visible, and pale, as though he had been badly frightened. Unusually quiet for remainder of the evening. Tried to ascertain info from Doug about what had troubled him, but he became agitated at that point and so I did not pursue the matter.*

'The entries since then have noted that he has been generally quieter, and avoided leaving the hostel area. Mind you, last night there was a request for his 'woman' story, and by all accounts he told it with his old gusto. So perhaps he's returning back to normal.'

Mills looked at his watch. 'Right, I'll go and have a word with him. I take it nobody witnessed anything that might explain what exactly took place the other night?'

'I asked one or two who were down in the town, but they said that Doug wasn't in any of his usual spots. Bit of a puzzler, actually.'

Douglas Marley was smoking heartily out the back, in the small courtyard. It seemed impossible to Mills that this man was only forty-five years of age. He looked as ancient as his old headmaster, Frederick Wise, though with a sight less to show for the stresses and strains of life that had carved out his features.

Mills asked if they might go somewhere more private, but Marley said that as there was nobody else around, he didn't have any problems staying where he was.

'I got no secrets to keep from the police – or anybody else. Fire away, if you have something to ask me, I don't mind.'

He spent a few minutes trying to build a rapport with the ancient forty-something, but though the man was genial enough, the detective doubted that his efforts were achieving very much. Douglas Marley, he thought, was one of those men with a naturally high wall, and circumstances had likely given good reason for him to work on strengthening that wall.

Here was a man who could give an impression, thought Mills. Appearing open, but at the same time loath to give anything away. The genial smile was a mask that many wore, yet beneath it, in so many cases, when you knew how to look, lay a blazing intensity of fear and mistrust.

The DS got down to business, referencing the grim discovery that had been made only a few yards up the road from the hostel. Mention of the corpse of the schoolboy drew nothing at all from Douglas Marley, not even a flicker.

Mills switched track. He tried for a rendition of the infamous domestic violence incident, but Marley wasn't playing.

Running out of strategies, he decided to go for broke. He brought up the subject of River Trent High, asking what memories Marley had of Fredrick Wise.

'Never had much to do with him – except when we were in trouble, of course. He's probably dead by now. Don't think I'll cry, though, if it's all the same.'

Mills chose not to disabuse him of the notion that his old headmaster was dead. Marley looked as though he could do with all the good news he could get, regardless of legitimacy. He moved on. *Howard Wood*?

'Pillock, he was, looking back.'

'In what way?'

'In every way. You blame the kids for what they do, but he's the one who's supposed to be responsible. It's what they get paid for.'

Mills was having trouble following.

'Do you mean bullying?'

'Bullying? What's that got to do with it?'

'I'm not sure what point you're making, Mr Marley.'

'I'm not making any point. I'm just saying, that's all.'

The surliness was setting in.

'Football fan, wasn't he?' asked Mills. 'Stoke City.'

'Do you follow them? You sound local enough. Not a Vale fan, are you?'

Mills laughed. 'Yes, I follow them, when I get chance. I hear that you were a big fan, you and Mr Wood. And *Steven Jenkins …*'

Marley tightened up at the name, the twinkle of suspicion that had never gone away becoming brighter and somehow more dangerous.

Two other men were coming out into the courtyard, and Mills suggested to Marley that they take a wander down into the town. 'You can show me your favourite benches.'

'What? You must lead a sad life. No crimes want solving?'

Marley was laughing. Catching the attention of the two other men who had entered the courtyard, he said, 'Listen up: this one here wants me to show him around my favourite benches.' Turning to Mills, he said, 'You want to get yourself a *real* hobby, mate. Or a proper job.'

Mills, believing that the interview was over, got up. Then Marley surprised him. 'Actually, now you mention it, I could do with stretching my legs. I don't know, the things you get asked to do nowadays. What a bastard life.'

***

In the churchyard behind St Luke's, Marley selected a bench from the two vacant ones and the two men sat down. Before Mills could start up a conversation, Marley said, 'Look, I don't want no trouble. I've seen too much of that. One or two of 'em in school might have picked on that lad who went missing, but I don't know much about that. I kept myself to myself. Best way.'

Surprise, surprise, thought Mills, but he took the sliver of opportunity anyway.

'He was a Chelsea supporter, I believe.'

'Who was?' said Marley, as though challenging Mills to expose the traitor without delay.

'The boy who went missing. Alan Dale. And one or two of the boys from your class may have picked on him because of that. Steven Jenkins was one of them, I understand. Who else do you remember?'

Marley stood up. 'I've heard enough about all this crap.'

'Phillip Swanson was there too,' said Mills.

'Was where? What are you talking about?'

'Sit down, please, Mr Marley.'

'I've heard enough. *Was where?*'

'Just up the road from the hostel. Bottom of The Stumps. My colleague spoke to Robert Wild last night, and he believes that you were there too?'

'Wild, what does he know? He wasn't ...'

'Wasn't what, Mr Marley? Wasn't ... *there?*'

'I want to go back. I've had enough of this. Harassment, that's what this is. I've got my rights and I'm making a complaint against you. You can get solicitors at the hostel.'

'Who did you see down here, Mr Marley?'

'Here?'

'Where we are now, this churchyard? You were here a few evenings ago. Or were you somewhere else? Not in your usual place? Why was that?'

Marley didn't answer.

'Steven Jenkins is dead, did you know that?'

'What?'

'He was murdered.'

'Murdered? Why?'

'We think that someone doesn't want the police finding out who was down The Stumps with Alan Dale on the day he died. What do you think about that, Mr Marley?'

'What should I think? I don't know anything about any of it.'

'Who else was there? A summer evening, June, 1972. You were fifteen years old. There was you, Jenkins, Swanson – who else?'

Marley was already making his way through the churchyard, back towards the town. Mills grabbed his arm, and swung him around.

Looking Marley square in the face, DS Mills flinched. *My God,* he thought. *That's pain there in his face, and so much fear.*

'I don't know anything,' said Marley. 'I wasn't there, I tell you. I keep myself to myself, and always have done. Why don't you leave me alone?'

'I want to know what happened. I want to know what happened to Alan Dale.'

'I told you, I don't know anything.'

'You played your part, that evening, in 1972. You played your part, torturing a timid little boy – and I want to know who was there with you, and I want to know what happened.'

Mills saw the pain and the fear turn to anger.

Marley pushed him away and made off, with a surprising turn of speed.

DS Mills took out his phone and rang Tyler. The DCI would probably appreciate being the first to hear that his sergeant had lost it, and that there was a complaint on the way.

***

'Harassment, you reckon?'

'Probably that.'

'Nice work, DS Mills. I'm at the school. We've had some interesting information back from interviews with some of the old girls from the class of '72. Two make mention of your friend Hillman. Two, separately and unprompted, on the subject of bullying brought up Hillman.'

'In what way? Do you mean that incident when he and Jenkins—'

'The suggestion is,' cut in Tyler, 'that a few years earlier, at junior school, Martin Hillman was top dog, at least in his class – though it might have stretched some way beyond that. The two old girls who pinpointed him were in his class all through junior school. And they paint a picture of a bully and a troublemaker, though one who quickly learned how to make the less intelligent kids do his dirty work for him, and carry the can.'

Mills started to ask a question, but Tyler hadn't finished.

'One of the girls suggested that with the rougher lads, it was generally a case of what you see is what you get. She said that Hillman gave her the creeps and she reckoned that Hillman's mother was even scarier. 'A right old witch,' was how she put it, 'and nasty with it."

'Did the two girls attend River Trent High?' asked Mills.

'They did indeed. And these two had already marked Hillman's card, and so they knew what they were looking for.'

'You make them sound like a couple of sleuths.'

'On the whole, I would say that girls, and women, are the more observant, and with more reliable memories. You see, contrary to what some have said about me, I do pay attention on the diversity training. Anyway, they both of them stated that Hillman remained a manipulative character, still pulling strings, ever more adept at keeping his own face out of the spotlight. If you weren't looking out for his involvement, you probably wouldn't notice it.'

'Keeping his head down and getting on with his work.'

'On the face of it.'

'These "old girls" – they didn't have an axe to grind?'

'It's not clear why they should. No angles have emerged, should we say. I'm doing some more digging and later I have another interesting appointment lined up.'

'Sir?'

'Robert Wild's old flame.'

'Pamela Scott? You've located her?'

'She lives in a place called Bradeley and works as a mobile hairdresser. I may have a trim while I'm finding out what she remembers from that day. I mean, apart from what Robert Wild might prefer to *think* she remembers, if you follow me.'

'I think I do, sir.'

That sarcasm, thought Tyler, as he ended the call. It was sometimes difficult to establish beyond all reasonable doubt.

***

Tyler smiled as the headteacher entered her office bearing a stack of files. He finished off another fine cup of tea and, as usual, complimented her on the standard of refreshments at the school.

She had already suggested that DCI Tyler might like to have his own name placed on the outside of her door, and that in turn she could try to find some private space at the police station. It might help, she said, in her efforts to attend to her own paperwork.

'Point taken,' he said. 'But you wouldn't like the company. And anyway, I think *Miss A. Hayburn* suits that door perfectly.'

As they worked through the files the detective suddenly broke off.

'Just one aspect of the name that perplexes me,' he said.

'What name?'

'Yours.'

'And what perplexes you about my name?'

'I wonder,' said Tyler, 'what the 'A' stands for?'

CHAPTER TWENTY-TWO

Why hadn't Sheila Dale come forward all those years ago? She had seen the marks on her brother. She'd heard his story about the savagery of his classmates – why hadn't she gone back to the school, demanded to see Wise, called the police? Why hadn't she raised holy hell?

To Tyler the answers seemed ludicrously clear.

What would an uncaring bastard like Fredrick Wise have done? Another round of thrashings, perhaps, to further inflame the situation? As for the police … in those days, those dark-age days of thirty years ago, you didn't involve the police merely because a child was being bullied to death. It was all a part of growing up.

Being, or becoming, a *man*.

Tyler looked at Miss Hayburn and thought: *things would have been very different, even back in the day, with a person like you in charge. Someone who knows the meaning of compassion.*

He watched her moving through the files; through the boxes of archived material with an eye that didn't miss a trick. That disarming smile had built many a bridge over troubled waters, he had no doubt. Here was a diplomat, and at the same time a natural leader, and one who didn't have to resort to the weaponry of the battlefield to maintain civilisation.

She looked up from her labours and caught his eye. The two of them quietly exchanged question marks, and then she said, 'Well, I do believe that we've found something.'

It had been a shot in the dark.

That punishment records had been kept at all was one thing. That they were still intact, buried deep in the school archives, was certainly stretching it. Wise, for whatever reasons, had kept meticulous records, and here, in red ink, under June, 1972, a relatively quiet month on the discipline front, it seemed, the names of Steven Jenkins and Martin Hillman stood out for all who might one day seek to find them.

'I wonder,' said Tyler, 'that Hillman had no recollection of the occasion.'

'No recollection?' echoed Miss Hayburn, still going through the pages. 'My goodness, Mr Wise was certainly prolific,' she observed. 'Jenkins alone must have made two dozen visits. How can you not change under that kind of pressure?'

'They made them tough in those days,' said Tyler.

'They must have,' she said. 'Douglas Marley was a regular, too, and Robert Wild put in a few appearances. But Jenkins seems to have the class record, by the look of things.'

'And Hillman just the one visit?'

'Looks like it. For "*obscene language*". Same as Jenkins, on that particular day.'

'No direct mention of bullying, then?'

'No mention of that word anywhere.'

'Not surprising, when you think about it,' said Tyler. 'A dirty word for a headmaster, and especially one like Wise. The man was a fantasist. He wanted the world to believe that he was running the perfect establishment. A kind of "not on my patch" mentality, don't you think?'

'I couldn't possibly comment,' said Miss Hayburn.

'But that's the impression you're getting?'

Tyler looked at the entry written in the book, dated close to the time that Alan Dale's torment had been brought to its climax, prior to him *going missing*.

'It might have been Hillman's only visit, but Wise certainly didn't pull any punches that day,' said Miss Hayburn. 'He must have had a downer on bad language, if nothing else.'

'So how could Hillman have forgotten about it? It isn't credible. I mean to say, Jenkins, alright, one visit might have blended in with another.'

'Is that significant?' she asked.

Tyler felt a sudden uneasiness. 'I'm not sure at this stage. We still have a long way to go with our enquiries.'

It was too easy to run off at the mouth in this woman's company. She was too good a listener, and her manner so deceptively casual that he imagined her making an exceptional interrogator, should the situation, the opportunity or the motivation ever arise.

He wondered if the way forward might be to pile all of the information gathered so far on to her desk, and ring her back in a couple of hours when she had solved the case and identified the guilty party.

Tyler excused himself to make another phone call.

***

Maggie Calleer answered. She asked the detective how he was getting on with his investigations. 'I want to jog your memory about Martin Hillman,' said Tyler.

'Hillman? You surprise me.'

'Life, I find, can be full of surprises.'

She asked what it was that he needed to know. His immediate concern was would she be at home for the rest of the morning. Miss Calleer agreed to wait in for his visit and to have the kettle on stand-by.

Finishing the call Tyler stepped back inside the headteacher's office, to be informed that Howard Wood would not be in school for the rest of the week.

'Is that good news for the school, or bad?' he asked.

Miss Hayburn was once again unable to comment. And when Tyler suggested that she already had done, she kept a straight face, and said, 'Then how remiss of me, DCI Tyler.'

She opened up another file and showed the detective some photographs from the school archives. Among them was a photograph of the entire school, dated June, 1971. In pride of place was Fredrick Wise, in those days sporting a regal moustache that reminded Tyler of official portraits of Chief Superintendent Berkins. That same no-nonsense austerity, though in fairness, in real-life Berkins was hardly the ogre that Wise appeared to have been. Official photos of people in positions of authority seldom brought out their most endearing features, reflected Tyler. Even in the rare cases where such features existed in the first place.

Wise may have been limited in his functioning as a pastoral minister to the children in his care, but he looked every inch a threat and a deterrent. Perhaps that was the point. Perhaps that was how the man earned his considerable pay.

DCI Tyler recognised the narrow face of Howard Wood in the same photograph, despite the long hair which had since given way under the relentless march of the intervening years. He was wearing a red pullover and Tyler asked Miss Hayburn if the man was still known to be a Stoke City fanatic.

'I believe so,' she said, cautiously. 'If not quite as devout as he once was, by all accounts.'

'Did Maggie Calleer tell you about his football interests?'

Miss Hayburn laughed. 'On the occasions I get together with Maggie, we usually find something more interesting to talk about than football.'

'Or Howard Wood.'

'You don't give up, do you?' she said.

She pointed to a young woman with fine long hair, positioned on the opposite side of the assembled in the photograph. 'That's Maggie.'

Tyler could see her now. He wasn't sure whether she had looked impossibly young for her age back then, or if the years had taken hold of her dramatically since. The kindness and the perceptive quality that she exuded were present at both ends of the thirty year line, and again he wondered whether Alan Dale might have survived the horrors of school had Calleer continued to be his class teacher and Miss Hayburn had held the higher reins.

'Alan Dale,' said Tyler, pointing to a smiling face next to Calleer. He looked again at the date on the photograph: June, 1971. 'The year before he died.'

'A lovely looking lad,' said the headteacher. 'He looks so bright, and yet …'

'Something sad in there, too, don't you think?' said Tyler. 'Sad, or frightened?'

'It's difficult to tell, when you know things about someone. Do we see the sadness because we expect to see it, or is it actually there? You know, Maggie would have seen it, if it had been.'

'But could she have done anything about it?'

'You shouldn't underestimate her.'

'I wouldn't do that. But she would have been up against it, with the likes of Wise in charge.'

'*In your opinion.*'

'In my opinion, of course.'

'*Hindsight.*'

Tyler looked again at the face of Alan Dale.

Miss Hayburn was right. The sadness, the apparent tinge of fear – most likely his own projections and nothing more. The savages were already through the gate, and entering the field of what had once been a young boy's happy and carefree life. But the shepherd was still keeping her flock safe. It would take the likes of Howard Wood, and the utter dereliction of duty, and perhaps even sadistic encouragement – yes, in the end, nothing less than that – to allow the savages to descend on their prey, and to see the hopelessness begin to take hold of poor Alan Dale.

'Are you okay?' asked Miss Hayburn.

Tyler nodded, swallowed hard and pointed to the boy next to Alan Dale. Anthony Turnock, Alan's friend. He too was smiling. 'Yes, you're right,' he said. 'It isn't sadness and it isn't fear. *Relief.* You can tell the ordeal was almost over for another year.'

Miss Hayburn raised her eyebrows.

Two along the row from Turnock was Steven Jenkins, striking an attitude for the camera; challenging the viewer, all these years on, to dare to look into his eyes. 'Could I take this photograph?' he asked. 'I'd like somebody to have a look at it. I will return it, of course.'

'No problem,' said Miss Hayburn. 'And pass on my best wishes to Maggie, if you would be so kind.'

Tyler looked at the headteacher, and not for the first time, with great admiration.

***

As Tyler got into the car his phone rang.

'No complaints in from the hostel yet?' he asked.

'Funny you should mention that,' said Mills. 'The officer in charge contacted me a few minutes ago. Douglas Marley collapsed after I left. They've taken him to hospital. He was asking for me, apparently.'

'What do you make of that?'

'I'm not altogether sure. Thought I'd be the last person he'd want to see, the way he was carrying on.'

'Better not disappoint the man then.'

Tyler ended the call and set off for Kingsley Holt.

***

'The boy next to Jenkins is Martin Hillman,' said Maggie Calleer, taking her reading glasses off again. 'But why are you so interested in Hillman?'

Tyler looked again at the photograph. Hillman was the enigma.

Jenkins, as full of attitude as he had expected; Robert Wild, posing, with a twinkle in his eye that no amount of excess through the years could eradicate; Douglas Marley, betraying a natural toughness as unforced at it was uncompromising; Phillip Swanson, looking nervous, as though the camera was pointing directly at him and him alone, finding him out, exposing him to the light.

But Hillman?

Something in that expression. Am I looking too hard? Seeing what isn't there?

What am I seeing?

'I've been perusing Mr Wise's old punishment book,' he said at last.

'That probably makes interesting reading,' said Calleer.

'Martin Hillman got his name in the book and yet has no recollection of the event.'

'Thirty years can do things to the memory.'

'But are you likely to forget something like that?' asked Tyler.

'I wouldn't know.'

He told her of the alleged incident, Hillman and Jenkins tormenting Alan Dale and running into Wise, who wasn't amused at the language they were using.

'Of course, this was the year after they had left your class, so there's no reason why you should have been aware of it at all.'

'Who told you this?' she asked.

'I'm afraid I'm not at liberty to divulge that information at the present time.'

'I was being nosy. I apologise.'

'And I'm sorry for the cloak and dagger. There's something about these enquiries that brings out my formal side.'

'Are you referring to the untimely death of Steven Jenkins?' asked Calleer. 'I mean to say, he might have been a bit of a monkey in his youth, but who would do such a thing? Was he tangled up in drugs or – I do apologise, I can't seem to help myself.'

'I think your curiosity is understandable, in the circumstances.'

'One day you're here asking about Alan Dale, and in no time you're back investigating the murder of his classmate.'

Tyler waited for the inevitable question. It was framed on her lips, but by force of will she held back.

'Okay,' he said. 'Can I come back to Hillman? Something doesn't quite add up. Martin Hillman was, by all accounts, a hard worker who never got into trouble. Except that, according to at least one account, he did get into trouble, serious trouble, and for bullying Alan Dale. Now, of course it's possible that the person giving this account is mistaken. Except that there is a written record, detailing both crime and punishment.'

'I'm surprised they've kept hold of records like that.'

'It took some unearthing. Probably end up in a museum one day. So, given that a visit to Mr Wise would have been a traumatic affair, not easily forgotten, wouldn't you agree that it is odd that Martin Hillman has no recollection?'

Calleer made no response.

'Okay, from what I've heard,' said Tyler, 'for the likes of Steven Jenkins and Douglas Marley, a visit to Mr Wise was part of the average week. Such treatment may have been routine for them, though I doubt even that.'

'But for Hillman, this was an event. He was not used to it. He was either not used to getting into trouble because he was a good kid, in which case he might have felt an amount of righteous indignation for the severity of the punishment, or else he was simply not used to getting caught.'

Calleer nodded. 'I think you've got that part right,' she said. 'I think you might have hit the nail on the head.'

'That Hillman was not used to getting caught?'

'That is what surprises me. Not that he could sink to bullying but that he could actually have been caught.'

She picked up the photograph again.

'What is it?' asked Tyler.

'I should have said last time. There was a rumour.'

'What kind of rumour?'

'It was about Howard Wood. There was an allegation made against a pupil in his class. The whole thing was hushed up.

'The point I'm trying to make, is that the rumour suggested Howard Wood put himself on the line to defend the pupil against the allegation. It was out of character for Mr Wood to stand up for anybody. Beer and football were all he seemed to care about.

'I went into the staff room one day, and a couple of teachers were talking. They stopped when they saw me, but I heard the word blackmail and I heard the name Wood. I never knew any more than that, and doubtless I never will.'

Tyler took a few moments to digest the possible implications of what had just been said. 'Are you telling me that Hillman blackmailed Wood?'

'I'm not saying anything of the sort. What I've told you is as much as I know.'

'But you have your thoughts on the matter, clearly.'

'Oh, I have my thoughts. But they're still only thoughts.'

'And you have no idea what the allegation was – against Hillman, presumably – or who made the allegation?'

'Again, only rumours.'

Tyler waited.

Calleer breathed deeply and said, 'A boy was expelled, I don't recall his name. The boy had made the allegation, I think, against Martin Hillman. But then the thing was completely turned around and the boy ended up being expelled. It was all very hush-hush.'

Tyler looked again at the school photograph.

'Martin Hillman has an oddly mature quality about him, wouldn't you agree? An air of, what, *cold detachment*, perhaps? Was he a cold fish, ahead of his years?'

'In some ways I think he probably was,' said Calleer. 'It was always difficult to weigh him up, certainly.'

'What else can you tell me about him?'

'His mother was a solicitor. She had a formidable reputation, I believe. From what I know of her – and I met her a couple of times, at parent evenings – the news that Wise had thrashed her son would likely have met with a lawsuit, even back then.'

'And Wise would have been aware of this?'

'I don't know. He might have been. But if he was, why go ahead and risk it?'

'Maybe he felt that it was his moral obligation.'

'I doubt that.'

'You don't remember Mr Wise as a man of moral integrity, then?'

'You're trying to put words in my mouth.'

'My turn to apologise.'

'All I can tell you is that Martin Hillman was, as I've already suggested, something of a dark horse. He was a boy I never came close to understanding. He didn't get involved in the usual kinds of trouble that might have been going on, but I never had him marked down as a saint either. To put it bluntly, he was the sort who simply *doesn't get caught*.'

'But even those types get unlucky once in a while,' said Tyler. 'Sooner or later.' Tyler pictured the scene: A boy makes an accusation against Hillman, and Hillman blackmails his own teacher to turn the accusation around and get the boy expelled. Hillman's mother is a solicitor, and a fearsome one. She would set the world on fire to protect her son.

And then one day young Martin turns the wrong corner at the wrong time while in the process of verbally abusing Alan Dale and Wise beats the living crap out of him for the language used, and without even stopping to consider the possibility of a complaint or worse. Hillman, rather than letting his mother loose on Wise, realises that for once he has come unstuck. Maybe he is embarrassed, and maybe he hungers for a more physical revenge: one that he can personally be involved in.

Old Testament-style revenge. An eye for an eye.

Maggie Calleer was still looking at the photograph.

'You're probably right,' she said.

'What's that?' asked Tyler.

'That even the Hillmans of this world do get caught, sometimes.'

She looked about to say more, and Tyler eased back, giving her the time and space.

'You know,' she said at last, 'I remember feeling incredibly sorry for that boy once.'

'Hillman?'

'His father was also a solicitor.'

'He has my sympathy,' said Tyler.

'He abandoned Martin when the boy was very young. Martin and his mother had to move out of their fine home and into something far more modest. There was a lot of speculation doing the rounds, staff-room gossip. His mother drank, apparently, and by all accounts it made her moody and unreliable. It also ate into what money was available to lavish on her son.'

'He was indulged, then?'

'Possibly she felt she owed it to him. Bought him things to make up for the guilt she was feeling over the split-up. God, listen to the amateur psychiatrist, will you? I'm back in the staff-room. Ignore me, please. Obviously, I have too much time on my hands these days.'

'I'll ask Miss Hayburn if she'll take you back on.'

'You think I haven't asked her myself? I'm joking, by the way.'

'You say Hillman's mother drank?'

'A few of the teachers noticed it on her breath at a parent evening. She could be quite explosive if anybody said anything negative about her son.'

'When you heard the rumour about Hillman blackmailing Wood, you put two and two together.'

Calleer looked uncomfortable.

'And what did two and two add up to, Miss Calleer? Were you thinking that Hillman had reason to despise drink? That Wood was a drinker and Hillman caught him when he was on duty? Maybe Hillman's mother put him up to it. One drinker can usually sniff out another ... so I'm told.'

The interview was over.

From his car, Tyler watched Calleer close the front door. Underneath all of those layers of kindness ran an undercurrent of melancholy, he thought. Perhaps born of guilt, but who knows? It pained him to witness such a thing. She didn't deserve to carry the burdens she undoubtedly bore. That was no kind of justice.

He looked again at the photograph.

So many stories woven into it. So many possibilities.

When Martin Hillman made the trip to see Mr Wise that day, was he picking up the tab for what he was doing to Mr Wood? Was Wise delivering a warning that nothing would be tolerated that might threaten the reputation of the school, and bring its captain into disrepute?

Or was it all a stroke of bad luck? Hillman opening his mouth to abuse Alan Dale as Wise was turning the corner and nothing more to it than that.

But somebody had to pay.

Was that somebody Alan Dale?

CHAPTER TWENTY-THREE

Pamela Scott was blonde and vivacious and everything that Tyler tried not to look for in a woman. Her neat and tidy semi-detached property was set back off the main road through Bradeley, and after this visit it would be a short drive back to Hanley to find out what exactly the chief superintendent wanted to speak to him about in person.

Before Tyler even had chance to make himself comfortable, Pamela Scott said, straight off, that she was a little bit up against the clock as there was a client needing major hair renovation over in Smallthorne.

She had the knack, he thought, of making that appointment sound infinitely more important than the meeting he himself had to look forward to, with a moustached man who would no doubt *not* wish to while away the afternoon making small talk about hairstyles and whatever else fired up the middle-aged females of the north.

'You want to talk about my schooldays, then?' she said, beaming away at the detective as he took his place on the three-seater without a drink.

'I believe that you attended River Trent High, Miss Scott.'

'We used to live over that way,' she said, as though needing an excuse. 'Didn't learn much, to be honest. Not in the academic meaning of the word, anyway.' She giggled slightly as she said it.

'Do you remember Robert Wild?'

The giggle was replaced by an eruption of laughter. 'I remember him alright. Is that why you're here? I should have known. What's he been up to now?'

Tyler tried to focus the woman's attention on the summer of 1972.

'We had a bit of a thing going, me and Robert – no harm in it, know what I mean?'

She winked, and Tyler recalled Wild's own irritable eye.

'We used to hang around that park for a bit, have a laugh, that sort of thing. We never did any harm, though. Robert was a bit of a lad, sort of thing, but he was harmless. What's he done, anyway?'

Tyler thought for a moment, and then decided to cut to it.

'Do you recall that a young boy went missing from your school around that time? His name was Alan Dale.'

'It was in the papers recently, wasn't it?'

'You don't recall it happening at the time? June, 1972?'

'That's thirty years ago! Bloody hell, mate, give me a break. Hang on, now you mention it, there might have been something. The police were around the school. That was him? The same thing?'

'That was *Alan Dale,* yes.'

'You saying Robert Wild had something to do with all of that? He wouldn't have got involved in anything like that, not Robert, I'm sure of it.'

'Involved in what, exactly?'

'Well, you know – don't they say that boy was, well, killed?'

Tyler didn't answer.

'I wasn't in Robert's class or anything like that, you understand. Or that boy who went missing – I was a year older than that lot, due to leave school, I was. Nothing to do with me, any of that. I've got a kid of my own now, two of them, as a matter of fact. Me and Brian aren't married but we're respectable enough and—'

'Thank you, Miss Scott, but I'm not for a moment suggesting that you had anything to do with anybody's death.'

He waited for her to settle down. As the agitation subsided, a moment of clarity emerged. 'There *was* something going on round about then, now you mention it. One time me and Rob were going along the top path of that park, after school, and there were some lads going down the side.'

'The Stumps, you mean?'

'I think that's what they called it. Don't know why, though. Anyway, I remember 'cos I knew one of the lads. He was in my class. Dammers, his name was. Paul Dammers. I had a bit of a thing for him too, you see – not that I was a slapper or anything like that. But I wanted him to see me with Rob. Try and get him going and all that. But they were mucking about. Now I think about it, one of them was crying.'

Tyler saw the scene coming to life as Pamela Scott's face became animated with the memory.

'Rob was shouting over to them to pick on someone their own size. He was trying to impress me, and show them he'd got a girl, I reckon. We didn't hang around, but I can picture it now, them knocking this kid around and him crying. But we had other things on our mind, know what I mean.'

'You say they were knocking him around?'

'You know, a punch and a kick. He was telling them to stop and that was just making them worse. That's how it goes, I reckon. You know what lads are like.'

'And they were going down The Stumps, down the path adjacent – by the side of the park?'

'I know what adjacent means, I'm not that thick. I did go to school some of the time, you know – for all the good it did me.'

Tyler took from his pocket a small photograph of Alan Dale.

'Was this the boy you saw crying, Miss Scott?'

She looked briefly at the photo. 'Could have been, but like I say, it was a long time ago and I had other things – actually, I have seen that picture before.'

'This is the photograph issued to the press. You've possibly seen it in the papers or on the television.'

She looked at the photograph more carefully. 'This is the boy who went missing back then?'

Tyler nodded. 'Is that the boy you saw being taken down by the park?'

The gravity of the situation appeared to be dawning.

'You mean – you think they killed him – that day?'

'That's what we're trying to establish, Miss Scott.'

She looked once again at the photograph. 'I think it probably was him, yes. Good God.'

'Can you remember who any of the other boys were that day? How many of them were there? You've already mentioned a Paul Dammers.'

'Paul was there, definitely.'

He took out the school photograph.

'Fuck me, look at that!'

'Any one you recognise, Miss Scott?'

'I'll say. Look – that's me – there! Look at that haircut! Hey, if you ever get tired of the police, you could blackmail me with that. I'd never work as a hairdresser again after that got out. Fucking hell! And that's Robert – ahh, he wasn't a bad one. We had some times, though, I'll say that.'

Tyler asked if she recognised any of the others in the photograph. Pamela Scott looked carefully, spotting Alan Dale again, and pointing him out. 'Some of the others look a bit familiar,' she said. 'There's Paul – Paul Dammers. He could be a laugh, know what I mean?' Then, placing her finger below the image of Steven Jenkins, she said, 'I've seen his face recently, I'll swear it.'

Tyler gave her the news.

'That's it, that's where I've seen him. Good God, half the class have been murdered! Wasn't the teacher, was it, getting his own back on the little shits?'

Tyler pointed to Maggie Calleer.

'I remember her. She was nice. Best of the bunch, I'd say. You don't think it was her, do you?'

He placed a finger beneath the image of Howard Wood.

'God, yes, him too. Bit of a wanker – sorry. Bit of a weasel. None of the girls liked him, at least I didn't. Always going on about football and Stoke City. Don't think he wanted to be there any more than we did.'

'Do you remember his name?' asked Tyler.

She couldn't recall it.

Tyler reminded her.

'That's it, yes: Wood. I think some of the boys thought he could be a bit of a laugh; a bit laid back, know what I mean. But I think he was one of them who had favourites. If he liked you, you were alright. Never had anything to do with him myself.'

'Did you witness any bullying at school, Miss Scott?'

'There's always plenty of that, isn't there. With kids, I mean. I never got picked on, if that's what you mean.'

'Was Howard Wood a bully, would you say?'

'Not with me.'

'Did you ever see him bullying any of the other kids?'

'I think he would take the piss a bit, that sort of thing. Try and humiliate the boys that he didn't like. Probably the ones who didn't get off on football, most likely.'

Tyler drew his finger beneath the line of children from Alan Dale's class, but Pamela Scott was already shaking her head. 'No, don't know them. Robert might. Have you tried asking him?'

Tyler tactfully suggested that he would bear that in mind.

'You've already spoken to him, haven't you?' She smiled, and the smile became a devilish grin. 'He remembered me!'

The detective tried to maintain a poker face.

'He fucking well remembers me! He gave you my name, didn't he? He *should* remember me, what we got up to.'

Then she turned and glanced at the photograph that stood on top of the television set. Brian and the two kids, by the look of it. Putting a hand to her lips, she said, 'But enough said about that, eh? Know what I mean?'

As Tyler stood up to leave, Pamela Scott made a last attempt at being helpful. 'You should try talking to Paul Dammers, I reckon. He was there that day, no question about that. He'll remember me, too – you can bet your life on it. Now he was football stupid the same as Wood. Got done once for vandalising school property with red paint. Must have been early that morning, or done it the night before. We came in and it said RED IS THE COLOUR across the front entrance. Bit handy, too.'

'Handy?'

'With his fists. Mind you, Rob could handle himself a bit. He didn't care. Paul was all mouth really. Stand up to him and he backed off. Preferred picking on the easy ones. We were both in Mrs Thing's class. Everson. Right old cow, she was.'

'You wouldn't know where we might find Paul Dammers?'

'It was a long time ago last time I saw Paul. But if you catch up with him, tell him – no, on second thoughts, better not. Don't think Brian would appreciate it.' She stood up to show DCI Tyler out.

'Say, keeps you lot fit being in the police these days by the look of it,' she said, giving him a once-over.

'Sorry? Oh, I see. One tries.'

The laughter roared out of her. 'You'd better keep going, babe. Brian's back later and he's bigger than you.'

More laughter followed Tyler out through the storm door.

Getting into his car he glanced back and caught a look on Pamela Scott's face. A look, he thought, of trepidation. As though for her the penny had finally dropped.

Had the realisation taken shape, wilting the lewd smile? Tyler wondered. The realisation that she may have given the police the name of the person who had killed Alan Dale? The person she had thought only of being remembered to … and by.

CHAPTER TWENTY-FOUR

At the City General in Hartshill, Mills was having trouble getting to see Douglas Marley. The man had been rushed from the hostel to the intensive care unit and it was looking every bit like a cardiac job.

Marley was in and out of consciousness, touch and go. Mills got the okay to remain at the hospital and Tyler made his way back to Hanley.

Entering the station, he was met by DC Brown. Another result: they had found Paul Dammers alive and well and living practically under their noses. He earned his living as a probation officer these days and was based just around the corner.

'Off sick at present, sir,' said Brown. 'Lives in Hartshill.'

'How long's he been off?' asked Tyler.

'A few days.'

'Now that *is* interesting.'

As Tyler entered Berkins' office he wondered if he might not pop up to Hartshill afterwards. A case of two birds and one stone: he could visit Dammers and see how DS Mills was finding hospital hospitality.

***

The moustache was looking formidable and Chief Superintendent Berkins had both hands on it as Tyler took a seat.

It was like this.

It was all well and good touring North Staffordshire and chatting to all and sundry about schooldays and so on and so forth, but there didn't appear to be any progress whatsoever being made on the Steven Jenkins murder investigation.

Tyler pointed out that so far there had been no substantial leads at all on the case, and that increasingly it was looking to be a professional job. The key, he said, might indeed lie in the Alan Dale case.

'And indeed it might not,' barked Berkins.

Tyler indicated that as progress was being made on the Alan Dale case, progress suggesting that Steven Jenkins may have been at least partly responsible for Alan Dale's death, it would be illogical not to pursue some connection, given the timing of the Jenkins murder.

'It's not logic I'm looking for, it's results. Look, I'm going to have to come up with another statement and, frankly, the blandness is starting to wear a bit thin. You're a good officer, Jim, and I can see that you're thorough enough.

'In a nutshell: I'm glad to have you aboard, but either we have something or we haven't. And if I'm to keep up any expectations of a result, then I need something to back that up or else we're all in for a visit from the Almighty. You know what I'm talking about.'

I'm new around these parts but I'm not stupid, thought Tyler. He was aware of the reputation of Charles Bollocks-for-Breakfast Dawkins – though even a high-flying dick-in-the-air like him couldn't reasonably expect results out of thin air, regardless of whose dangly bits were on the line.

'Forty-eight hours,' said Tyler, somewhat hopefully.

'Twenty-four,' said Berkins. 'And that's both off the record and non-negotiable. So I wouldn't waste another minute of your valuable time arguing over lost causes.'

***

DC Brown finished the call from the coroner's office and missed Tyler by seconds. The post-mortem had revealed Jenkins to have been a very sick man indeed. Liver cancer.

Did Jenkins know?

Brown looked up the contact number for the dead man's GP.

***

At the City General Tyler could find no sign of Mills in the waiting areas for intensive care, and the sergeant's mobile appeared to be switched off. Tyler considered a visit to Dammers, to save some time, but thought better of it. He checked with reception. There were no messages.

Banging a fist on the steel edge of the reception desk earned him a cautionary look from the bespectacled dragon behind the desk, and the promise of a bruise later. The side of his hand was aching already as he made his way to the coffee machine, but he was damned if he was going to ask the desk-monster for an ice-pack.

The change in his pocket was a coin short of whatever putrid solace might have been on offer. The receptionist, eyeing him carefully now, would no doubt have change for a fiver. But was it worth it? Any anyway, the more he thought about it the more he was convinced that there was nothing less than a twenty left in his wallet.

His aching hand was taking his mind off his thirst. He tried his sergeant's mobile again, and this time Mills answered.

'Where are you?'

'About ten yards behind you, sir.'

Mills emerged from the prohibited area. 'Fancy a coffee? Looks like you could do with something.'

'Let's not go there.'

The coffee was every bit as bad as Tyler had anticipated, but the burn on his tongue was taking his attention away from the pain in his hand and the anger fermenting steadily in the parts of his brain not preoccupied with physical pain.

There was nothing happening, no reason for Mills to remain at the hospital. The two officers headed for the exit and out towards the car park.

'So how is Marley?' asked Tyler.

'Things are getting interesting.'

'They need to get more than interesting, and fast.'

'Sir?'

'You were saying …'

'After I left Marley at the hostel, he went into a panic attack quickly followed by cardiac failure. Then he started shouting for me. At the hospital—'

'Could you skip to it,' said Tyler. 'Interesting though your account is.'

'His breathing's bad,' said Mills, keeping the slight out of his voice as best he could. 'But he was able to indicate that somebody had been to see him down in Stoke the other night, near to the church.'

'Did he say who?'

'Like I say, he's having difficulty breathing, and they have to keep giving him oxygen. They only let me see him at all because he kept asking.'

'*Did he say who?*'

The ferocity startled Mills. 'No, sir. He did not.'

'You obviously made a big impression.'

'He's terrified. Whoever came to see him has put the fear of God in the man. I think he's convinced they'll come back for him.'

They were out on the car park. 'I want you to come with me. Let's go in yours,' said Tyler.

They got into the car. 'I thought Marley hadn't been seen in any of his usual haunts that evening?'

'That's the thing, sir. Whoever visited Marley in his usual spot, asked him to walk with him. They went over to the other graveyard, across the road. You don't get many over there. Bit of a muggers' paradise. Whoever was with Marley either wasn't aware of that, or else wasn't fazed by it.'

'But who, dammit?'

Tyler smacked at the dashboard, spilling the dregs of the flavourless coffee onto his jacket and earning a fresh wave of pain. He lay back in his seat and draped his other hand across his forehead.

'You alright, sir?'

'No.'

'Can I—'

'Probably not. Unless you can supply me with the two things I need at this precise moment in time.'

'I'm not following you.'

'I'll spell it out: I need a beer and a whisky chaser on repeat prescription – and that's one thing. And I need a face that I can put a fist through. The clock's ticking. Let's see Mr Dammers, shall we?'

***

Paul Dammers lived in a quiet cul-de-sac, in a smart semi with a generous stretch of land, front and back. And he was giving DCI Tyler a bad case of déjà vu.

The tell-tale signs of stress that had been so evident on the face and in the manner of Phillip Swanson, were here too and in equal abundance. This one wasn't a smoker, though Tyler found himself wishing that the man was. It would have given Dammers something to do with those hands before he ended up hypnotising him *and* his sergeant.

Social work and probation were not good for the health, it seemed. Something clearly wasn't.

In the catalogue lounge, the detectives strode over familiar ground, revisiting the school, the park, The Stumps, teachers, pupils …

Tyler decided against remembering Pamela Scott to the man. It was hard work enough without the digressions.

Dammers went through the usual moves: didn't recall Alan Dale, vaguely remembered the police coming to the school because someone had gone missing, didn't have anything to do with kids from other years, occasionally played football in the park but wasn't that interested, etc., etc. Mrs Everson's class, old battle-axe, blah blah.

'You were in Howard Wood's class the previous year?' asked Mills.

'He was alright, Mr Wood. Bit of a laugh.'

'Was that because you shared an interest in football, Mr Dammers?' asked Mills. 'In Stoke City?'

'I suppose we did, yes. I still watch them.'

Progress, thought Tyler. *You don't get many admitting that much, at least not in the course of the current investigation.*

'Do you see Mr Wood at the match?' asked Mills.

'He still goes, does he?'

'You've not seen him recently?'

'No, why should I have done?'

'He lives close to here. Did you know that?'

Dammers shook his head, but he didn't look at all convincing. Tyler decided it was time to bring up that old flame after all.

'Pamela Scott? No, I don't recall the name.'

'She remembers you. She seemed to think that you and a younger lad, Robert Wild, may have been jostling for her attentions.'

Dammers puffed out his cheeks, as though the effort of memory was proving too much. 'It was a long time ago, but I don't know that name.'

'Nor Robert Wild?'

Another shake of the head, but betrayed by the eyes.

Tyler thought of something, and asked if he might be excused for a moment. Out in the car he made a call back to the station. He spoke to DC Crawley.

'Everson, yes. Get on to the school and check if they have any current contact information. Do your best on this one, quick as you can. Oh, and while you're on to them, ask if they can look something up in Mr Wise's old punishment book.'

'Sir?'

Tyler heard the suppressed laughter bubbling around the edges of Crawley's voice.

'I'm looking for any reference to Paul Dammers around the time of Alan Dale's disappearance, or before.'

'Anything you say, sir. Oh, by the way. DC Brown would like a word.'

'Put him on then. It'll have to be quick.'

'He's just popped out of the office. I'll—'

Tyler ended the call with a warning to the DC about the dangers of wasting police time.

In the house, Mills was treading water. Dammers was telling the detective that he hadn't been off with stress before, but that it was a stressful job and he'd been doing it a long time.

'So,' said Tyler, re-joining them. 'What do you recall about Steven Jenkins?'

***

At the station, DC Crawley was telling his colleagues about the latest mission.

'Sounds a bit kinky to me,' said PC Henderson, widening her eyes. 'You'd better let me handle it.'

'Kinky?' said Brown, entering the room through a wall of solid laughter. 'Tell me and tell me immediately. All details are relevant. I want *everything*.'

When the merriment had died down sufficiently, Crawley made the call. They put him through to Miss Hayburn. Now the pressure was on.

DC Crawley stuttered out his request, trying to avoid catching the eye of PC Henderson. But the headteacher seemed unwilling to impart information down the phone, and Crawley, his hand covering the mouthpiece, relayed this back to the bank of grinning colleagues.

'I could send one of our PCs down to the school,' said Brown, winking towards Henderson.

It wouldn't be necessary. The information was for DCI Tyler. 'One key fits all locks,' said Crawley, his hand once again covering the mouthpiece. 'Maybe she's got a thing for Tyler. It takes all kinds to make a world.'

Crawley suddenly coloured up. 'Sorry,' he said, looking into the mouthpiece as though he had seen a devil hiding inside it. 'I was talking about …'

He let it go, wrote down the information, thanked Miss Hayburn profusely for her trouble, ended the call and said a silent atheist's prayer.

The laughter at the spectacle of Crawley's self-induced humiliation broke all records for that day. 'Big breakthrough,' he said at last, addressing DC Brown. 'Paul Dammers got a pasting on the day after Jenkins and Hillman. Vandalism. No further details.'

'The plot thickens,' said Henderson. 'Can't police work be absolutely fascinating?'

'Look, can you follow up on this Rosemary Everson while I give the vital information to the DCI.'

'Did you tell him about Jenkins?' asked DC Brown.

In a short time, Crawley had travelled a long way from laughter.

***

Tyler was asking Dammers about Jenkins. At least he had the good sense to admit knowing that a person with that name had recently been found dead in extremely suspicious circumstances. It was a start.

'So, when you heard the news, did it jog anything?' asked Tyler.

'Did you recall him from school days?' clarified Mills.

A little seemed to be ebbing back. Jenkins was in the year below, Dammers believed, again underlining that he'd had little or nothing to do with the younger ones.

'He was in Mr Wood's class?' asked Tyler.

'Might have been.'

'Anyone else from that class spring to mind?' asked Mills.

'No, like I say …'

Mills rolled off the list: Swanson, Hillman, Marley. Paul Dammers seemed to start at the sound of each name.

And then a mobile rang.

Tyler listened to what DC Crawley was telling him, and ended the call. He looked at Mills. The news about Jenkins would have to wait.

'Did you have much to do with Mr Wise?' Tyler asked Dammers.

'Not really.' Then Dammers, appearing to recognise that the officer was holding a card, modified the statement. 'I was in trouble, maybe once or twice. That wasn't unusual at that school. Wise was a bit of a disciplinarian.'

Dammers was working hard trying to dampen down the rising atmosphere in the room, but his nervous smile didn't come close to infecting the company he was keeping.

'What sort of things were you in trouble for, Mr Dammers?' asked Tyler.

The dregs of the smile disappeared, but Dammers still clung desperately to a poor imitation of an easy-going attitude, until it packed up altogether and went the way of the smile. The final, unconvincing shrug of the shoulders came as something of an obituary to the death of cool.

'It was—'

'A long time ago?' suggested Tyler. 'Do your best. We've got all day.'

But they did not have all day, and Tyler came like a howling wind at last to the man's aid before he took his nails all the way to the elbow. 'Bullying? Fighting? The details in the book kept at the school are a little brief, but we are working on them. Here's a theory, just a theory. You and Robert Wild were both after the same girl. He made a fool of you, a younger lad stealing your girlfriend. You had to save face, bit of a dust up, Mr Wise gets wind of it and he takes no prisoners.'

Tyler caught Mills' quizzical look out of the corner of his eye; but his focus remained squarely on Paul Dammers.

The stressed probation officer was looking relieved. Had the DCI provided a scenario that he could subscribe to, true or otherwise?

'It was something like that, I think,' said Dammers. 'You know how it is, kids.'

'Hang on to that one, then. But maybe you prefer this?'

Tyler was on a roll. Bluffing could get to be a habit, as long as it came off and didn't blow up in your face. And anyway, bluffing was one thing; imaginative extrapolation from the facts such as they are … something else entirely.

'The fat kid gets the shit kicked out of him for some reason as yet unclear. Except that there doesn't have to be a reason. Maybe you were feeling a bit off that day. Maybe it really was girl trouble and somebody had to suffer. Either way, the fat kid gets the treatment, and somebody stands up for him. But who would do that? In a hell-hole like River Trent High in 1972, who would risk it for the sake of a fat kid?

'*Alan Dale, perhaps?*'

'*That's bullshit. I never touched any fat kid.*'

'*One more try. How about vandalism? A can of red paint? Red is the colour.*'

Dammers was trembling. 'I don't know what you're talking about.'

'You had nothing to do with the younger kids, except picking on them. Bullying wasn't an issue high on the agenda of Fredrick Wise, so it was the fox in the chicken coop syndrome. You knew Jenkins from watching Stoke City. You'd stand with Howard Wood, and he'd supply the booze and the cigarettes.'

Tyler paused for a moment, but Dammers wasn't saying anything.

'You didn't like people who didn't support your team, and you didn't like creeps who stole your girlfriends. You couldn't do much about the latter, but there was a nice little scapegoat in Mr Wood's class. A kid having the nerve to admit to not being a Stoke City fan, even though he hadn't the first clue about football and couldn't have cared less for anything but the colour.

'And you heard about what happened to Jenkins and Hillman and you wanted to make a stand. And somebody grassed you up and so now all three of you had something in common – courtesy of Mr Wise. *The need to pass something on.*'

'I don't know what you're talking about.'

Tyler signalled to Mills. It was time to read out some rights and take a trip down to the station together.

Yet Tyler was under no illusions. Bringing in Paul Dammers for the murder of Alan Dale would not keep the powers off his back for long.

CHAPTER TWENTY-FIVE

At Hanley Police Station Paul Dammers was demanding to see a solicitor.

'Probation officer,' Mills told DC Brown. 'Taking his own advice. He'll want everything by the book, no doubt. Make sure there's an interview room set up.'

'Will do. By the way, Rosemary Everson died of a major stroke about two years ago. Don't know if Tyler had anyone lined up for that?'

Tyler rounded the corner. 'Sorry to break up the party, but have we got anything from the lists of people present at Hillman's "meetings"?'

'We have most of it back,' said Mills. 'I'll show you when you're ready, sir.'

'Show me now.'

Tyler strode off and Mills turned to Brown.

'Is he all right?' whispered Brown.

'Let's hope so,' said Mills, hurrying off after Tyler.

Handing over the folder containing the feedback, Mills mentioned the death of Dammers' old teacher, Rosemary Everson.

'I doubt she would have told us much,' said Tyler. 'But you never know. Anyone else made mention of Dammers?'

'Not really. We could widen the focus.'

'Not sure we have the time. What have we got here, then?'

Hillman's information regarding meetings around the time of Steven Jenkins' death, and particularly the late and lengthy meeting that served as his alibi, was meticulous and thorough. Mills remarked that it was the kind of work that might be expected of such an ambitious man.

'Or somebody with something to hide,' said Tyler. 'Has anybody spoken with any of these people yet?'

Mills nodded. 'And everything appears to be legit in the cross referencing. Unless we're talking about a conspiracy involving half the population of two counties.'

'I get the point, Sergeant.'

Mills looked at Tyler long enough for the DCI to sense the scrutiny.

'What is it?'

'I know you're under pressure at the moment, sir.'

'Yes. I am. *And*?'

Mills hadn't been sure about Tyler to begin with. The DCI had arrived under a cloud of rumour and suspicion, and it was easy to be mistrustful of a new face. Tyler didn't seem the type who went out of his way to make friends, but all the same Danny Mills had sensed a beating heart beneath the sharpness.

Jim Tyler wasn't like others he came across, ambitious types from bigger cities, full of procedure and little else. The man was a maverick, but he had integrity and a passion to nail those guilty of the gravest deeds, irrespective of all other concerns. Tyler, he thought, was a fresh wind blowing, and no bureaucratic machine bent on glory, as some had suggested prior to his arrival.

'Are you making a point,' said Tyler, 'or shall we get on?'

Mills lost the heart to say anything. The moment was not conducive, and, he thought, likely never would be.

'In that case, perhaps we can get back to Martin Hillman, and what exactly you meant when you said that we have something.'

'It's not much.'

'Do you have anything, or don't you?'

'We think Hillman was here a few days ago.'

'I thought you said his alibi was solid.'

'It is. He was in Derby for a business meeting on Sunday night, when Jenkins died. But he was here, in Stoke-on-Trent, earlier that weekend.'

'How do we know that?'

'A couple of things, sir. DC Brown spoke to one of the alibi folk – a phone conversation an hour ago. An ex-pat.'

'A what?'

'A woman by the name of Julie Hammond. She's living and working in Derbyshire, apparently, but she was born and raised in Longton.' Mills smiled. 'She joked about asking Hillman where her oatcakes were.'

'Are you deliberately talking in riddles, or have I over-worked you?'

'Oatcakes. The local delicacy. You must try one.'

'Yes, I will, no doubt. What's your point?'

'Julie Hammond hadn't met Hillman before. She heard he was from Stoke originally and so broke the ice with a remark about him bringing oatcakes back from their mutual homeland, as it were.'

'And no doubt Hillman broke his cover by announcing that he'd brought a dozen!'

'Not quite. But she reckons he let slip about returning from Stoke but forgetting the oatcakes, and then tried to back-track.'

'What's she do, this Julie Hammond?' asked Tyler.

'I don't think she actually said.'

Tyler thought for a minute. 'Anything else?'

'We checked out his mother's grave in Newcastle-under-Lyme cemetery. There were fresh flowers, sir.'

'Could be another relative. A friend.'

'Could be, of course, but doubtful, as far as we can tell. No relatives, certainly. We made some enquiries. One or two in the Hartshill area remember the family.'

'And?'

'One of the neighbours recalls that Hillman went a bit 'off-the-rails', as they put it. They knew about his dad leaving, the upheaval, and allowances were made.'

'And this was when?'

'It was before he moved up to River Trent High. By all accounts, he settled down and his old neighbours were proud that he's doing well for himself.'

'Local lad makes good,' said Tyler. 'Look, I'm sorry. Tell Brown and the rest of the team that I appreciate their efforts. It's good work, really, it is.' He paused for a moment, letting the words ring in the air. Then, 'I think we need to speak to Mr Hillman.'

'That's not all, sir. I rang the hospital. Marley's stable at the moment and he's been asking to see me again. And we might have some CCTV footage from the churchyard. I'm having that checked out.'

Tyler looked at his watch. 'Get yourself up to the hospital. You need to see Marley. I'll deal with Dammers when the solicitor gets here.'

'What about Hillman?'

'Ring me from the hospital. We may be bringing him in, but that depends on what we get. He could make us look stupid. We're walking a fine line. Anything from that GP yet? Did Jenkins know he was dying?'

'Brown's onto it.'

'One more thing: this Julie Hammond. Anything strike you as odd?'

'How do you mean?'

'Not a business rival, is she? Or from the opposite political party?'

'We could check.'

'This oatcake story – it's like something out of Miss Marple. Look, I'd like you to contact her yourself and find out a bit more. Go and see her if you need to.'

Mills turned to go.

'Again, sorry about earlier. There's a good team here.'

'I know that. And, sir …'

'What is it?'

'Take it easy.'

***

At the hospital Mills was allowed to go straight through. 'Be careful, though,' said one of the staff as Mills was about to enter the side ward where Marley lay. 'He may be off critical, but he's convinced he's dying. You'll probably get the death bed speech.'

Marley appeared lifeless, thought Mills. As pale as the vegetarian meal that his wife had rustled up and left in the fridge for his supper the previous evening. A rack of ribs would have been more of a welcome home, but minus the beer, what was the point. She was on a diet and so was he.

And talking of speeches, she'd given him the one about the stress of being a police officer and the importance of looking after yourself and eating healthily and cutting down on just about everything that made life worth living.

They had kids, she kept reminding him. He had a responsibility to take care of himself for their sakes. She had a point; of course she had a point. But did she have to keep making it?

Sitting down at the side of the bed, Mills looked at Douglas Marley and wondered again how somebody could look so ancient after a mere forty-five years on the planet.

He spoke the man's name, and Marley's eyes jerked open. A nurse followed him into the room, checking the fluids and consulting with a machine issuing beeps and lines across a small screen. When she was done, she turned to Mills. 'Not too long,' she said, before leaving them to their privacy.

Mills didn't dwell on the ambiguity of the remark and was starting on the pleasantries when Marley cut him short.

'They were warning me off saying anything.'

'Who was warning you, Mr Marley?'

'There was five of us. That day, down by the park. And we had that kid with us. We were only kids ourselves.' He looked at Mills, and there was desperation about him, pleading to be understood, forgiven.

'You had Alan Dale with you?'

Marley nodded. 'That lad that went missing. The one they found.'

'Can you tell me who the five were, Mr Marley? *Doug.*'

Marley's breathing started to labour.

Mills said, 'Steven Jenkins, Phillip Swanson, Martin Hillman, Paul Dammers ... you?'

Marley nodded, struggling to get his breathing under control. Mills thought about calling for the nurse. A few more questions would do it. Nail it.

He pressed on.

'Who killed Alan Dale, Doug?'

Marley took a minute to steady his breathing. When he spoke again, it came in gasps. 'It wasn't like that. We were having fun – to start with. Just a game, you see. And then one of them started up about football. Stoke City.'

'Red is the colour?'

Marley looked at Mills. 'You know about that?'

'But I still want you to tell me.'

Marley looked away, his chest rising and falling more steadily. Even the voice, when it kicked in again, had become easier, as though the storm was passing.

Marley told a tale that sounded close enough to the account Sheila Dale had given to Tyler.

'We went too far, but we didn't kill him. He was crying and we left him. I've felt bad about that day for the whole of my life – and that's no shit.'

Looking into the man's eyes, Mills couldn't help but believe him.

'There was a big game going on the following evening. A few of the lads went to the match. Some charity game, but with stars from the past and what have you. So, the next night there was a game organised in the park. I was playing. I was no good, but I was having a laugh. The ball went over by the railings and I went to get it. Three of them were with that lad again.'

Mills noted that Marley didn't like speaking the boy's name.

'Alan Dale?'

Marley nodded. 'Him. They were taking him back down the path. He was crying but they wouldn't let him go. One of them shouted to me, "Time for another reminder".'

'Reminder?' said Mills.

'It's what Wise, the headmaster, used to say when he was going to set about you. "Time for a reminder." Anyway, I thought the lad – I thought he'd had enough, so I shouted back, "Why can't you leave him alone".'

'What happened next?' asked Mills.

Marley's breathing started to labour again. 'I went back to the game. I didn't give it another thought until the next day, at school.'

But the next day was Saturday, thought Mills. He was about to raise the point when Marley said, 'No, wait a minute. It was weekend. Must've been the Monday. There was no sign of him. I was looking out. He wasn't in class. I wondered if they'd gone too far and he'd ended up in hospital or something. I asked one of them. They said if I knew what was good for me, I'd forget the whole business and let it stay forgotten. Not long after that the police came to the school and I didn't tell them anything.'

Marley's breathing was deteriorating.

'Who were the three, Doug? And who warned you off?'

'Me and Swanson were in the game. He'd seen them taking the lad back down the path, same as me. They warned him off too.'

'*Who warned you off, Doug?*'

'The older one.'

'Paul Dammers?'

Marley nodded. His chest was rising and falling rapidly in an effort to breath, and the sound was like a saw cutting into bone.

Mills was already on his feet to summon a nurse.

One last question.

'Did Dammers visit you by the church the other night?'

Marley was shaking his head.

'Nurse,' shouted Mills, opening the door out onto the ward.

He turned back to Marley. 'Not Dammers?'

Marley was gulping at the air, his face mottling as he fought to breathe.

'Nurse! *Nurse!*'

The sound of footsteps running towards them.

'Who was it, Doug? Who frightened you so much ..?'

The nurse flew into the room, the doctor not many seconds behind. And then Mills was ushered out as the battle began to save what was left of Douglas Marley's life.

CHAPTER TWENTY-SIX

Chief Superintendent Berkins congratulated Tyler on his work, even reprising the speech about having every faith in him and about the bright road ahead. But no sooner had Tyler started to fill him in on the details, that same faith appeared to wane, and the road ahead quickly lost its lustre.

'To say that it's a bit thin is the understatement of the century. An experienced probation officer – he's going to know the ropes and he's going to end up hanging us from one. His solicitor will handle our respective occupational funerals.'

Tyler raised the subject of Martin Hillman.

'No, absolutely not. You need a lot more than you've got so far, Jim. A sight more. An MP – God above.'

Tyler thought better about pointing out that Hillman was not quite an MP yet, and that such things still depended on a well-established democratic process. Still, it was no secret that bureaucratic organisations naturally feared the most powerful bureaucrats. And MPs, or those within touching distance of such office, were among the most highly feared of all. They knew the networks of pensions at stake, and could ring up chief superintendents and beyond, even the likes of Charles Dawkins, for that matter, and practically hold an organisation to ransom.

Nobody liked to admit it. In a day and age of 'justice and equality for all', the official line stated that everybody was treated with the same impartiality in the eyes of the law. It was the politically correct thing to say, and the politically prudent. To even suggest otherwise, despite the deep suspicions of the general public, was to place your neck, along with your pension, firmly into the noose.

But the eyes of the law saw what they wanted to see; what was convenient to the preservation of the machine. *Being afraid to acknowledge this,* thought Tyler, *doesn't stop it being true.*

***

Tyler took the call from Mills.

'Douglas Marley died a few minutes ago, sir.'

'Did he tell you who visited him in the churchyard?'

'No, I'm afraid he didn't.'

The whole thing was falling apart.

Tyler let his head fall into the hand that wasn't holding the phone.

'Any news from Jenkins' GP, sir?'

Through splayed fingers, Tyler answered. 'Jenkins knew he was dying. They discussed treatment options. There weren't many. The prognosis was poor.'

Tyler's hand, the one not holding the phone, had taken on a life of its own. Massaging his eyes, trying to keep what constituted mind and body together.

It was now or never, as the old song went. Double or quits.

'Sir?' sounded Mills' voice down the line. 'Are you okay?'

Tyler knew that once he had actually said it, once the words were out of his head and spoken aloud, that it would happen. It would be the end of a career, one way or another. Quite possibly a number of careers, and most likely his own.

Like the cursed sword of legend being drawn from the sheath, it could not return until it had drawn blood.

He took a breath that might have reached as deep as any that Douglas Marley had taken, and spoke into the handset.

'We're bringing them in,' he said.

'Who, sir?'

'*All of them.*'

CHAPTER TWENTY-SEVEN

So many clocks were ticking.

Chief Superintendent Graham Berkins had left the building, unaware of what had hatched inside the mind of DCI Jim Tyler. But he would be back soon enough. If no-one else beat him to it, someone on Martin Hillman's behalf would bring Berkins charging into the building, demanding to know what the blazes was going on.

As things stood already, Dammers and his brief were likely to make fools of all concerned. Someone would have to pay for that, and Tyler was under no illusions about who the main contender was likely to be.

So now he had played the bigger, far riskier hand, raising the stakes again. The chance of a red-faced department and the need for a fall guy from within had been magnified to the power of God-knows.

It was, Tyler knew, a multiple bluff with odds stacked so badly that no professional gambler would have entertained the idea for a second. Dammers had to be still present at the station when the others came in. But his brief wouldn't see his client delayed a moment longer than the rules stipulated. Any extension was unthinkable without good, solid reasons.

For this insane thing to work, timing was everything.

And a good dose of gambler's luck.

Tyler looked at the clock on the wall, attempting by force of will to hold the hands back. Failing, he set about busying himself in preparation for the long night ahead.

***

Swanson was the first in, arriving even before Dammers' solicitor. The omens, for a few minutes, even seemed favourable. It might be enough, thought Tyler, to convince Paul Dammers that the gang had been rounded up and the truth about to be exposed.

Then the call came through from DS Mills.

Hillman was stirring up a hornet's nest over in Derby, and the soft-spoken threats were serious indeed. Nevertheless, the law was the law, and, ass or no ass, whatever the consequences later on, *Martin Hillman was coming in.*

'And don't spare the horses,' said Tyler, ending the call.

Phillip Swanson hadn't seen the merits of legal representation yet. It wouldn't hurt to have a little chat straight off. Tyler asked that Swanson be taken straight into one of the interview rooms. 'Make sure he and Dammers catch sight of each other, though,' he told the duty sergeant.

Mills was following up on some phone calls and it was the turn of the oatcake woman, the 'ex-pat' whose remarkable powers of observation had rung a false note, at least with Tyler.

She answered her mobile on the first ring.

'Julie Hammond? Sorry to bother you again.'

Mills listened carefully as she answered his questions, explaining again how it had struck her that Hillman seemed to have a preoccupation with time. How he had been 'suspiciously keen' to establish the precise timing of his arrival for the meeting, and drawing attention to the lateness of his eventual departure.

'I remember thinking: is he trying to impress somebody? Let them know how hard he works? I probably wouldn't have thought any more about it.'

'But for the "oatcake" business.'

'Well, you start putting this and that together.'

Tyler was right, thought Mills. There was something odd going on. *Who was this Julie Hammond?* There was something that she wasn't telling.

'Do you think,' asked Mills, 'that Mr Hillman might have been establishing an alibi?'

'For what, do you think?'

This is cat and mouse, thought Mills.

There was a heavy pause, and then Hammond said: 'I believe that you are investigating the murder of Steven Jenkins?'

Mills hesitated. 'I need to speak to you in person,' he said.

'Is there any particular reason for that?'

'You will need to complete a statement.'

'I will need to check my diary and get back to you,' she said.

'Can I ask,' said Mills. 'What do you do for a living?'

Following the briefest of pauses, she said, 'If you have your diary to hand, we can arrange a time that suits us both.'

***

Downstairs the desk sergeant had a promising observation for Tyler. The eyes of Paul Dammers had apparently 'popped out of his head' on seeing Phillip Swanson.

'They didn't acknowledge each other, but they're certainly not strangers.'

Swanson was smoking heartily as Tyler entered the interview room, the ashtray already filling up nicely.

'We meet again so soon, Mr Swanson. You recognise your old school friend, I take it?'

Swanson pulled heavily on his smoke.

'How can I help you?'

His voice was all over the place, the same as his hands, while his eyes moved from the detective's face and back to the ashtray, setting a pattern that would continue throughout the minutes that followed.

Tyler sat down opposite, with a mute DC to make up the numbers.

'We've spoken to a lot of your old school friends lately, Mr Swanson. Matter of fact, we have another one coming in shortly. But we'll come back to that. Do you remember that chap out there? Been a few years, has it, or have you seen him more recently?'

'I'm not sure who he is,' said Swanson, unconvincingly.

'Familiar, though?'

Swanson nodded, cautiously.

'His name is Paul Dammers. He's helping us with our enquiries. He was at River Trent High the same time as you. The year above, but he knows all the people that you used to know. He works as a probation officer, interestingly enough, though possibly not for much longer.'

Tyler watched Swanson's reaction carefully. If anything, the fear had intensified. But was he ready yet, ready to try and save his own skin?

'It appears that Douglas Marley had a visitor. Bit of a character was old Doug, by all accounts. Shook him up badly, this visitor.'

Tyler eased back in his seat, presenting the calm façade of having all of the answers already. He glanced across at DC Clarke, and wondered what she was making of all this. She appeared almost as nervous as Swanson, he thought.

'I wonder who his visitor could have been?' said Tyler.

Phillip Swanson took down another heavy lungful of smoke, but didn't say anything.

Tyler weighed up the options, and then rolled off the names from that long-ago day in June, 1972.

'And none of you seems to be in the best of health at the moment, I'm sorry to say. Steven Jenkins is dead, Douglas Marley … in hospital, you off sick, Paul Dammers also on the sick – even your old teacher, Howard Wood, he's sick, too. You are a suffering lot, aren't you? Cursed, almost, you might say.'

Swanson lit up another cigarette.

'Something not agreeing with you, Mr Swanson? Oh, and I missed somebody out, didn't I?'

Tyler leaned forward and Swanson edged back in his chair, as though trying to get away from the relentless, accusing presence of the detective.

'So, who have I missed out? He'll be here any time now, but let's see if you can remember, shall we? See if you can work it out.'

The silence thickened.

'Good career, social work. Very noble and worthwhile, I imagine – protecting children. Don't know what your boss is going to think, though, when she finds out that you had a hand in killing one. May have been a long time ago, but even adolescent *child killers* aren't welcome in the profession these days, so I'm told. Be a pity to carry the weight of somebody else's baggage through the rest of your life.'

The crack came so fast that Tyler practically heard it. It announced itself as a deep moan from within the broken figure sitting before him.

'I didn't do anything.'

'Didn't do anything, Mr Swanson?'

'I was down The Stumps when they were hitting that kid but I didn't—'

'You mean Alan Dale?'

Swanson nodded, taking in another lungful of smoke.

'Hitting him?'

Swanson gave his account of the events that day.

'So, who was doing the hitting?' asked Tyler.

'Jenkins.'

'Anybody else?'

Swanson was thinking about it.

'Hillman?'

'No.'

'But he was there, wasn't he?'

'He might have been, I don't know.'

'So, who *was* there?'

Tyler suddenly felt like a midwife at the anticipation of a long and protracted delivery.

Swanson appeared to ponder, intermittently looking from Tyler to ashtray and back again.

'Mr Swanson?'

The agitation was increasing, and Swanson appeared ready to burst open with it. At last Tyler said, 'Listen: I will name them and you will say whether they were there or not, do you understand?'

Tyler raised his voice, and spoke more slowly. 'Mr Swanson … do … you … under … stand?'

Jenkins, Dammers, Marley, Swanson himself – yes, they were there, all four of them. But at the name Hillman he again hesitated.

Tyler repeated the name. Swanson was shaking, head to toe.

For the final time, Tyler asked the question: *was Hillman present*?

'*Mr Swanson?*'

The man looked into Tyler's eye.

'I'm scared.'

He let the man light another smoke, and regain a modicum of composure. Then he asked him, 'Okay, Phillip. If Jenkins was doing the hitting, what were the rest of you doing?'

'Dammers was holding him,' said Swanson. 'Me and Doug were joining in the singing. We never actually hit him.'

'So that makes it all right, then?'

Swanson didn't answer. He pulled heavily on his cigarette.

'Did any of you, apart from Jenkins, assault Alan Dale?'

'No.'

'You didn't actually kill him that evening, did you?'

'We didn't kill anybody.'

'No, you didn't. Not that evening. You went back another time to finish the job, didn't you?'

'I wasn't there that second time.'

'But you knew about it? So, where were you?'

'In the park. There was a game.'

'You saw them taking Alan Dale back down the path, isn't that right?'

Swanson was looking down at the table, nodding frantically.

'Jenkins, Hillman and Dammers?'

'Jenkins and Dammers were there. I don't know about Hillman.'

'You've had a visitor recently, I believe. Someone doing the rounds – someone from the past giving you all a briefing in the wake of the discovery of Alan Dale's corpse. Hillman just turned up, out of the blue, did he? Where did he visit you?'

'I didn't see Hillman.'

'Who, then?'

'I spoke to Dammers. I had a phone call. He said that he'd been talking to Howard Wood.'

Tyler felt the glow ignite inside him.

'When was this, exactly?'

'After the report about the dead boy being Dale. Wood was expecting a visit from the police and Dammers told him to play it cool.'

Tyler's heart was thumping in his chest, and he tried to keep the effect of it out of his voice.

'He'd been to see him?'

'I don't know. I think so.'

'But he didn't come to see you?'

'He was on the phone a long time, and I thought I'd convinced him that he had nothing to fear from me.'

'That you could keep your mouth shut? That you could handle the *authorities*?'

Swanson lit up another. 'Something like that. But then he turned up.'

'How nice for you. And did he say anything about visiting Jenkins or Marley?'

'No.'

'Had you seen Jenkins recently, or any of the others?'

'None of them, I told you that.'

'Howard Wood?'

'Why would I?'

'The occasional match, perhaps? Relive old times? Matter of fact, it wouldn't surprise me if Wood hadn't suggested coming forward. Help the police out – funny how a discovery of a corpse like that can do wonders for the memory. It was *such a long time ago; a bit of harmless fun.* Get your stories in first because, after all, *you didn't really do anything,* right? Not even withholding valuable information at the time – and for thirty years afterwards.

'And perhaps you took it upon yourself to alert Dammers or maybe Hillman directly. Let them know that there was a weak link or two in the chain. Maybe you saw Steve Jenkins. Maybe *he* made the suggestion about coming forward. Some interesting possibilities around Steven Jenkins, wouldn't you say – considering he ended up getting his throat cut so deep that it practically took his head off.

'I'm in the territory, am I not, *Mr Swanson?*'

Swanson buried his head into his arm and began to weep, while Tyler watched with disdain.

***

When Tyler came out of the interview room, followed by a somewhat bemused DC Clarke, barely back off sick leave, and looking about ready to jump back overboard, he needed a gallon of tea. But when the desk sergeant gave him a list of messages his thirst was instantly forgotten.

Everything appeared to be moving at the speed of light.

Mills had come in and from his account Hillman had not been good company. Berkins had already caught wind of events and expected a call from Tyler immediately.

Tyler said that the chief superintendent would have to wait as there were more important matters to be dealt with first.

He took a stunned Mills into his office to give him the update following Swanson's interview.

'You're shaking, sir.'

'What's that?'

'You don't know it – you're bloody shaking.'

Mills went to organise an urgent drink and then he helped Tyler into a chair.

CHAPTER TWENTY-EIGHT

Tyler came round and Danny Mills' face was the first thing he saw.

'What happened?'

'You fainted. Some people will do anything to get out of returning the chief's call.'

Tyler groaned. 'You know, I was starting to like this city.'

'Make the call, sir.'

'I don't expect that Berkins will be overly impressed with our methods of late. Mine in particular.'

'Why don't you find out?' Mills gestured towards the phone.

'You could book me a hospital bed for the night, Danny. Put me in Douglas Marley's old bed. I can wait to see which visitors I get.'

'They don't have to worry about him opening his mouth now, sir.'

'I'm sorry. That was in poor taste.'

'I think we'll get over it. Now, if I were you, I would make that call. He's probably on his way over as we speak.'

'No point in wasting a phone call, then. And as for being me – you wouldn't want that.'

Mills, filling up Tyler's cup again, lowered his head towards him. 'Have me for insubordination if you like, Jim. But first up – *make that fucking call.*'

Tyler conceded defeat, laughed hysterically for about thirty seconds, and then he picked up the phone.

Berkins sounded glad to hear from him.

Mills listened as Tyler attempted to explain his actions to Chief Superintendent Berkins, impressed as he heard the detailed account of the interview with Swanson and the complicated possibilities and permutations likely to follow. Mills thought he heard Berkins making noises about somebody getting himself a job as a confidence trickster, as Tyler held the phone away from his ear.

When the call ended, Mills said, 'Not happy, then?'

'Somewhere between apoplectic and certifiable. But they hedge their bets at that level. Secretly, I think he was full of admiration, and at the same time soiling his pants. If it works out, I've done nothing wrong, and he can bask in the glory. If it doesn't, he's going to want a head in the basket. And all he has to do is ask. So, place your bets.'

'Come on, let's get this show on the road.'

'Are you up to it?'

'No question about it. I have to be.'

***

Dammers didn't say anything while the technicalities of the interview were explained to him. He appeared strangely more confident in the interview room than he had done at home. It wasn't the first time that Mills had witnessed that phenomenon; a person was often most vulnerable in their private space, and more guarded.

And in the case of Paul Dammers, dealing with the police at home was no doubt alien, whilst dealing with them here was like putting on your work clothes. Doing what you got paid to do and not taking it too personally.

His manner suggested that he knew the process as well as the solicitor sitting next to him. Mills wondered if that arrogance wasn't going to let him down hard.

Tyler recapped carefully the conversation that had taken place at Dammers' house earlier in this long day of days. The punishment at the hands of Wise for vandalism, corresponding with the beating, that same day, of Alan Dale on The Stumps.

Dammers neither denied nor confirmed anything, leaving it to his solicitor to interject. 'Have you brought in my client merely to have fun assassinating his character, DCI Tyler?'

Tyler conjured up the day when the five of them had taken Alan Dale down The Stumps to show him what happened to a kid who supported the wrong team. Tyler painted a vivid picture, all the time watching Dammers' reactions to the trip down memory lane.

There was fear in his eyes, fear but not a modicum of shame. And the fear was kept in check, thought Tyler, by the knowledge that his solicitor knew the word 'evidence' as well as he knew the word 'proof'.

And in the knowledge gained through a career in probation work: that the odds were always, *always* going to be stacked in favour of the offender and not the victim when it came to which version of the 'truth' would ultimately prevail.

'Do you intend backing up any of these old stories, or shall we begin the process of demanding a formal apology for my client *now*, perhaps – for subjecting him to these rather unsavoury allegations?'

Dammers was still to speak, but Tyler had finished the knuckle-cracking and was about to insist upon it.

'A number of people – ex-pupils from your school – have given testimony that you held Alan Dale down while he was repeatedly beaten. Do you deny that, Mr Dammers?'

Paul Dammers looked at his solicitor, but the question was deemed a fair one.

'Whose testimony?' he said at last.

The question surprised Tyler. After all, Dammers had seen Swanson here at the station already. Did he want to see how many cards the police were holding before committing himself?

'Phillip Swanson,' said Tyler.

Dammers didn't even blink at that.

'Douglas Marley.'

Not a flicker.

'We have Martin Hillman waiting outside, and we will be talking to him directly.'

The mention of Hillman's name and the suggestion of his presence appeared to come as a shock, but still Dammers didn't exactly fall to pieces at the news. Tyler asked the question again, and Dammers looked again to his solicitor.

'Will you please answer the question,' said Tyler.

The solicitor whispered something into the ear of his client, and a moment later Dammers asked if he might take a break. Tyler spoke to the tape machine, announcing that a short break would now take place before the interview resumed.

Outside the door, he took Mills to one side.

'We only have Swanson and Marley's testimony and one's dead and the other's a nervous wreck. Push too hard and fast and he'll play safe. We can't trust to Hillman opening up.'

'He won't know that Marley's dead, sir. Not yet.'

'Time to spin the wheel and see what colour our probation officer and his brief are placing their money on. God, talk about a den of iniquity – MPs, probation, social workers and solicitors. We pulled out a royal flush this time, Danny-boy. Talking of which ... make a start on the messages while I pay a visit.'

When Tyler came out of the gents, he made his way to the CID office. Mills was waiting and he was beaming. 'We have a result from the CCTV, sir.'

'Dammers?'

'*Hillman.*'

***

Back in the interview room, Tyler switched on the tape machine and announced the resumption. And then he repeated the troublesome question: was Dammers prepared to admit that he was present that afternoon, holding Alan Dale while he was assaulted?

Dammers glanced at his brief, and then turned back to Tyler.

He nodded.

Tyler pointed toward the recorder.

'Could you please speak for the tape, Mr Dammers.'

'Yes, I was there.'

'And did you hold Alan Dale while he was assaulted?'

'I don't believe so.'

'You don't believe so? Mr Dammers, did you or didn't you hold—'

'It was a long time ago. I can't imagine that I would have done, though.'

'Do you recall who was assaulting Alan Dale?'

Tyler again observed the face of the gambler, trying to weigh up which hand to play. It was always useful to have a scapegoat in situations like this one. To confess to the lesser charge and hide behind the 'real' culprit. Even better if the scapegoat was conveniently deceased.

'I think it was Jenkins.'

Bingo, thought Tyler. *Surprise, surprise.* No doubt when the news got out that Marley was dead, *he* would figure more prominently in the accounts too, particularly when it came to allocating the violence.

'Steven Jenkins was the only person assaulting Alan Dale?'

'I think the whole thing was his idea.'

'So why did Steven Jenkins wish to inflict such a beating on a defenceless child, Mr Dammers?'

'I think it was because of the football thing, like you said. But like I say, it was a long time ago.'

'And you think that was fair and reasonable, do you? He doesn't support your team, so you—'

'DCI Tyler, I believe that my client has already answered your question.'

'Yes, thank you. So, Mr Dammers: Steven Jenkins assaulted Alan Dale, but there were five of you present. Six including Alan Dale, is that correct?'

'I'm not sure.'

'Did you hold Alan Dale while Jenkins assaulted him?'

'It may have been one of the others. I was there, but—'

'So, who else *might it have been*?'

'I think it might have been Swanson.'

'Are you sure about that?'

There was a lightening of tone as Dammers said, 'Actually, it could have been Marley. It was one of them, maybe both of them. Like I say, it was—'

'Yes, Mr Dammers. A long time ago, I realise that. So, what about Martin Hillman? What part was he playing?'

Dammers seemed to lose the lightness of a moment ago. 'I don't particularly remember him being there. I mean, he might have been, but I'm not sure about it.'

'I see. So, let's move on to two evenings later, shall we.'

Tyler painted the scene once again. A fine summer's late afternoon, a game of football organised in the park. This time only three of them present to torment Alan Dale.

'Another beating, was it, or something more this time? Alan Dale had a fractured cheek, aside from the injuries that actually killed him.'

The solicitor interjected, and the immediate brightness reflected again in the face of Paul Dammers.

Tyler continued. 'You were there that second evening, Mr Dammers? Along with Steven Jenkins and Martin Hillman?'

Dammers glanced towards his solicitor.

'Will you please answer the question, Mr Dammers,' said Tyler.

Dammers turned back to the detective. 'We were just messing about, not meaning to do any harm.'

'You fractured the boy's cheek.'

'Detective Chief Inspector!'

'Please go on, Mr Dammers.'

'It was Steven Jenkins who punched him.'

Ah, the dead man again, thought Tyler. 'And was there any particular reason for this vicious assault on a defenceless child?'

'As far as I was concerned, we were just mucking about.'

It sounded too thin, and Dammers knew it. He went on, 'I think Steve – Jenkins – had a bee in his bonnet still, about the football.'

'About Dale supporting a different team?'

Dammers nodded.

'For the tape, please, Mr Dammers.'

'Yes, because of that.'

'And about the fact that he had been punished by Mr Wise, which he may also have blamed Alan Dale for.'

'Yes, possibly that as well.'

'But not Martin Hillman?'

Dammers looked blank.

'Martin Hillman didn't have a grudge, despite the fact that he too had been punished "on account of Alan Dale"?'

'I don't know about that.'

'But he was there, wasn't he? The three of you had gone to all that trouble to take Alan Dale back down the path. Except that this time what you had in mind was far worse.'

'Detective Chief Inspector—'

'This time the beating was just a warm up exercise, wasn't it? Get the party going?'

'DCI Tyler, I think that my client has helped you as far as he is able with your enquires. And now if you don't mind …'

'We've almost finished,' said Tyler. 'So, if you could bear with me for just a little longer.'

Tyler turned back to Dammers. 'You're still not sure of Hillman's involvement, on either occasion?'

'Like I said, it was a long time ago.'

Tyler felt his hands making fists under the table, and at the same time he recognised the relief coming into the eyes of Paul Dammers: the man was starting to believe that he was home free. That all of the significant cards had already been played.

'Cast your mind back, a final time, to that second evening, Mr Dammers. Steven Jenkins, for whatever reason, hit Alan Dale in the face, fracturing his cheek. Alan Dale was never seen again after that day, until his corpse was found recently. He died in that place. You, along with Steven Jenkins and Martin Hillman, were the last *people* to have seen him alive.'

Dammers was licking his lips.

'You have something to say, Mr Dammers?'

He had something to say, alright; his eyes were filled with it. 'The one thing that I do remember – was the girl coming.'

'Girl?'

Tyler caught Mills' eye, but all it reflected was his own bemusement.

'We went when we saw the girl coming.'

As Tyler tried to re-assemble his scattered thoughts, he heard Mills ask, 'Do you know who this girl was?' And then Dammers strident reply: 'No, but I think she looked familiar. Didn't the boy have a sister?'

CHAPTER TWENTY-NINE

'They all seem to want to keep Hillman out of it,' said Mills, when Tyler returned from speaking on the phone again with Berkins.

'And that includes Berkins,' said Tyler. 'He's on his way over. He'll be in time to pin a medal to our chests or else roast us.'

'Where's your money?'

'Don't know about you, but I'm not strictly the medal type.'

'I think you underestimate yourself.'

'I just work from the evidence available.'

Mills laughed. 'Talking of which – what do you think about this "girl"?'

'I'm not sure what to think,' said Tyler. 'A mystery girl would be a handy distraction.'

'I don't believe he intended it to be much of a mystery, sir.'

'Come on,' said Tyler. 'Let's not keep the VIP waiting.'

***

Martin Hillman did a good line in petulant charm, thought Mills, as the players took up their places in the interview room. Mills thought back to that old school photograph. The look of what Tyler had referred to as 'cold detachment' peeping through the mask. And that same meticulous parting of the hair, cut at an MP's length all those years before; as though signifying a premonition or else a master plan.

Hillman appeared to be feeling in good company next to his solicitor, and Mills wondered if it was a Freudian thing, Hillman's mother being a solicitor, even his runaway – or perhaps driven away – father. But maybe that was a conundrum for some professorial type thinking of churning out a new thesis on the workings of the human mind with reference to the great Sigmund, and not for a detective sergeant who recently did a one-day course on applied psychology for the academically challenged.

Still, Mills couldn't help thinking: had Hillman's mother cast the die in the mind of her young son – that there wasn't a problem in life that could not be smashed away by the services of the right kind of legal representation?

Maybe she had a lot to answer for, God rest her soul.

Mills was snatched from his reverie.

Tyler switched on the tape and proceeded to make the preliminaries sound like the rising of the final curtain.

***

The formalities completed, it was speech time. The manicured brief had his money to earn, and wasted no time setting about doing so.

His client, 'being a man of serious integrity and standing in the community', would 'naturally be more than willing to assist the police in the execution of their duties in any way possible.' His client would be 'particularly keen to offer his assistance when the matter involved the investigation of a serious crime.' It was, however, 'in nobody's interests to use heavy-handed techniques and outrageous stunts in a ham-fisted attempt to conjure something up where evidently substance was notably lacking.'

It was, thought Mills, a consummate speech, but still not worth whatever this suited con-man was charging.

It was, thought Tyler, the biggest load of tosh that he had heard in quite a while, and further indication that the night ahead was going to be hellish.

Tyler made no comment on the speech, giving it a few seconds' silence before launching into a concise résumé of the established facts concerning the final ordeals suffered by Alan Dale. No other names were mentioned at this stage, and the effect seemed to Mills rather like an intricate sketch minus the colour.

Throughout the résumé, Hillman maintained a countenance of mild indifference silently echoed by his solicitor.

Tyler threw down his first question.

'Were you, Mr Hillman, involved in the incidents that I have described, on either or both of the days in question? The days in question being June 14th, 1972 and June 16th, 1972.'

Hillman looked toward his counsel, and it seemed to Mills that nobody could give a simple answer to a simple question anymore, not when you were paying the person sitting next to you the kind of money that a police officer could only dream about.

If some tacit command had passed between the two men, it was not apparent; yet when Hillman turned back to face Tyler, something had changed.

'I was there,' said Hillman.

'On both days?' asked Tyler.

'Yes. On both days.'

'And what was your role in the events that transpired on those two occasions?'

The solicitor interjected at this point, demanding that Tyler clarify what exactly he wished to know. Tyler maintained the question, but the interruption had served to warn the client not to be drawn by broad questioning into saying more than was required.

Mills had seen people give entire life stories in answer to the vaguest questions. There didn't seem to be much danger of that happening here, though.

Hillman thought and then said, 'It was a nice evening. I'm talking about June 16th, though actually both evenings were pleasant, as I recall. It was not unusual for youngsters to use the park in the summer. There was something going on, and I was naturally inquisitive.'

This is going to be like pulling teeth, thought Mills. Hillman and his counsel could spin things out for hours, wearing out the interrogator and at the same time giving the illusion of being abundantly helpful.

Winding down the clock.

Thirty minutes in and the detectives were still no wiser than at the outset. Hillman was speaking in long and leisured sentences, saying virtually nothing, while his solicitor was raising objections every time Tyler tried to short-cut the routine and move the thing forward.

Around the hour mark, Hillman's counsel started to make good use of the crusted jewels on his wrist that collectively resembled a watch. It wouldn't be more than a minute or so before he started asking how much longer Tyler intended keeping his client.

Anticipating this, Tyler offered a break. A comfort stop, he called it. It would also give him time to review his strategy and get another opinion.

They went for it. It was the first positive sign that Hillman and Co didn't know all the tricks.

***

DC Brown was putting in quite a day himself, though he didn't baulk at organising the refreshments. In the CID office, he was asking Mills how it was going, and Mills said, 'Slowly.'

'What's Hillman said about being on CCTV?'

'We haven't got to that yet.'

'What's Tyler playing at?'

'Now that *is* a question.'

'What's a question?' said Tyler, entering the office.

'Just thinking out loud, sir,' said Mills.

'About anything in particular?'

'It was me,' said Brown. 'I was asking what Hillman was saying about the CCTV footage – placing him in Stoke the other night. I suppose we're all a bit uptight about the situation.'

Tyler nodded. 'I appreciate that. And I appreciate all of the hard work that this team has put in. Whatever the outcome of all this, I want you to know that, okay.'

'Thank you, sir,' said Brown.

'Berkins not shown yet?' asked Tyler.

'He rang a short time ago,' said Brown. 'He wanted to know if there had been any *developments.* He wants you to ring him as soon as you've finished with Hillman.'

'He's staying up all night, is he?'

'I wouldn't like to speculate, sir,' said Brown.

'I want you to organise something for me,' said Tyler. 'I want you to make sure that Hillman sees Dammers and Swanson.'

A question-mark formed on Brown's face.

'It makes an interesting party trick when the entertainment's delayed. I saw an inspector pull it off once. He's a chief superintendent himself these days, but don't let that put you off. It's really quite simple.'

***

Hillman and his solicitor were waiting for the detectives to join them back in the interview room when the lights went out.

Dammers and his representative were waiting in a room further down the corridor, while Swanson, whose now-requested legal rep had unfortunately been involved in a minor road traffic accident and was delayed, was attempting to break the world smoking record in a room of his own.

The desk sergeant, joined by DC Brown, showed Hillman and his brief out of the pitch-dark room. A technical hitch, Brown explained; they would have to use a room further down the corridor.

The solicitor seemed on the point of saying something, when they passed an open door. Hillman had already seen the occupant, chugging on a cigarette as though his life depended on it. Swanson looked up, and for a moment the two men locked stares. The desk sergeant and DC Brown observed as Swanson, the breath appearing to be temporarily trapped inside his smoky lungs, nodded and weakly said, 'Hi.'

But Hillman didn't return the acknowledgement, and turned away abruptly.

'I think we can use this room,' said Brown, pointing toward another open door further down. He let Hillman turn the corner into the room before shouting, 'Oops, we *are* busy this evening. Sorry about that.'

Dammers turned to see Martin Hillman standing in the doorway. He couldn't help but betray recognition, though he managed not to speak. Hillman turned to his brief, who in turn addressed the two police officers. 'I take it you have a room that is not already occupied?'

Hillman was finally shown to an unoccupied interview room and told that the interviewing officers would be along soon. DC Brown waited in the corridor while the desk sergeant went to inform Tyler of the juxtaposition.

Almost immediately Tyler arrived apologising profusely for the inconvenience, and asking if they would mind returning back to the original interview room as the problem with the lights had now been rectified.

He noted that Hillman looked less controlled now, more distracted, as though all of his powers of concentration were being eaten up trying to mind-read the situation and its possible implications.

Hillman walked back up the corridor, in the company of his choosing, with Tyler right behind him. Martin Hillman scarcely turned his head as he passed the two open doors, but Tyler looked in through both portals and saw a deepening fear resident in each.

With Hillman back in the original interview room, Tyler again apologised for the inconvenience, and asked if they would like drinks. While this was being organised he said to Mills, 'I think Dammers and Swanson have come up to the boil. Let's boogie.'

***

The interview had moved on to formal, and Swanson was told that, of course, he was at liberty to wait for his solicitor or be provided with an alternative, though by the look of things he was going to have to be patient. Swanson's nerves were ragged enough. He wanted to get this over with.

'So, Mr Swanson, as you can see we have practically the full set. Douglas Marley is too ill to join us, but we have a statement from him. Now, I want to know who approached who about keeping quiet about the circumstances of Alan Dale's death. I want to know whether it was Hillman, Jenkins or Dammers who actually killed Alan Dale. And I want to know who killed and/or arranged the killing of Steven Jenkins.'

Tyler addressed the shattered wreck before him, observed Mills, with controlled incandescence. And there was no doubt about it: Swanson was ready to sell his soul and anything else required to make this nightmare end.

Swanson spoke. 'Dammers came to see me. I told you that. He was talking about what had happened all those years ago, down by the park. He said that the police would be nosing around again, asking questions. He said that they'd already been to the school and were trying to talk to Howard Wood. But if we kept our cool, nothing would happen.'

Swanson tried to light another cigarette, but his hands were shaking too badly and he gave it up.

Mills said, 'Finish telling us what you have to tell us, and I'll light one for you.'

Swanson went on. 'He said that he'd spoken to all of the others from that day, and that everyone was going to play ball. I asked him if he was sure about that and I could tell he was holding something back. I've been doing my job a long time, and I can tell when somebody's being straight. I think he knew that he had to tell me, or else it was just creating another possible problem.'

'So, what did he tell you?' asked Tyler, slowly, calmly, betraying nothing of the furious energy building inside. Mills was sensing it, though, nonetheless.

'He told me that Jenkins was a problem. That he was bottling out, but that it could be taken care of.'

'Did he explain what he meant by that?'

Swanson reached for his cigarette packet, put it back down. 'He didn't explain and I didn't ask.'

'But you had an idea that something might happen to Steven Jenkins?'

'Yes. I didn't think they'd kill him. I thought more of a warning or something.'

'They? You said *they*, Mr Swanson?'

'Did I?'

'What was Martin Hillman's part in this?'

'I don't know. When Dammers was telling me about the others, he never mentioned Hillman.'

'Why is everybody so afraid of Martin Hillman?' asked Tyler.

'I don't know.'

'And Douglas Marley? Was he a problem?'

'How do you mean?'

'Martin Hillman made a special trip over to visit Marley. Did you know that?'

Swanson started to sob.

Tyler let him.

Then he repeated the question.

'I knew that Marley had a lot of problems – I knew that through my job. Dammers asked me if I'd had any contact with Marley, which I hadn't. He wanted to know how the land lay with him.'

'What do you mean by that, Mr Swanson?'

'Dammers said that when he visited Marley, he had gone along with what was said. But he had the feeling that Marley couldn't be trusted. He said something about needing a second opinion.'

'And you thought that might mean Hillman?'

'I don't know anything about Hillman.'

'Who killed Steven Jenkins?'

Mills took out a cigarette out of the carton on the table, placed it between Swanson's dry lips, and lit it. 'Nearly over now,' he said.

Tyler asked, 'Do you think Martin Hillman was in any way responsible for the murder of Steven Jenkins?'

Swanson was shaking and crying. Taking a heavy pull on his cigarette he said, 'Hillman never got his hands dirty.'

CHAPTER THIRTY

'Mr Dammers, why did you visit Steven Jenkins?'

'I never visited him.'

'Arranged to meet him, then?'

Dammers didn't answer.

'You were doing the rounds, weren't you? You had a call from Martin Hillman, and he wanted you to look up some old school *chums* on his behalf. Phillip Swanson, Douglas Marley, Steven Jenkins, and even your old teacher Mr Wood. Wood and Swanson were solid enough, so you believed. *But Douglas Marley …*'

Tyler made the motion of a boat crossing a stormy sea. 'A bit rocky, but nothing that a pep talk from a real master couldn't put right, eh? Jenkins, on the other hand – he was always the bolshie one, wasn't he? Hated authority; hated being told what to do. Had kept his nose clean for quite some time, working here and there for whoever would take him on. Usually falling out with his employer, sooner or later – the nature of the beast, you might say.'

The solicitor asked if Tyler intended keeping them enthralled with his wild speculations all evening, or if there was a point in sight. Tyler didn't even acknowledge the interruption.

'Have you spoken to Martin Hillman during the last week or so?'

'No.'

'Have you had any recent contact with Steven Jenkins?'

'No.'

'With Douglas Marley?'

'No.'

'With Phillip Swanson?'

'No.'

'With Howard Wood.'

'No.'

'At least two of them say that you did.'

'I didn't.'

'Did you assault Alan Dale?'

Dammers laughed. 'I already told you: that was Jenkins.'

'When you left Alan Dale for dead?'

'Detective Chief Inspector!'

Tyler nodded toward the brief. Were they programmed to continually remind a detective of his rank, he wondered.

'When you … *left Alan Dale*, you say that a girl was coming up the hill. Do you know who this girl was?'

'I don't know. But she seemed familiar. I'd seen her around.'

'Earlier you intimated that she may have been Alan Dale's sister.'

Dammers shrugged. 'I heard that he had a sister.'

'How? From whom? And when?'

Dammers seemed flustered for a moment and Tyler feasted on it. It was one thing throwing out neatly barbed accusations, quite another to find your arrogant façade pricked by them.

'She found him alive?' asked Tyler.

'He was alive when we left; we hadn't really hurt him that much.'

'A broken cheek bone? A savage beating? Your work as a probation officer must be quite interesting.'

'Really, I must object. And as you clearly have no evidence at all linking my client to the alleged crimes, I must insist that you conclude this *interview* without delay.'

'Mr Dammers, where were you last Sunday evening and in the early hours of Monday morning?'

Dammers smiled. 'I was at the office and then out for the evening.'

'Working Sundays?'

'Catching up on paperwork. We're very busy, you know.'

'Anybody at the office with you, or do you prefer to work alone?'

'As a matter of fact, a colleague was with me.'

'And do you make a habit of working that late, and at the weekend?'

'Unfortunately, needs must. It's not a nine-to-five job. You must know how it is.'

'And you can supply the name of this colleague, Mr Dammers?'

'Kay Shields.'

'Probation officer?'

'Yes.'

'And where did you go when you left the office?'

'We went for a drink'

'A local pub?'

'Yes, and then on to a club.'

'On a Sunday evening?'

Dammers smiled. 'We're in the twenty-first century now, I believe.'

'You go to a lot of clubs, Mr Dammers?'

'Is this relevant, DCI—'

Tyler held a hand up to the brief, and looked directly at Dammers.

'Occasionally, but I wouldn't say often.'

'Where did you go after you left the club?'

'To my house.'

'Alone?'

Dammers shook his head.

'Is that a 'no', Mr Dammers?'

'Kay was with me.'

'Did she stay the night?'

Dammers looked at his solicitor, who nodded.

'Yes, she did.'

'And she would be willing to make a statement to that effect?'

'You'd have to ask her yourself,' said Dammers.

Tyler wrapped up the interview amid threats of a serious complaint.

Along the corridor, he leaned with his back against the wall. Mills said, 'Did I miss something in there, sir, or are things as bad as they look?'

'I thought the musical chairs went a treat. So, it hasn't been a complete washout.'

The two officers looked at each other before breaking into grins.

'So, what now, sir?'

'We check out Kay Shields, but I'll guarantee her alibi's as rock solid as Hillman's. You get the picture, don't you?'

'Pretty much.'

'Go on then. Let's see if it makes any more sense coming out of your head than it does running around in mine.'

Mills took a moment to collect his thoughts. 'Well, I think it's like this: Dammers met with Marley but couldn't be sure how trustworthy Marley was. He may have met with Jenkins too. Hillman also meets with Marley and possibly with Jenkins. He decides Marley's okay, but can't trust Jenkins. The hits had been provisionally arranged, but two would look *too* suspicious, and so he took a chance on Marley but couldn't risk Jenkins. Both Hillman and Dammers already have their alibis set up corresponding with the provisional hit.'

Tyler thought for a moment. 'Any money that Kay Shields is a wet-behind-the-ears type eager to impress her supervisor with some serious overtime, not to mention— no, I don't need to go there. Dammers would have set her up neatly, I'm sure of that. Hillman has his own alibi. It stinks of contrivance, of course.'

'Do you think Hillman arranged the hit?'

'He could have farmed it out. Paul Dammers, by my reckoning, would have the contacts. But I bet it comes down to Hillman's money. Depends on how far you take the idea of not getting your hands dirty.'

Brown came over with the message that Berkins' car had arrived outside.

'It's now or never time again,' said Tyler. 'Everything we have adds up to nothing. I don't know about you, but personally I would rather be hanged for a sheep than a rat.'

With a look of confused foreboding, Mills followed the DCI back towards the interview rooms.

***

Hillman's brief made a lot of noises about complaints, and when he'd finished Tyler started in with another terse evocation of a June late-afternoon thirty years ago.

'Do you recall that afternoon, Mr Hillman?'

Hillman sighed, heavily and with obvious theatricality. 'As I might already have mentioned, I occasionally went down to the park. I did so on the occasions that you have specified. The weather was very pleasant.'

'Were you involved in beating Alan Dale?'

'I was not.'

'Paul Dammers, Phillip Swanson, Douglas Marley – you remember them, Mr Hillman?'

'Vaguely. Two of them were in my class at school. I kept myself to myself in those days, and I certainly did not spend my free time tormenting the likes of Alan Dale.'

'I have been speaking to Paul Dammers and Phillip Swanson this evening, Mr Hillman. They both say that you were there on the afternoon in question.'

'I was. On both occasions, I've already told you that.'

'Earlier you said that there was something going on and that you were 'naturally inquisitive'. You never actually stated what that was.'

'There was a game in the park, as I recall.'

'And that would have interested you?'

'Perhaps it was the good weather. The approach of the school holidays, maybe. I remember being in a buoyant mood. I think the game was cancelled and re-arranged on the later evening.'

'Mr Dammers and Mr Swanson recall that you were with the Dale boy, taking him down The Stumps.'

'Then they have obviously been mistaken.'

'How could that be?'

'The passage of time, perhaps? How should I know?'

'Douglas Marley also remembers you being present.'

'Then he's mistaken, too.'

Tyler paused for a moment. Hillman appeared to be on confident form as usual. It was time to see how solid that wall of confidence was.

'DS Mills spoke to you at your home – about being punished by Mr Wise, along with Steven Jenkins, for an incident at school involving Alan Dale.'

Hillman said, 'I have already stated that I was never punished for anything.'

'Do you realise, Mr Hillman, that we have documentary evidence of that punishment taking place?'

Hillman looked hard at Tyler, but remained silent.

'Wise documented all incidents in a book kept in his office. According to an entry made in that book, by Mr Wise, you and Jenkins were physically chastised.'

'Then there must be some mistake. He clearly wrote down the wrong name.'

The confident swagger was still there, but the eyes betrayed a trace of uncertainty.

'When did you last have contact with Steven Jenkins?'

'I haven't seen him in thirty years.'

'What about Phillip Swanson, Douglas Marley, Paul Dammers?'

'I saw two of them a few minutes ago.'

Mills watched the smugness glow across Hillman's face.

'And before then?' said Tyler, maintaining his calm.

'Again, it must be thirty years.'

'And when were you last in Stoke-on-Trent?'

'Oh, quite a while ago I should think.'

'Not within the last week, then?'

'No.'

'Are you quite sure about that, Mr Hillman?'

'Quite sure. I have nothing here apart from the grave of my mother.' His face quickly assumed the gravity of pathos. 'I must confess, with the somewhat busy life that I lead these days, I have sadly neglected my duties there.'

Mills could certainly see a rosy career as a politician stretching out before Martin Hillman.

'Once this business is over, I will make it my priority to visit Mum's grave. I take it I will still be welcome?' he added with a sneer.

Mills eyed the DCI, who was managing not to respond to the provocation. The manipulative audacity of the man deserved a firm kick in the guts, thought Mills.

Tyler delivered it.

'You were in the city a few days ago, Mr Hillman.'

The solicitor pointed out that if the DCI intended calling his client a liar, he had better have some evidence to back up the allegation.

'You came to see Douglas Marley. To make sure Marley kept his mouth closed when the police started making enquiries about Alan Dale.'

Hillman eyeballed Tyler. 'And did the same people tell you that who remembered me 'tormenting' Alan Dale? There seems to be a lot of hearsay doing the rounds, for some reason, though not a lot of substance.'

Tyler asked Mills for the envelope. Mills passed it on as Tyler told the blind tape machine what was happening. Then he removed the still images, and looked at Hillman. He could see tiny beads of perspiration forming on the politician's brow.

'Bit of a backwater, Stoke, wouldn't you say?' said Tyler. 'According to some.'

Hillman said nothing.

'Well, times appear to be changing. A Cultural Quarter, an Electoral Mayoral system – even healthy options as toppings on the traditional oatcake. Isn't that true, DS Mills?'

Mills confirmed that there was no deceit in the statement.

Tyler let the connotations reverberate around the 'oatcake' reference.

'Yes, your little alibi meeting – and didn't somebody at the meeting refer to your trip to Stoke to buy oatcakes?'

'Really, DCI Tyler. Are you conducting a serious investigation here or is this some Famous Five adventure?'

A glare from Tyler indicated that the brief wasn't being as witty as he imagined.

Hillman clearly remembered.

He looked as though he was frantically trying to weigh up the damage. But all the time his eyes never left the back of the cards that Tyler was holding.

The DCI placed three images on the desk in front of Hillman.

'And now the city even has CCTV, and what's more, loaded and operational. You take a good photograph, Mr Hillman. I'm sure it will hold you in good stead for your future career.'

He turned the stills around so that Hillman could take a good look.

Each of the three images was clear, and unmistakable: Hillman and Marley, occupying the same bench in the churchyard.

'You appear quite engrossed in this one,' said Tyler, tapping the middle still. 'Agitated, one might even say … threatening.'

Tyler sat back. 'Dated, naturally. And the ones of you and Jenkins ought to be with us shortly. I'm told they're equally impressive.'

Hillman's brief asked for a few minutes to speak to his client in private. Tyler and Mills left the room and instantly the desk sergeant descended.

'The chief wants to speak to you, sir. *Urgently.*'

***

The moustache appeared formidable, fronting as it did a face burning with stress and rage. 'It seems that I arrived a little too late,' spat Berkins.

'Sir?' said Tyler.

'I was in two minds to come into that room and terminate the interview before any more damage was done. This farce has to stop while we still have a police station.'

Tyler told the senior man about developments.

'Hillman's sweating buckets in there. He's lied and he's got to come up with something fast. They'll be limiting the damage, and whilst I'm not exactly expecting a full confession, at least regarding the murder of Steven Jenkins, this could be the start of the entire filthy web untangling.'

Berkins was looking far from convinced.

'Jim,' he said. 'There's something you're not telling me. In fact, there'd better be.'

Julie Hammond hadn't come clean yet, but Tyler was fairly certain that he knew where the missing pieces of the puzzle were hidden alright.

Berkins didn't need telling how poor cross-border communication could be, and he didn't need it spelling out about the risks involved in undercover operations. If this wasn't played right, Hillman was going to wriggle out through the holes, and everything Hammond had presumably worked for could end up being compromised too.

Berkins wasn't the first senior officer that Tyler had upset in recent times and he likely wouldn't be the last. As for Hammond – he was saving her for another day.

***

Tyler bolted down a mug of tea so fast it gave him heartburn. Mills asked how he had gone on with Berkins.

'He's not quite hit the ejector seat, but we're coming in on a wing and a prayer.'

'Bit of a risk – that bluff about the pictures of Hillman and Jenkins?'

Tyler smiled. 'You don't approve?'

'Will Berkins, though?'

'Let's just say that the subject of CCTV is dear to his heart. He stuck his neck out to get that equipment into the town centres, and he stuck it out even further to make use of *covert* recording equipment in Stoke churchyard.'

'Sounds like he's gone up in your estimation.'

'The man's an archangel, always said it. Actually, the truth is, there's a lot worse than Berkins out there. The man goes to church. Deterring the bastards desecrating those graves isn't enough for him though. He wants to catch them *bone-handed.*'

'Marley thought the churchyard was a safe place because of the cameras,' said Mills.

'And Hillman didn't think Stoke would pay to have them operational. Which is why Hillman thought the churchyard was as good a place as any to meet Marley when he took his evening stroll into town. But then Marley was a regular there, and Hillman didn't want to risk anyone seeing the two of them together, and so they moved on to the less well-frequented part.'

'What does Berkins want us to do with Hillman?'

Tyler shrugged. 'I wasn't kidding about being on a wing and a prayer. Having said that, forget what I said about ejector seats. If we end up making him look stupid he's going to want to see us hitting the ground in a ball of flame. But he won't be complaining if we manage to pull it off. If we nail this piece of shit.'

'That's very reassuring, sir.'

***

Hillman had regained his composure to an extent that surprised both detectives. Either the man was a true Houdini, or else chief of chiefs, the Almighty Charles Dawkins himself had finally left the golf course and was busily re-ordering the rules on which the world turned.

Hillman's brief spoke first.

'My client wishes to change some of the details of his previous statement.'

Hillman was back on. Apparently he had, after all, popped over to see Marley – and, yes, Jenkins too.

Mills could hear Tyler's heartbeat even above the sound of his own.

'I received a telephone call from Steven Jenkins. I have no idea how he tracked down my number, except that I am a reasonably high-profile character these days and I know a lot of people.

'Jenkins was worried that the discovery of the corpse of Alan Dale would bring the police to his door. He sounded frightened and he pleaded with me to meet him. I did not want him coming to my house as I was naturally worried about a man I hadn't seen for thirty years suddenly finding out where I live. So, I agreed to meet him in a neutral location – but you know all about that.'

Tyler was itching to know where. In what fantasy land the imaginary second set of covert CCTV cameras was 'located'.

'Why didn't you alert the police?' asked Tyler. 'Jenkins was acting very suspiciously wouldn't you say?'

'I can see all that now. But, to be honest, the man sounded desperate.'

'What did Jenkins want?'

'He remembered me from school. Thought that I was somebody he could trust to give him some advice. He said that he had bullied Alan Dale in the past, but insisted that he didn't kill him or anything like that. He wanted me to act as a character witness should the police visit him and take matters further.'

'And why did you visit Douglas Marley?'

'Jenkins asked me to. He thought that Mr Marley might, for some reason, believe it had been Steven who was responsible for the boy's death. He wanted me to talk to Douglas Marley. He said that I was obviously a good communicator, which I took as a compliment, of course. I wanted to be helpful. That is my nature. As it turns out, perhaps I have been a little naive. We must all learn our lessons in life. Personally, I never stop learning.'

Tyler was about to challenge the whole ridiculous fabrication, when he recognised from the light in Hillman's eye that the coup de grace was about to be delivered.

'He also wanted me to ask Mr Marley about the girl.'

Tyler glanced at Mills. The two detectives, in that brief exchange, gave Hillman too much, and they knew it.

'Girl?' said Tyler.

'Jenkins told me that he had been mucking about down by the park. That Marley had been with him. They were teasing the boy—'

'*Teasing?*' said Tyler.

'His words, not mine. I wasn't there, after all. Jenkins said that the boy – this Alan Dale – started crying, and so they left him alone at that point. But they saw a girl coming up the hill.'

'The Stumps?'

'I think that's what they call it, yes.'

'Jenkins didn't say who this girl was?' asked Tyler, his tone hard and sardonic.

Hillman ignored the tone. 'He didn't say. But he wanted me to ask Marley about her.'

'Mr Hillman, if any of this is true, why did you not come forward before now? Why did you not impart this information to DS Mills when he interviewed you previously?'

Hillman shook his head, the weight of remorse finely judged and immaculately executed. Here, thought Tyler, sat a man who could stand in front of a mirror and believe that he looked upon a future leader of nations.

'I ... really don't know. I was trying to make sense of the business, and at the same time I was suspicious.'

'Suspicious?'

'Of Mr Jenkins' real motive. Marley's too, for that matter. You see, I wondered—'

Hillman broke off.

'Mr Hillman?' said Tyler.

'You may find this somewhat fanciful,' said Hillman.

'Try me,' said Tyler. 'You never know.'

'Well, the truth is – I wondered if they were not trying some implausible plot to, well, to blackmail me.'

Blackmail? Thought Tyler. *A neat twist.*

Hillman, who may have been blackmailing Howard Wood thirty years ago about his lunchtime drinking – turning the thing inside out and upside down. He had to hand it to the smug bastard, it was rich work.

But why was Hillman even raising the subject of blackmail?

There was something else going on here, thought Tyler. There was another piece of the puzzle, and Hillman was hedging his bets. Preparing for something?

'Yet you still chose not to report any of this?' said Tyler.

'I have no doubt that I would have done, of course. But then I heard the news that Steven Jenkins had been murdered, and to be honest, I didn't know what to think about any of it. I still don't, if the truth be known.'

If the truth be known.

It took a man like Hillman to deliver a line like that, in this situation, without batting an eye.

Tyler knew, beyond doubt, that this man before him was a liar. Hillman had been there on both days in June, 1972, down by the park, tormenting Alan Dale, and likely instigating it. Arranging the killing of Steven Jenkins to keep his mouth shut, even throwing in a bag of cocaine for good measure.

Jenkins had been a chancer, his fingers in this and that over the years – but dying over a drugs deal? Tyler didn't think so. He preferred the sound of blackmail, Jenkins playing the angles; a dying man having one parting shot at the prize.

Intimidation to quieten Marley, Swanson and possibly Howard Wood too. Conspiracy with Dammers to keep the secret of what had happened to Alan Dale all those years ago, and Jenkins playing his own game.

It stacked up, and Tyler's mind hurtled around the possibilities left to him. He could feel the nose of the plane already tilting towards the ground, and he glimpsed the hard earth coming up to meet him.

If Dammers cracked, the whole thing would unravel and Hillman would be stuffed, regardless of his cleverness, his ruthlessness, his contacts and his empire. Dammers was a paler, slighter version of the same creature and, above all, he was afraid of Martin Hillman.

Paul Dammers was the type to sell his own mother's skin and bones if there was something to be made from the sale; but he would put his head beneath the blade before he would betray the real monster.

There was no question left to ask in the presence of this *thing*. Hillman had destroyed lives and would doubtless go on doing so all the way to the top of the hill. And as it stood, there was nothing that could be done to stop him.

Tyler could have walked out of that interview room and kept on walking; but there was one question left to ask. He felt his stomach tighten and turn.

'You asked Douglas Marley about this "girl"?' said Tyler.

Victory was on Hillman's face now. It was bursting out like a sunrise.

'Naturally I asked him. That's partly why I went to see him, like I said.'

Hillman was going to make the detective work all the way to the finishing line.

'And what did he tell you, Mr Hillman?'

'He said that she was someone he had seen before.'

'Did he know her name?'

Hillman was loving it.

'If I remember correctly now ...'

Tyler's hands were curled tightly into fists – fists that he longed to smash into the centre of that arrogant facade, and give Hillman a taste, a mere taste of what he, one way or another, had given Alan Dale.

Through clenched teeth, glancing first at DS Mills, who was looking tense enough to be having precisely the same thoughts, Tyler spat out the question. '*Do you know the name of the girl?*'

'Got it,' said Hillman, grinning around the room. 'Dale.'

Tyler was falling towards the looming Earth.

Hillman and Dammers had the same ace card.

'Dale?' said Tyler, and the question sounded lame even to him.

'Marley said he thought the girl was the boy's sister.'

For an instant the inevitability made Tyler want to laugh.

CHAPTER THIRTY-ONE

Sheila Dale answered the door and the two detectives followed her into the now familiar front room. She didn't offer to make a drink and for once it was the furthest thing from Tyler's mind.

'Miss Dale,' he said. 'Do you want to tell me exactly what happened on the day your brother died?'

She sat down. Tyler and Mills sat opposite.

And then she began.

On Friday, June 16, 1972, the day Alan died, she had gone to the market in Stoke to buy fresh meat. She usually went on a Saturday morning, more often than not the two of them together. But on that day she had broken with routine.

'The truth is,' she said, 'I had no reason to go to market that day. I can't explain why I went. The day before, I had followed Alan home from school. After what had happened to him at the hands of those … I followed him home.

'Nobody bothered him that day. He went straight home. But I think he had a feeling. My brother was not stupid. He was angry with me, saying that he didn't need his big sister walking him home, and that I would only make things worse for him. He made me promise that I would never do it again. And I promised.'

She broke off, the pain of that promise as raw as it had been all those years ago.

'He said that they would leave him alone now; that they'd had their fun. He made me believe that for his sake, but I doubt that he believed it himself.'

'So, what happened on that Friday?' asked Tyler. 'What happened on the day that Alan went missing?' He cleared his throat unnecessarily. 'On the day your brother died.'

'Around about the time that school finished, I walked down to the market.'

'Which route did you take?' asked Mills.

'I went down Honeydew Bank and into Stoke. While the building work was underway we avoided The Stumps. I told myself that the reason I was going to market on Friday was so I could show Alan that I wasn't following him. That if I came back with the meat, he would know I'd been somewhere else. Do you understand that? I had to let Alan know that he could trust me. I didn't want to be responsible for adding to his burden.'

'But you didn't return the same way, did you?' said Tyler. 'Instead of returning up Honeydew Bank, you went towards the bottom of The Stumps.'

Dale nodded.

'Why did you do that, Miss Dale?'

She closed her eyes for a few moments. The two detectives watched her, each trying to imagine what she was seeing in the wretched darkness.

'When I left the market, I felt compelled to go to that place.'

'Place?' asked Tyler, knowing.

'The place they took him, two days earlier. Ever since I had seen those marks on Alan, and he told me what they had done, I couldn't get the images out of my head. I still can't.'

'Miss Dale, I know this is difficult, but I need you to tell me what you saw next. Please, take your time.'

Tyler had, many times, recited the cliché that the English language is the most expressive of all languages. At that moment he cursed its inadequacies, along with his own.

'As soon as I reached that place, the bottom of The Stumps, I knew why I had gone to the market, the real reason. It wasn't that I wanted to prove something to my brother; it was because I feared for him.'

'Animals like that don't stop. They keep going and if nobody stops them, something has to happen.'

'I was fooling myself, playing games with myself. Nobody else was going to do anything to save my brother.'

Tyler sat silently, alongside Mills, the two of them knowing that there was nothing left to do or say except wait for this woman to tell it in her own way and in her own time.

'I could hear noises as I came to where they had blocked off the path. I knew they were there. Then I heard a shout and I saw them running away. I went under the barrier and when I came to the site it looked deserted.

'But then I heard a sound, a cat or something, I thought. An animal trapped, possibly injured, or dying. I thought of those devils running away and I imagined that they'd been torturing some poor creature.

'And I admit – I was relieved.

'I pictured Alan sitting at home, safe and well, the weekend to look forward to and school almost over. I imagined him one day becoming something in this world. I imagined my brother putting all of his troubles behind him, stronger because of all that he had gone through.

'Alan was a very special person. And for those moments I saw him fulfilling his potential. Becoming the person he was destined to be, and who we would all be so very proud of.

'I thought I would find the injured animal, take it to the vet, and return home with the fresh meat and a tale to tell. Over tea I could tell Alan and Mum and Dad about the poor little thing that I had saved, and we would do something special together that weekend. Celebrate that school was nearly over for another year, and that maybe things were set to change.

'And then I saw him. He was lying in the dirt and rubble. I could see that his face was bleeding. He was a mass of bruises and cuts, but his face, his poor face …

'He was crying when I found him, but when he saw me he stopped. Even then he tried to hide it from me – can you believe that? He tried to smile, as though to say, 'Fancy seeing you here and what's that you've got for tea?'

'He saw the anger in my eyes, he must have. I told him that this had gone too far, that he was leaving that school right away. We would tell Mr Wise we'd had enough of his school for bullies and make sure the entire city knew what he was running there and that it wasn't safe for decent children.

'Alan was trying to tell me I had it all wrong. That he had been playing. Fallen over and bashed himself up a bit – that's what he said, exactly how he put it: *bashed himself up a bit*. If you had seen him – nobody should have to endure that. Nobody could go on enduring that.

'He picked himself up off the ground and made to dust himself off, like it was nothing that a good wash couldn't put right. He was a brave boy, was my Alan, and nobody bore what he had to. He still wouldn't give in, wouldn't admit what they had done to him … and let us take him away from that place.'

Mills took a long, deep breath.

Tyler asked: 'What happened, Miss Dale?'

The tears were falling, and then they stopped, replaced by a gaze into the distance, where a screen invisible to the two detectives showed the eternal re-run of that horror from which Sheila Dale might never escape until the day they buried her.

'When Alan stood up I saw a glimpse of the future. *Alan's future*. I knew that all my earlier imaginings of him living to survive this; of him becoming a man – something in this awful world – I knew that it was all wishing on stars. That boys like Alan are never allowed to live, to thrive, to become what they have it in them to become. That it would all remain unfulfilled because the only road left for him to walk down was paved with nothing but more pain and suffering.

'I walked towards him, and his smile faded as though he had seen something terrible approaching. I saw the terror in his heart for the first and last time and it was awful, too much for anyone to bear. He took a step back and then, too late, I saw the ditch behind him, the huge trench into which they would pour the foundations of their precious new building.'

The gaze was crumbling, and the catch in the throat announced the storm that was waiting to come down.

'I shouted his name, but he was gone. The scream inside me wouldn't come out, and I stood at the edge, looking down on his broken body. I called his name, but I knew he was gone.'

***

Mills made the drinks while Tyler stayed to try and comfort Sheila Dale; but all he could do was watch impotently as she turned herself on the spit.

As the storm lashed down inside the room, he thought about his own trials. About the ghosts from his past and the fantasies of retribution and justice that had haunted him for as long as he cared to remember.

Never had he come close to witnessing such overwhelming pain and grief, though he had many times looked into the glass and believed that he had seen the real thing.

Mills came back in with the drinks, but the two officers said not a single word, merely looking at each other, listening to the rawness of it, not caring to intrude until the savage ferocity showed signs of subsiding.

Mills made a call, requesting that a couple of local officers be dispatched, as it didn't seem prudent to leave Dale to her own company. While they waited for the back-up, she sipped at the tea that Mills had prepared and insisted she drink, and at last Tyler asked her why she had not reported the events at the time.

'I saw him lying there, still and at peace,' she said. 'And all I felt was relief: simple, selfish relief. I would not have to worry about my brother ever again. His suffering was over, and he was in a better place. I told myself all of those lies until my head was filled with them, and then I crawled back under the barrier and I went home and I said *nothing*.

'Can you believe that?

'I let the hours pass, Mum and Dad going out of their minds – and the longer I left it, the harder it was to break my silence.

'I went to bed and I cried the whole night and every night since. The police came and all I could tell them was that something terrible must have happened because Alan had never done this before, not coming home. I was sure they would find him quickly. The work would start up again, his body would be discovered and they would find out what had happened. Then they'd round them up, destroy their lives the same as they had destroyed Alan's.

'But the days passed and nothing happened. I went down to look. They'd already started on the foundations and I knew Alan would never be found. I knew then that his story would never be told because I hadn't the strength or the courage.

'I could still have come forward, I know that. I was scared for myself. People would think that I had killed him. You're probably thinking the same thing now.

'I thought of what that would do to my parents, and to me. I couldn't bear it. I left them what little hope they had, and did everything to nurture that hope. I tore myself in two trying to believe it myself.

'In my darkest hours, I kept myself sane imagining that in time the truth would come out and that his killers – because they did kill him, one way or another – would be brought to justice. Even more than that, I hoped and I prayed that one day they would wake up knowing what they had done and that the knowledge, the burden of it, might destroy *them*.

'And the years passed … and I think you know the rest.'

'And thirty years on,' said Tyler, as if to himself, 'a boy and his dog opened everything up. The whole rotten can of worms.'

'As soon as I heard about the body being found, I knew I would make my confession at last. That I would finally do what I should have done all those years ago.'

'Yours is not a confession,' said Tyler, glancing at Mills as he said it.

'Oh, but it is. All the people I deceived, all of your time wasted. If I had an ounce of the courage that my brother had, I would have told you everything straight away. I would have come forward the day Alan died – no, none of that would have been necessary. If I had that much courage I would never have let it come to that. I would have done something to protect my brother.'

Mills stretched out a hand and placed it on the woman's arm.

'Alan would have been proud of you,' he said. 'And so would your parents.'

'For keeping silent for thirty years? If there's any justice, I will burn in hell with the rest of them.'

CHAPTER THIRTY-TWO

Chief Superintendent Berkins was not a happy man. He was taking great pains to explain to DCI Tyler why he was not a happy man. Tyler kept his peace, waiting for the nutshell.

'In a nutshell: Martin Hillman is, to use the words of his legal representative, *treated like a common criminal* and yet he still manages to point you in the direction of the person who, to my mind, is clearly culpable. But do you bring Miss Dale in? Or is it tea and sympathy with a couple of PCs from Leek, no doubt making us the laughing stock of that station along with the rest of Staffordshire and I don't know where else.'

Tyler had heard enough. 'I think that Sheila Dale is deserving of nothing more than our sympathy.'

'Detective Chief Inspector Tyler!'

Tyler wanted to ask Berkins if he was training to be a solicitor, because it didn't take a detective to work out that shouting 'Detective Chief Inspector' practically every time he opened his mouth was the first sign.

'Fact: according to Miss Dale, she was the only person present at the scene when her brother died. Is it not at least a possibility that she killed him?'

Tyler was about to interrupt.

'Let me finish,' said Berkins. 'Fact: when her brother's body was found – and she clearly never expected it to be – she came forward, but not before. Thirty years she has sat on the knowledge of what happened to her brother – thirty years! And when she does come forward, it is to provide us with the map of a wild goose chase, no doubt hoping that something might turn up to let her off the hook. When it doesn't, she tries Plan B: a confession that falls short of actually confessing that she killed her brother.'

Berkins sighed heavily. 'Come on, Jim. You've been in the job long enough.'

'I don't buy it.'

'That doesn't stop it being a possibility that has to be seriously considered, though, does it. When Alan Dale died, she was *there*. The two of them, brother and sister. No-one else. Her word that he fell and wasn't pushed – not to mention the fact that she left him there to rot.'

'You've allowed feelings to intrude, Jim, and I believe that has impeded your judgement.'

'Would we be having this conversation if Hillman wasn't one of the names that came up?'

The chief superintendent, like many in his position, could do a good line in looks that might break the balls of a lion. Unleashing a textbook example, he said, 'Would you like to reconsider that question – while you still have the chance?'

Tyler apologised, and his apology was accepted, not in words, but with a gratuitous twiddle of both ends of the moustache.

'And for the record, Jim, I do not give a fig for MPs or aspiring MPs. If they break the law, I want them brought to justice. By the same token, neither do I care for the emotional outpourings of 'so-called victims' looking for a way out at somebody else's expense, do you understand me?'

'Perfectly.'

'Dale comes in: Perverting the course of justice and the murder of Alan Dale.'

Treading the finest of lines, Tyler said, 'You don't think that she had a part to play in the death of Steven Jenkins, *sir*?'

'I think we will leave it there for now, DCI Tyler.'

'Are you suggesting,' said Tyler, 'that the death of Steven Jenkins is unrelated?'

'We don't know who killed Jenkins. But, it seems clear to me, that we have a good idea who killed Alan Dale. The problem appears to lie in convincing the detectives.'

***

When Tyler returned to the CID office he found Mills looking ready to burst. He was holding a letter. Tyler read it, all the time his hands shaking. Neither detective said anything. Then Tyler said: 'Scotland! At least that explains the second-class stamp.'

Mills then told him that the 'oatcake woman' was urgently awaiting his call. Tyler began to laugh, and he went on laughing until a cascade of tears was washing down his face. 'The time for oatcakes is past,' he said, somewhat enigmatically.

But he made the call anyway. He had to thank somebody for something.

***

Julie Hammond sat opposite Tyler in the third-floor office at Hanley Police Station. She'd driven over on business and called Mills on spec. Was it a good time to call in and have that chat?

'You might want to put it like that,' Mills had told her.

Tyler wondered if he had ever sat in the presence of so much determination, so much energy. She looked to be in her mid-thirties, with a personable smile that seemed to him to belie a rugged thirst for justice.

'So, do you mind telling me,' said Tyler, 'who you are, exactly?'

The woman grinned, and there was fire in those eyes. 'DS Hammond, Derbyshire CID. But tell another living soul what I'm about to tell you – and I will have to kill you.'

DS Hammond had been keeping a keen eye on Martin Hillman for some time. Suspicions regarding corruption in office, illegitimate business dealings, allegations of money laundering and possible links with a significant drugs syndicate.

Working undercover, she had used an operative to attend one of Hillman's late-night meetings on a previous occasion. The same night, it turned out, that a business rival had been assassinated in what had been assumed to be a drive-by shooting over drug territory.

And so, when Hillman had been planning another apparently less-than-urgent meeting at an ungodly hour, she had made it her business to be there in person, and to find out just how important the meeting really was.

She blew it with the oatcake business and realised that she would never be trusted to move into the inner sanctum. Hillman knew that everyone present at that meeting would have been interviewed by police, and so it hadn't necessarily put Hammond at risk. But it had made him cagey.

Hearing about the Jenkins murder in Stoke-on-Trent, bells had been ringing over Derbyshire. There was a Hillman–Dammers connection already documented and it went way back. Dammers was even living in the old Hillman house.

Tyler listened, and then he exploded.

He was investigating one and possibly two murders and there was intelligence out there and so no, frankly, he didn't accept all of that cop-undercover-cloak-and-dagger bollocks.

Julie Hammond let him have his say.

And then she accepted his apology.

The investigation into Hillman was ongoing. The man was dangerous and lives were still at risk. Undercover officers sometimes died in the course of their duties.

Tyler re-assured her that nothing had been said, and that nothing would be said, that might in any way compromise her work or that of her team. 'Will you get him – in the end?' he asked.

'We'll do our best. We'll cause him some damage, something beyond inconvenience, I should think. But more than that, who can say?'

Hammond asked how things were going Tyler's end, and he smiled, thinking about the letter. 'Actually,' he said, 'we're about to bring him back in.'

CHAPTER THIRTY-THREE

Hillman quoted chapter and verse all the way from Derby, but when he walked into the interview room at Hanley Police Station and saw the look on the faces of DCI Tyler and DS Mills, the silence fell like a guillotine blade.

Tyler didn't show the letter straight away. There was a tangle of meetings and alibis to wade through first, to get the juices flowing.

Hillman's solicitor, on serious time now, was earning every penny of it. Blocking this, questioning that; threats of bringing the department to its knees for the disgraceful way it was treating his client.

Tyler took his time constructing the scene:

Dammers had made contact with Jenkins after the discovery of the body of Alan Dale. On the face of it, he was making sure that everybody had their story straight when the police came knocking. And Jenkins had his story straight, and there was no question about where that story was going to get Martin Hillman.

Hillman was leaning forward. The lack of speculation, the firm certainty in Tyler's tone, was something he had not encountered before, and he didn't like it.

'He told Paul Dammers that as you had once been well accustomed to blackmail – meaning that you had used the noble art on your teacher, Howard Wood – you would understand what was being offered.'

The solicitor objected, but this time it was Hillman who shut him up.

'What are you talking about?'

Tyler went on. 'Jenkins told Dammers that he wanted to meet with you to discuss a proposition. A once-in-a-lifetime *business deal.*'

The phrase, clearly a quotation, stung Hillman, and he flinched but said nothing.

'You met him at an arranged location and he showed you a letter he'd written.'

The shock registered as Hillman tightened, the colour draining from his face.

'The letter was long and detailed. It started off with some background: about an allegation made against you at River Trent High that resulted in the expulsion of the boy who had made the allegation. And how you blackmailed Howard Wood and used him to turn the allegation around.

'The letter moved on to an account of what happened on Wednesday, June 14, 1972, when five boys took Alan Dale down The Stumps. The letter suggests it was your idea, Mr Hillman. That it was in fact retribution for being punished, along with Jenkins, for an incident involving Alan Dale.'

Tyler watched the fear and uncertainty moving around on Hillman's face.

But still, thought Tyler: *it wasn't running as deep as it ought to.*

'Jenkins referred to you as a sadist. For the others, it was merely 'fun', but you *really* enjoyed it. *You* beat Alan Dale that day, didn't you? You took a stick from the allotments and you beat him without mercy. You took Howard Wood at his word and you branded that boy with the stripes of Stoke City, reminding him while you did it that '*Red is the colour*'. Though it had nothing to do with football or Stoke City for you, did it, Mr Hillman?'

Hillman was as pale and silent as a corpse.

And yet.

'Jenkins goes on to recount how, two days later, three of you decided to have some more *fun*. The others were bored with it, but you couldn't let it go. You wanted your pound of flesh – you wanted blood for what had been done to you by Wise. And while Alan Dale was begging you to stop, you called on Steven Jenkins, like he was your *hired assassin*, to shut Dale up. And he did, punching him in the face while you stood there and laughed.

'But then someone disturbed the party. Alan's sister. You fled, but Steven Jenkins was curious to see what would happen next, while you and Paul Dammers were busy getting as far away from the scene as possible – a trait that you have gone on to develop into something of an art.'

Hillman's solicitor objected, Tyler acknowledging the objection with a scowl, before continuing.

'From the cover of the park bushes, Jenkins watched Alan Dale fall into the trench. He fell. He was not pushed.'

Hillman, coming slowly back to life, frowned. 'Are you suggesting that, in the end, nobody *actually* killed Alan Dale?'

'And yet,' said Tyler, 'it seems that nobody was more responsible for his death than you.'

The solicitor earned some more of his fee with another loud objection.

'I imagine,' said Tyler, 'that Howard Wood will admit to being the victim of blackmail all those years ago, when he is shown this letter.'

Tyler placed the letter down on the table. 'Skeletons in the cupboard, Mr Hillman. Not what the electorate want to hear, is it?'

Hillman's eyes fixed on the letter.

'So, Jenkins decided to blackmail you. He had nothing to fear from the revelations penned in his own hand. Jenkins did occasional, casual, labouring work. Being involved in a bullying episode thirty years ago, regardless of whether it ended in the tragic death of an innocent boy, would hardly make much difference to his career prospects. But it certainly would to yours.'

Tyler read from the penultimate page: '*I was always impressed with the way you had the balls to blackmail your own teacher and get away with it. It made me think that maybe one day I might try it myself. When the police came to the school I even thought about having a go at blackmailing the kid's sister, leaving like she did and him not getting out of that hole.*'

'*I even went and looked and he was dead. I thought she'd gone to get help but then when we found out he was reported missing I*' thought, 'Steven, there's some money to be made here.' Except I didn't have the confidence you had. I approached her a couple of times and she told me to go to the police if I had something to say. You could have persuaded her though, I'm sure of it. Surprised you didn't think about it to be honest. Maybe you did.

'Over the years it would occur to me every now and again. Find out where she was living and turn up and get a few quid out of it. But something else always came up and I never got round to it. Story of my life.

'But now I finally got around to making a quid or two out of the business. You doing so well and all. I don't know that I would have thought about it but for Dammers coming around and playing it heavy. You want to get yourself some decent heavies. Like me heh heh!!!'

Tyler turned over the final page.

'You can keep this copy for old times' sake. Everybody likes a bit of nostalgia. And if you ever get fed up paying out, look at it, from time to time, to remind you of its value. And I'll keep my copy, and I'll do the same.

To old times.

Steven Jenkins, always your friend.

***

'Did he tell you how ill he was?' asked Tyler.

Hillman didn't answer.

'The imminence of death sometimes produces great courage. He had nothing to lose. If you paid up, he could afford to bow out in a blaze of glory. Or maybe he thought you would make it a quicker death for him.'

Hillman looked to the man sitting next to him, and for the moment neither said anything.

'He kept two copies, as it turned out,' said Tyler. 'Because the one assumption that I'm prepared to make is that there was a copy in his flat, and that copy was taken on the night he was killed. The other copy he left with a person he could trust, with instructions where to forward it in the event of his death. He had more faith in the postal service than I do.

'Still, better late than never, wouldn't you say, Mr Hillman?'

Hillman sat for a few moments, staring at the letter. Then he sat back and started to laugh.

'Something funny?' asked Mills.

'Is that all you've got?' said Hillman. 'Is that it?'

'What were you expecting?' asked Mills.

'Well, from the smug look on both of your faces, I was thinking that you might have something resembling evidence.'

He looked to his brief, who nodded, and then he turned back to Tyler. But he let the man he was paying do the talking.

'I will be writing a letter shortly myself, on behalf of my client. Now, if you will excuse us, I believe that we all have work to be getting on with.'

***

Chief Superintendent Berkins wanted a word. The word turned in to many words, and they came out like gunfire.

When he'd finished he waited for Tyler to speak.

'Everyone is scared of Hillman.'

'Is that so?' said Berkins. 'Based on what?'

Tyler sighed. He was sick of talking about it. What was the point? When it came down to it Berkins was right. There was no point to argue. An abundance of conjecture and speculation amidst certainties in his own mind that could not be proven – he needed evidence; he needed one of the horses he was backing to come in on the home straight and cross the line.

It was time for action; either to put the cuffs on Hillman or else find a rougher, more elemental kind of justice, if not for Steven Jenkins and everyone else that Hillman had stamped on through the course of his mean life and psychopathic rise to power, then for Alan Dale.

Tyler wanted a drink, and badly. He wanted to start drinking and keep on until he passed out and woke up on another planet, in another lifetime.

'Do we have any idea who forwarded the letter?' asked Berkins.

'I doubt we ever will. Hillman likely suspected the existence of a third copy, but went ahead and arranged the hit anyway, as a lesson and a punishment. Hillman even raised the subject of blackmail himself, but the shock was still there nevertheless, when he actually saw us with the copy. There's a lot of dirt in that letter. It raises a lot of questions. It doesn't hang him but he could do without it.'

'It doesn't *prove* anything,' said Berkins.

'Hillman was responsible for the murder of Steven Jenkins.'

'I don't need – I shouldn't need – to tell you, the coinage we deal in, that the courts deal in, is *evidence*. And anyway, why would Jenkins effectively sign his own death warrant?'

'A posthumous claim to glory, a belated act of heroism, greed, desperation, spite – who knows what Jenkins was thinking?' said Tyler. Then: 'Maybe he wasn't alone in keeping tabs on Hillman.'

'Meaning? There was something else that you were going to tell me, Jim,' said Berkins.

Tyler told the man what he needed to tell him about the undercover operation on Hillman.

'Where does all this leave your investigation, Jim?'

'I think Dammers set up the hit. I intend putting a tail on Dammers.'

'To what end?'

'Dammers can lead us to the hit man, I'm certain of that.'

'I don't know,' said Berkins. After giving the matter some thought, he asked Tyler what he intended doing with Miss Dale, who was already waiting downstairs to be interviewed and formally charged.

Apologise on your behalf? Thought Tyler, but didn't say.

***

As Tyler entered the CID room, he asked Mills, 'How is she? What's she saying?'

'I've never seen anybody so relieved to be brought into a police station. I think if we gave her the option of being hanged here right now she'd take it. She wants to be punished, sir. She's waited all her adult life for it. I think, when we let her go, she's a high suicide risk.'

Mills took his notebook out and showed a page to Tyler. 'What she said earlier.'

A society that creates conditions in which a child can be terrorised daily and nothing is done. A police force who gave up too easily the first time, and who would have done so again but for me. And who am I? Alan deserved better than me.

'I suspect,' said Mills, 'that Berkins might prefer Sheila Dale's summing up not to be made public.'

'To hell with Berkins.'

Mills was right though. There was nothing Dale wanted to hear but the pronouncement of her own death sentence, and not even Chief Superintendent Graham Berkins could organise that.

Tyler sat down opposite the woman and asked Mills to arrange for some tea.

'For what it's worth,' he said, 'many have already found justice, one way or another.' But even as he said the words, he was questioning on what level he believed them.

Dale looked at him, the cynicism etched deeply into her. He told her as much as he could. He told her of two deaths, the ruined careers.

For a long time, she didn't say anything. 'I don't need to know,' she said at last. 'I don't *want* to know. A lot of people are responsible for the death of my brother and maybe no-one more than me. I'm glad people are suffering, but they will never know suffering like Alan did. Those teachers, children, that school, this city – the whole evil nest should burn for what was done. They can rot in hell with the so-called *good people* who did nothing.'

Dale blotted her eyes.

'What they were planning to build in that place – they should scrap it. Do you know what they should do? The one thing that would make this city remember its shame – if it ever wants to be proud again? They should build a monument, like they do to honour the war dead. Remind people that this should never be allowed to happen again.'

The tea arrived but nobody felt like drinking.

CHAPTER THIRTY-FOUR

Tyler spoke again with Julie Hammond. It was clear enough to both of them that the key to nailing Hillman lay in the hit on Jenkins. The previous hit – coinciding with another well-documented, well-attended meeting arranged by Hillman, again a good distance from the scene of the crime – had been linked to the Greater Manchester area. A rival of Hillman had been shot to death. A knife in Hanley and a gun in Salford, but it amounted to the same thing in the end.

Hammond's team were tailing Dammers. Berkins couldn't afford an officer to go on any further wild goose chases, but Tyler and Mills were putting in unofficial overtime to subsidise what Hammond could offer, and between them they'd got Dammers covered around the clock.

They couldn't keep it up much longer. Other cases were flying in thick and fast. Dammers was staying clear of Derby and Hillman wasn't stupid enough to go near Stoke-on-Trent for a good long time. *Hillman's poor mother's grave,* thought Tyler, as he sat parked around the corner from the cul de sac where Dammers lived, and where Hillman and his mother had once lived.

Tyler was about to call it a night. A member of Hammond's team was due to take over. It was midnight when Dammers got into his car, accelerating north along the D-road, towards Junction 16 of the M6.

Following discreetly Tyler wondered if this was a trip to Manchester, but he knew that was too good to be true. Strokes of luck like that didn't fall into your lap that easily.

Still, he played with the fantasy of Dammers leading him straight to a flat in Salford, the man opening the door to Dammers as Tyler turned the lights on full-beam. The two villains throwing their hands into the air, shouting, '*It's a fair cop, Guv. We'll come quietly.*'

Tyler's phone was ringing. It was Hammond.

'You can't sleep either?' she said.

'Afraid not,' said Tyler. 'I never can when I'm tailing low-life around the cities of England.'

'So I understand. Ever heard of Kieran Blake?'

'Should I have?'

'He lives in Salford.'

'And there's a connection to Hillman?'

'It seems so. He's been used as an enforcer before. Well, CID up there are playing a blinder. They've been watching the man for some time. Remember the drive-by shooting over that way? Well, there was another shooting in Rusholme, you probably heard about it. Drugs-related, but not gang-related, the way it was setup to look like, that's the thinking. There's definitely a connection to Hillman, I can smell it. And I'm not the only one. Kieran Blake could be the man.'

'Perhaps I'm on my way to meet him right now.'

'No need. He's just arriving on your patch.'

On cue Tyler saw Dammers fail to take the motorway slip-road, instead circling back in the direction of Stoke. He thought of Berkins, and accusations of goose chases.

'If this Blake is in the vicinity, do you think we should roll out the red-carpet?'

'I don't understand your protocols, but I think it would be rude not to have some kind of a welcoming party. What's happening, Jim?'

'Maybe Dammers realised he'd come out without his wallet.'

'Giving the tail the run-around?'

'I'm hanging back. If there's a tail on Blake I don't want to risk blowing it.'

'There's a tail, alright. They're on him 24/7 and I've never know liaison as good as this.'

'Perhaps we're finally learning to play together nicely,' said Tyler.

'Well, you never know. It would be about time.'

'Let's re-write the book,' said Tyler, letting Dammers' tail-lights grow smaller in the distance.

***

It was a short time later when Tyler's phone rang again.

'Looks like someone's rumbled somebody else. Dammers is back home making himself a milky drink with the kitchen curtains open, while Blake is heading back to Salford. If I were you, Jim, I would call it a night.'

'Damn.'

'Doesn't bode well, does it?'

***

Tyler couldn't sleep. He lay in his bed, in the early-hours darkness, counting the scumbags from his past, and watching each and every one transform into the image of Martin Hillman. If he could nail that one, perhaps he could leave the rest hanging on the same cross.

He wanted a drink.

N*eeded it.*

***

Jim Tyler's hands were shaking, his throat hard and dry. He got out of bed. The moment of his life was arriving, to and from which all roads converged. Putting on his running gear, he strapped the phone to his arm and hit the streets.

There was no such thing as silence in a city any more, whatever the hour; and yet a strange serenity could pick into the raging heart of the solitary runner as he clocked up the miles, wasting the energy that would otherwise consume him.

Without consciously planning any route, he found himself running back towards the place where Alan Dale had been found; and once there, climbing the broad sweep up towards Hartshill.

Tyler was halfway up the bank when he felt the phone vibrating against his arm. He stopped to check it. Julie Hammond was awake too, and with the same things on her mind: Hillman, Dammers, hired killers and justice. She was about to leave a message when Tyler answered.

Kieran Blake had slipped his tail.

Tyler was a mile away from where Dammers lived, and he could feel the adrenalin surging. He carried on up the bank, entering Hartshill.

***

Danny Mills was out of bed and hastily getting dressed. Hammond had messaged him. If something was cracking off, he was going to pitch in. It would likely amount to nothing, but he wanted to be close-by in case he was needed.

Mills hadn't been asleep. He'd spent an unpleasant evening arguing with his wife over whether it was time to change schools and be done with. Whether they would be subjecting their children to the bullying they were suffering, if they had been content to stay put. They'd gone around in circles before finally hitting the sack, only to lie in their separate silences a million miles from sleep.

The message had come as a relief to Danny Mills: a reason to get out of bed and begin the day, and gain some distance on everything.

He drove out towards the city.

***

Tyler moved discreetly, passing the cul de sac where Dammers lived. Surprised not to see any signs of surveillance. He jogged on, staying close, circling; uncertain of what exactly he was doing there.

He had reached the top of The Avenue when he noticed the Astra moving purposefully up to the top of the rise, passing him. The man driving – *Kieran Blake*. He knew it; recognised the eyes of a vulture, clocking him, registering his presence, and processing whether this man out running in the early hours of morning had to be taken into consideration.

Every rule stated that you shouldn't leap to conclusions.

And every instinct screamed that those same rules belonged only in the museums of the dead.

Once the car had moved on out of sight, Tyler began to back-track.

***

Mills was entering the city, with a few miles to go before he reached Hartshill. He thought about what he was doing. Whether he ought to ring Tyler.

But what was he doing, beyond going for a late-night drive? Blake had slipped the tail, but that didn't mean he was going to see Dammers. And if he was, that didn't necessarily amount to anything.

He pressed on, without urgency, wondering what the night would bring, doubting that it would bring anything at all. How long before this sorry saga was finally brought to an end, and the case closed in every last respect? Not long, he knew that. The ice was thin and getting thinner.

***

Tyler had trailed back but there was no sign of the Astra in or near the cul de sac. He kept moving. Either he had got it all completely wrong, or else something was on and Blake was taking no chances.

He heard the car coming towards the small recreation area behind the Co-op, dotted with trees and bushes and benches, rarely deserted during the summer months, but empty now. Tyler darted for cover and waited.

The Astra came into view slowly, its driver casing the corners and parked vehicles. It *had* to be Blake. And by the look of it, this was no social call.

The car moved past but Tyler didn't budge. Five minutes later and it came around again, from the same direction. The driver knew the territory, and he knew how to circle and what he was looking out for.

At last the Astra entered the cul de sac.

Tyler messaged Hammond. It was good work, and her team would take it from there. Tyler said to stay back; he would be the eyes and ears and give the signal once and if.

Paul Dammers was at the front door and the driver of the Astra was sitting behind the wheel. Then Dammers walked out towards the vehicle, carrying a small attaché case. He was opening the boot of the Astra and sliding the case inside, walking back now towards the house. As he passed the driver's window, something changed hands.

The engine of the Astra started up and Tyler signalled through to Hammond. Out of nowhere two vehicles descended on the scene, blocking the Astra's escape.

Tyler saw Dammers hurl an object across the neighbours' fence and dart inside his own property, while the driver of the Astra jumped from the car and began to run for it.

The officers split into two groups, three sprinting towards Dammers' house, and another three in pursuit of Blake. The man was fast, and Tyler wasn't in the mood to play the spectator. Blake was running back towards The Avenue, and already Tyler had outstripped Hammond's team for pace.

***

Mills drove up through Basford and was entering Albany Road, adjacent to The Avenue. He was about to pull over and liaise with Hammond before getting any closer to where Dammers lived.

In the distance he could make out two figures running at speed. It seemed a little late in the evening, he thought, to be out trying to break records.

As he cleared the brow of the hill to begin the long descent down The Avenue, Danny Mills blinked in disbelief.

And then he gunned the car down the hill.

***

Tyler was on the man, who turned and swung the first punch, catching Tyler across the jaw. The DCI rocked backwards but wouldn't go down. The man looked about to capitalise on the punch when he saw the car barrelling down the road towards them, and three officers trailing.

The distraction was enough for Tyler to launch himself again, taking the man down to the ground, catching another heavy blow as he did so. Tyler, dazed, managed to make a fist and aim it in the direction of the distorted features beneath him. He felt something give, a cracking sound, and wondered if it was teeth or knuckles.

Mills screeched to a halt and leaped out to assist, cuffing Blake as the cavalry descended.

***

Berkins sat across the desk from Tyler looking proud indeed. It had been an 'unprecedented, exemplary example of what can be achieved with hard work, determination and tenacity' and a 'textbook template in cross-border policing that will, undoubtedly, be used for years to come both on the page and in the classroom'.

The drugs, the cash, none of it was linking directly to Hillman, though. There were too many layers separating the man from what happened at street level, and Hillman had been careful to tie off any loose connections that might lead back to him. That's what the likes of Paul Dammers were for.

Kieran Blake's DNA showed, beyond a shadow of doubt, that he was Steven Jenkins' killer.

All eyes were on Dammers.

How far could loyalty stretch? How many years inside staring you in the face before the alternatives could be seriously considered?

The knock on the door came as Berkins was approaching the final crescendo of his finest speech.

Mills came into the room a little less apologetically than Tyler might have expected.

There had been a development.

Dammers was ready to talk.

CHAPTER THIRTY-FIVE

Tyler was dreaming of the perfect murder as the first light of morning crept into his room. He had travelled across country to be in the home of the hybrid man he had spent his life wanting to kill.

Except that everything had turned upside down. This man, this once-feared and fearsome creature, had shrunk to a withered, pitiful thing. Looking into the eyes of the teacher/headmaster/playground bully/neighbourhood thug – not to mention *Greenslade* – the rolled-up memory, clear as a bell and at the same time distorted by the prism of years – this thing that he had so wanted to destroy – a new emotion took control and Jim Tyler began laughing. And as he laughed, long and hard into the face of his old adversary, he watched it shrink and wither further; and the longer Tyler laughed at it, the more the devil thinned, until it occurred that if he kept on laughing, in the end the creature would die.

Death by laughter.

Tyler couldn't stop. He went outside, laughing as he walked down the road and all the way out of town, his face and belly aching with it; laughing so long and so loud that finally he woke up …

Sitting up in bed, the dream had started to recede, already a distant, half-remembered series of shimmering images that might have only seconds left to live out in the solid world. Other images, too, were clamouring for space; and Tyler realised that for the first time in years he had dreamed of a woman who was not Kim.

***

Mills was sitting in his car watching the school playground. He could see Harry at the far end, playing with boys from his class. Jessica was closer, talking with two girls. Both of his children looked absorbed in what they were doing. Both looked happy.

The window was down and Mills could hear the barrage of sound from the playground, though no individual voices. Then something cut through, the loud and unmistakable imitation of a police siren. Two boys close to Harry, running around making the noise. At first Mills thought that he had been spotted, despite the anonymity of the unmarked car, his plain clothes and sunglasses.

Danny Mills was out of the car, trying to get an angle on the playground game.

Was Harry crying?

Mills moved quickly to the perimeter fence.

As he recognised that his son was laughing, he heard a voice shout, 'Harry, look, it's your dad!'

One of the teachers was looking over. His cover was blown. Harry came running over. 'What do you want, Dad?' He was looking over his shoulder, back at his mates, embarrassed by his father's impromptu visit.

'You okay, son?'

'Yes, what is it?'

'No problems?'

'No, but there will be if you keep turning up here.'

Mills had to say something. 'I'm thinking of getting tickets for next season.'

It was done. There was no way back.

'Wow, great, Dad.'

And then Harry was gone, back towards the group of boys, to tell them his news.

Before he turned to leave, Mills caught Jessica's eye, and she nodded, discreetly.

It was time to go.

***

Tyler drove up to Penkhull in his running gear. He parked up at the top of The Stumps and zig-zagged around the nooks and crannies of the village for a good five miles. He finished off with a single circuit of the park, and by the time he got back to the car his mind was made up.

At the station Mills greeted his arrival with a mug of tea and the news that Howard Wood was on long-term sick, and enlisting the support of a staff counsellor. There were rumours that he was thinking of calling it a day.

'Should be struck off,' said Tyler.

'They do that with teachers?' asked Mills.

'I meant the counsellor – for listening.'

The two men looked at each other and then Tyler said, 'Okay, what is it?'

'It's just, well, my wife was asking – she'd like you to come to our house for a meal.'

Tyler smiled. 'Tell your wife that I would be delighted.'

'That's brilliant,' said Mills. 'She said to ask what kind of food you like.'

Tyler shrugged. 'Tell her not to worry. I'm an easy man to please.'

Later Tyler took a call from Maggie Calleer. 'The newspapers are making interesting reading these days,' she told him. 'It seems that if I want to catch up on how my old charges are doing, I only need to consult the tabloids. Did Martin Hillman really kill Steven Jenkins?'

The question was so blunt that Tyler found himself at a loss for a suitable response.

'It surprises you, then?' he said.

'Of course it surprises me. It surprises me that one human being would ever wish to kill another. Doesn't that surprise you?'

Now that was a question, he thought.

'So Hillman did kill him?' Calleer laughed, bitter sarcasm dripping down the wire. 'What am I thinking? I will re-phrase the question: so, did Martin Hillman *have* Steven Jenkins killed?'

Tyler could have given her the bureaucratic brush off that all good boys and girls of ambition learn at an early stage in their careers. Instead he said, 'Someone once told me that the person you mention would never get his hands dirty. I believe that person was right. Some bullies are like that, and it becomes a habit. It takes a keen eye to see the one making the bullets for others to fire, so to speak.'

'And my eye wasn't keen enough to see the real Martin Hillman?'

'Forty kids is a lot to keep your eye on. The quiet ones are easily overlooked. Also, I think he was … exceptional.'

'Thank you for your kind diplomacy. Though I'm not sure it's enough to get me to sleep at night.'

'I imagine there will be a lot of people having difficulty sleeping,' he said.

Before the call ended, Calleer said, 'Miss Hayburn spoke to me last night. She appreciates that you must be very busy, but that if you can find a spare minute – apparently there's a question of yours that she left unanswered.'

***

The man with the moustache was taking a holiday, the first in quite a while. And before he set off he wanted to formally congratulate Tyler on the way he had handled 'this singular episode in the annals of crime in the City of Stoke-upon-Trent.' It demanded – and it received – possibly the firmest handshake that Tyler had ever received, even from the moustached man. And it came with a buffet lunch.

Funny the way things turn out, thought Tyler. Someone even higher up the food chain had liked the way 'things had turned out' and didn't need to hear about the methods and misunderstandings along the way. They might become the stuff of legend, but more likely they would be allowed to sink without trace.

He thought of an old maths teacher who once said that the person marking your paper was assessing the working-out along the way every bit as much as the final answer. But in real life, a multitude of sins could be allowed and forgiven so long as the thing worked out satisfactorily in the end.

Careers and pensions safe.

The machinery and the bureaucracy clunking on.

A satisfactory outcome?

Five adolescent boys had grown into men with a grim, disgusting secret to keep them company along the paths they were to take in life. Jenkins was dead, Marley was dead, Dammers was looking at serious jail time, which might yet be negotiable if he helped to land the bigger fish, and Swanson was in pieces. Hillman might still survive it, that all depended on the priorities of a loyal right-hand man, though his political ambitions were, for the moment at least, in tatters; and even his business empire might never thrive at the same level again.

Who could tell?

But he was still a long way from justice.

It all depended on what you called satisfactory.

For the city fathers it made good press: A city on the rise, smashing down the old and rebuilding. A thirty-year-old mystery solved and the 'alleged monster' didn't even live here, flying the nest to be corrupted out in the wider world.

It was a lousy and a dangerous sub-text, though a convenient one.

Berkins was making heavy-weather of it. 'We try not to make a habit of initiating our detectives with cases like this,' he told Tyler, one hand on his moustache as he fumbled yet again for the closing, climactic line. 'I'm not saying that life around these parts can't be a challenge; but I do think that this 'episode' has been, shall we say, *extraordinary.*

'This city has a proud heritage, but, I believe, an even greater future. In a nutshell: we need people of talent and integrity to be a part of that great future.'

Tyler wondered if a band would strike up now, and whether protocol demanded he clamber to his feet and salute with a tear in his eye. Berkins' chest was puffed out like plumage and his moustache magnificent. If he was looking to kiss and make up, why didn't he just get on with it – if it came minus the kiss.

Then the second handshake and a closing smile cut directly from a Hollywood out-take and it was all done.

Tyler kept a straight face until he was out of the room.

***

With the tell-tale signs of the press lurking around the school, Tyler drove the unmarked car as close up to reception as he could, entering the building swiftly and without his jacket and tie. The receptionist showed him through to where he was going, though he knew the way well enough.

In the moments before she arrived, he thought back over the past days and wondered what revelation could still be waiting. Tyler's mind was on Howard Wood when Miss Hayburn entered her office.

'Oh, good of you to drop by,' she said, taking her seat opposite the already seated DCI.

'My pleasure,' he said. 'I hear that Mr Wood is still off. I believe that whatever is afflicting him may be terminal?'

'It better be,' she said. 'A guilty conscience often is. I read about the blackmail in the papers. Not going to do much for the image of this school, is it, pupils blackmailing teachers. And before you say, I appreciate that it was thirty years ago. But if that man were to walk back in here ...' she appeared to shudder, 'let's just say that a lot of good work has been undone.'

'There's no question of that, surely?'

'You would think not. But stranger things happen, believe me.'

There was a pause, and as Miss Hayburn looked at him, Tyler felt the need to keep the conversation going. 'I want to thank you for all of your assistance,' he said.

'Don't mention it. I'm glad it came to something – your passion and persistence. I don't suppose a case like this can have a happy ending.'

'I think they should terminate Wise's pension,' said Tyler. 'That would be a start.'

'On what grounds?'

'For doing more harm than good to the thousands who walked through this door. For setting everything in motion.'

She looked unconvinced. 'I think the likes of Martin Hillman were set in motion a long time before Wise entered the frame. I think that's how it works. But first causes are notoriously hard to prove.'

'I think Wise became the catalyst for what happened to one young child at least.'

'Perhaps.'

'I believe there was a question you left unanswered,' said Tyler.

'Indeed there was. You asked about my name. You asked what "A" stands for and I didn't answer.'

'I see,' said Tyler, clearing his throat awkwardly.

'Well, it stands for *Alison*.'

She stood up. 'And now I have to get back to running this school. So, if you have any further questions, you're going to have to ask them over dinner.'

***

Later, Tyler asked a favour of Mills, and the DS happily agreed. They had both finished for the day and drove together to a quiet street a few hundred yards from the village square in Penkhull. Standing outside a small property that even the estate agents suggested had 'potential', Tyler said, 'So what do you think?'

'Needs some work, by the look of it.'

'Rome wasn't built in a day, Danny.'

'True enough.'

'Time I made a start, though.'

'It's as good a place as any.'

'By the way, I meant to ask: did you get chance to visit Jenkins' neighbour?'

'I did, but she's sworn to secrecy. Five hundred words a minute and not one about Scotland.'

'Some things we are not meant to know.'

'I never doubted it. What do you reckon will happen with Hillman?'

'I think it's safe to say that he's blown this election.'

Mills smiled. 'He'll have all the angles weighed up and take the best route through. I'm not convinced that he won't sneak out of it. He won't be making MP though.'

'Not this year. But I wouldn't count anything out. When I first saw the state of Steven Jenkins' corpse I thought the job had been bungled. Too obviously a hit, and at the same time too bizarre, almost ritualistic the way the head was almost taken off. But that wasn't the point. It was a warning. I doubt Paul Dammers will have the bottle to disregard it. He'll be back one day, whatever happens, and that warning's transferable.'

Tyler nodded back towards the property.

'I'm going to put in an offer.'

***

Sheila Dale's house in Leek was up for sale and she was moving back to Penkhull. For her the exile was over. Building had started on the site where Alan had died, his remains finally laid to rest in the cemetery on the Hartshill/Penkhull border where his parents had been buried and where Sheila would one day join them. It happened to be the cemetery that housed the remains of Martin Hillman's mother, and barely fifty yards of gravestones separated them.

Tyler had set up a fund in Alan's name, for children who had been the victims of bullying, and asked Sheila Dale to manage it. He kicked the thing off with a charity run, and even Chief Superintendent Berkins had dug a hand into his pocket.

A separate fund was also in place, to erect a small monument at the bottom of The Stumps. Dale was keeping silent on the final wording of the inscription that would be chiselled into the base of the statue, and the local craftsman tasked with completing it was similarly giving nothing away.

Mills had approached Stoke City FC to organise a charity match to raise funds, and Tyler invited Dale to come along.

'I'm not a football fan, either,' he told her. 'But as I'm paying.'

***

The game was lousy, by all accounts, and it rained all day for good measure. Jim Tyler felt bad about subjecting Sheila Dale and Alison Hayburn to the torture, though Danny Mills and his family seemed to be enjoying themselves, pumping the air with raised fists as Stoke scored the last-minute winner against an all-star opposition.

***

On the day of the unveiling Jim Tyler wondered what the inscription would read. The nervous city fathers had been given a prior peek, had insisted on it, in case anything scandalous was in the air that might reflect badly on the city.

He stood next to Danny Mills as Sheila Dale held the string that would release the veil. There was a fair turn-out, he thought. Some ghouls present, naturally.

Mills spotted a familiar face in the crowd and a few moments later was introducing Tyler to Josh Smith. 'So this must be Stan,' said Tyler, patting the head of the black retriever. 'Unusual name for a dog?'

Mills winked at the boy. 'Don't worry about him; he's not from these parts. Where he comes from they've never even heard of Sir Stanley Matthews.'

When the veil dropped, the likeness of the statue to the dead boy caused a collective gasp.

But there was no inscription.

As the applause started up, Tyler caught the eye of Sheila Dale, and understood.

The local sculptor had captured what words never could: A boy with a light in his eye, looking with innocent defiance across the city. At peace, at rest, demanding that this never happen again.

The End

A Note from Bloodhound Books

Thanks for reading Red Is The Colour We hope you enjoyed it as much as we did. Please consider leaving a review on Amazon or Goodreads to help others find and enjoy this book too.

We make every effort to ensure that books are carefully edited and proofread, however occasionally mistakes do slip through. If you spot something, please do send details to info@ bloodhoundbooks.com and we can amend it.

Bloodhound Books specialise in crime and thriller fiction. We regularly have special offers including free and discounted eBooks. To be the first to hear about these special offers, why not join our mailing list here? We won't send you more than two emails per month and we'll never pass your details on to anybody else.

Readers who enjoyed Red Is The Colour will also enjoy

Those That Remain by Rob Ashman

Enter The Dark by Chris Thomas.

Acknowledgements

I would like to thank everyone who read earlier drafts of *Red is the Colour*. I'm so grateful for your time, effort and generous feedback.

I would particularly like to thank: Fiona, your enthusiasm for this book gave me the encouragement I needed; Kath Middleton, your suggestions, as usual, were good ones; and Nicola Findler, casting a police officer's eye over proceedings, and providing useful insights into police work. Thank you to Clare Law, my editor. And thank you to my publishers, Bloodhound Books.

This book is very much a work of fiction, and I have taken a few liberties with the history and geography of the setting, in service to the story that I wanted to tell.

Red is the Colour is the first in a series of novels featuring DCI Tyler and DS Mills.

Printed in Great Britain
by Amazon